W9-CBQ-183

Life Force

FAY WELDON

Life Force

VIKING

VIKING
Published by the Penguin Group
Viking Penguin, a division of Penguin Books USA Inc.,
375 Hudson Street, New York, New York 10014, U.S.A.
Penguin Books Ltd, 27 Wrights Lane, London W8 5TZ, England
Penguin Books Australia Ltd, Ringwood, Victoria, Australia
Penguin Books Canada Ltd, 10 Alcorn Avenue, Suite 300,
Toronto, Ontario, Canada M4V 3B2
Penguin Books (N.Z.) Ltd, 182–190 Wairau Road,
Auckland 10, New Zealand

Penguin Books Ltd, Registered Offices:
Harmondsworth, Middlesex, England

First published in 1992 by Viking Penguin,
a division of Penguin Books USA Inc.

1 3 5 7 9 10 8 6 4 2 JAN 3 1 1992

LIBRARY OF CONGRESS CATALOGING-IN-PUBLICATION DATA
Weldon, Fay.
Life force : a novel / by Fay Weldon.
p.   cm.
ISBN 0-670-84146-3
I. Title.
PR6073.E374L52   1992
823'.914—dc20   91-26870

Printed in the United States of America
Set in Fournier
Designed by Jessica Shatan

Dedicated to

NELL LEYSHON

without whom this novel could not
have been written in the form it is

NOTHING HAPPENS,
AND NOTHING HAPPENS,
AND THEN EVERYTHING HAPPENS.

Life Force

*L*eslie Beck came to see me the other day. He was carrying an oil painting under his right arm. In the past, his arms had always seemed too short for his body, but now he'd had to stretch the right one to contain the painting, and the left was keeping it company, so today he looked not wider than he was long, like a rugger player, but too attenuated for his own good, like the kind of basketball player who gets goals just by reaching over everyone else's head and dropping the ball through the hoop. Whereupon everyone cheers and shouts, though personally I can never see there's any merit in merely being taller than anyone else. Or perhaps Leslie Beck had just got thinner, and I had shrunk as well. At any rate, our relative sizes had altered, one way or another, in my favor.

Leslie Beck had never, it seemed to me, been quite tall enough for his wives: first Jocelyn, then Anita. Marriage is easier when the man is noticeably taller than the woman: it makes the balance of power, usually in the man's favor, seem a more natural state of affairs. Then there is less resentment against the male assumption of superiority. I am not married, so am in a position to notice these things without great pangs of anxiety and fear. In actual terms,

Leslie Beck had once been five foot ten and was now coming in at about five foot eight. Two inches can make a lot of difference.

Leslie Beck, I realized, must be pushing sixty. Perhaps his true nature was showing through, as natures in the end do; and I found I wasn't liking it. For though Leslie Beck's red hair seemed crinkly and plentiful, it occurred to me now that it was quite likely not hair at all but a rather expensive wig; and though his step was jaunty, I wondered if it might not drag the minute he was round the corner, and though he seemed to carry the painting without effort, it might have needed a pause and a couple of deep breaths before he pushed open the door to achieve that effect. In fact, I found I'd gone right off Leslie Beck, for no fair reason. Sixty happens to everyone, sooner or later. That is, if he's lucky.

"Hi, little Marion," he said.

"Why, hello, Leslie," I said. "What's that you have under your arm?"

"A painting by Anita," he said. "I thought you might be interested."

And Leslie Beck laid the painting, which was done on a proper, expensive, prestretched canvas, five feet by four feet, on the big desk which I keep clear for just such eventualities, and unwrapped it. Swathes of polystyrene bubble wrap fell to the floor and lay about like sheets of cracked ice subjected to unnatural forces. Leslie Beck was taking good care of this painting.

"How is Anita?" I asked. He paused. He looked at me. His eyes were still blue, though rather paler and more watery than once they had been. Now tears came into them.

"I'm being very brave," he said, "but she's dead."

And I looked around the gallery, the Marion Loos Gallery, just off Bond Street, my pride, my achievement, my family, the source of my income (such as it was, the country being in recession) and my security (such as it could be, with tides of violence and unrest lapping at our doorstep), and I was glad I had placed my trust in material objects and not in human beings. But the sun chose that moment to come out from behind a cloud and shine directly in through the plate-glass windows; and the paintings currently on exhibition, by a certain Scottish artist, William MacIntyre, which should have responded to the sudden light, at least in theory, by flinging back their own innate energy, matching solar power with human vision, failed to do so and just looked dull and as if no one were ever going to buy them, or could reasonably be expected so to do. I could see dust motes floating in the air and smell the exhaust fumes of the city traffic which had seeped into the gallery along with Leslie Beck. Nevertheless, appearing at that moment, the sun struck some kind of light right into my head and made me feel quite dizzy—not, I think, with grief for Anita, but with the revelation of some powerful allied emotion. Perhaps it was just dislike of Leslie Beck.

"I thought you'd know," he added. As if everyone would be familiar with the details of his life and times. He, Leslie Beck.

"I didn't," I said. "I'm sorry."

"Next time you have a group show," he said, "perhaps you'd hang it. What do you think?"

But I was not, for once, looking at the painting for "good" or "bad," or anything except its narrative. It was an interior; its subject was Leslie and Anita Beck's bedroom, which I remembered well, from the time she'd been off somewhere. Where had it been? Visiting children or ill parents—the likeliest thing. Some episode, anyway, in the kind of discursive family life other people have, but not me, never did have, nor, I imagine, ever will. I have cats, and they suit me very well.

"It is an unbearable tragedy," he said. "Just when Anita had finally discovered her talent."

"Quite so," I said.

"I thought in the six- or seven-thousand range," he said.

Aphra came toward us, so I didn't bother to say "You're joking." Aphra was hopping.

"Why, hello," said Leslie Beck appreciatively, the way men often do when Aphra appears. Aphra is twenty-four and has a great deal of dark brown frizzy hair which springs energetically from a perfect forehead and coils messily down over hunched and narrow shoulders. Her nose is too large and her mouth too narrow, but her skirts are very short and her energy level high, and no one seems to worry about details of feature, least of all Aphra. She was wearing black-and-white-striped tights, the stripes going down the leg, not round. Though from time to time I beg her to dress more calmly, so as not to offer competition to the paintings on the wall, she never will. Aphra bent down to rub her toe, which she had badly stubbed, and she folded her body easily in the middle, and Leslie Beck noticed that, too. Another age, another time, another place, he would have whistled.

"That's a nice painting," said Aphra. She had done a night-school class in fine art and felt entitled to pass opinions, though I asked her not to. It was true, though I wished it were not, that the paintings she liked most were the ones which sold first.

"My wife painted it," said Leslie Beck. "It's a study of our bedroom. It was on my suggestion that she started painting. She needed something for herself. You know what it's like for women. She'd never have started if I hadn't encouraged her."

"Well," said Aphra, "she certainly seemed to like your bedroom," and she hopped and limped on to do, or so I hoped, the mail.

And then Barbara came out of the stockroom, and Leslie Beck said, "Well, hello," in the tone of a middle-aged roué, and certainly not an elderly widower. Of my two assistants, Aphra, being in her twenties, was a less practical proposition than Barbara, or so Leslie Beck seemed to deduce. Barbara had a degree in fine art and a librarian husband and a small child, and the kind of gentle, puzzled look young mothers who have recently acquired this status tend to have. She was not too beautiful, not too young, and looked as if she were just waiting for someone to explain things and make her happy.

"Hello," replied Barbara, courteously and formally, and passed on.

"You know how to pick your staff," observed Leslie Beck, and I returned my attention to the painting. The same cream curtains, the same white cotton bedspread—but the good, expensive things do, of course, last. The wallpaper was striped. I had remembered it as floral: that, at least, had changed. I remembered the pleasure Leslie Beck had given me on top of the white bedspread, there being no time for us to open up the bed, and I remembered my envy of the softness of Anita Beck's pillows; but the memory was diffused, as if another person had inhabited the body whose legs spread open, welcoming and willing on another woman's bed, while Leslie Beck gave and took the amazing pleasure he felt was his to give and take.

Now, the painting was not my cup of tea, as the woman who had painted it had not been, either, she who had ousted Jocelyn and been the subject of Leslie Beck's complaints: her plainness, her dependency, her laggardliness and general dreariness—those qualities, in fact, I most hoped were least characteristic of myself. The painting was muzzy around the edges, photographic in attempt and achievement in the middle. "Why, look"—I could already hear the words at the opening—"you could almost pick up that comb and use it!" Well, I didn't want that kind of work on my walls, even in a corner badly lit in a group show: I had my pride; I did not want to make so easy a living. Such paintings sell well in the middle market, in the middle price range, but there's no fun, no risk, no outrage in thus playing safe. You could die of boredom—or, alternatively, promote Barbara to manager and just go home and wait for the source of income to dry up. As for the comb itself, old-fashioned and silver-backed, Anita Beck had simply failed to perceive what was invested in it, and I felt she should have. That was what painters were *for*. I had picked up that comb in my time, pulled it through my hair. Leslie Beck and my own urgencies had tangled it, both moving my head this way, that way, in and out of Anita Beck's soft square feather pillows. I'd needed a comb. Myself and who else: we had used the comb and then, no doubt, picked our hairs out of it, not so much out of concern for Anita, the second wife, as to save Leslie Beck embarrassment.

"It's not quite my style, Leslie," I said. "Not quite the gallery's style."

"Then that's a pity," he said. "I did think, since you were such a help to her in the past, and she was so fond of you, I'd give you the opportunity of first option."

"You're thinking of Jocelyn," I said, "not Anita," and it seemed to me he had to pause a little before remembering who Jocelyn was.

"Well," he said, dismissing all that, "you'll be interested to know Anita built up quite a collection of paintings over the last couple of years. You must come round and see them. She developed cancer of the liver. From diagnosis to death in three months. It was in her family. Her mother died of it. Dreadful. Anita painted mostly interiors, but a few landscapes. I was little by little widening her scope. Getting her out of the house."

"Poor Anita," I said.

"She had this amazing sensitivity," Leslie Beck said. "This response, this special talent. But very little self-confidence, left to her own devices. I like to think I helped her. Of course, I won't release all the paintings at once. I know the art market like the back of my hand. She's buried next to her mother, in the family vault."

"That's nice," I said. "All very close, as families ought to be."

I was not portraying myself as either sensitive or responsive, but I need not have worried. I could be as inane as I liked and Leslie Beck wouldn't notice. I hadn't remembered Anita as coming from the kind of family that boasted its own burial vault, on the contrary, but I suppose money can buy anything these days, even its own family history. Though "vault" might just mean the same shelf in the mortuary.

"I'll leave Anita's painting with you, anyway," he said, "to think about. Not one of her very best, but naturally I'm attached to it. Well, I am to all of them." Then he turned his back on the painting, and on its glinty wrappings still scattered all over the floor, and prepared to leave. More exhaust fumes leaked in as he opened the door, though I realized he could hardly be blamed for that.

He stopped in the entrance and looked back at me. He wore a very good gray suit and a cheerful, youthful tie. His cheeks were pink. He looked to me like a carnivore and a drinking man. I am a vegetarian.

"I don't know what I'm going to do," he said, "without her. How I'm going to live." He spoke loudly enough for both Aphra in the stockroom and Barbara in the back gallery—attending to some muddle about the price of a particularly small MacIntyre painting, which a prospective purchaser wanted measured, both with the frame and without, gross and net, as it were—to hear. "Dear little Marion," he said then, in a meditative fashion, "I think of you a lot, you know."

If he had not said it, I might have believed he was suffering from some kind of retrospective amnesia and could not be held accountable for what he said or did, or how he insulted his wife's memory, and I would have forgiven him. Had he forgotten me altogether, it would have been, I suppose, understandable, though not pleasant. But that he should both remember and still see nothing amiss in trying to sell me poor Anita's painting; and, more, that he had reconstructed the wretched woman's life to provide himself with a happy marriage; and, yet more, that though in love with his own grief he was so shallowly in love that he could still attempt flirtations with my staff—these things were intolerable.

"And in the end, you did so well for yourself," he said. "The

Marion Loos Gallery! Who'd have thought it! And all from our little spot of enterprise, or do you have a backer? Some nice rich banker?"

"No backer," I said, "no banker. All my own work. Please shut the door. You're letting the traffic fumes in. I get asthma."

"So you do," he said and smiled, and it almost worked. "I remember. But we had to keep that quiet, didn't we?" When he smiled he showed his teeth and looked young and mischievous and somehow in command again, as if his view of the world were the right one, the only civilized version around.

"Do you ever wonder?" he asked.

"I never wonder," I said.

"Some things," he said, "it's best to keep quiet about. But I'm sure you'll see your way to hanging Anita's painting. Times have been easier, as I'm sure you know."

His teeth were still regular, pointed and white. Once they'd put me in mind of some small, agreeable, nuzzling animal, or, as he became more imperative, something dangerous, some glossy fox, perhaps, rooting around and above me—a vision which would occasionally change, even in the middle of lovemaking, to one of the fox loose in the henhouse, tearing and slavering, blood and feathers everywhere, and then I'd lose my impetus, as it were, my capacity to be mindless, never my strong point, and have to pretend orgasm. He was easily convinced. And then he'd change sides and meld into the cock surviving the slaughter, straddling the dungheap, preening and crowing, "Clever me, clever me, how happy I am." What an act of trust sex is: thus to open the henhouse door to the fox, let alone bed down nightly with the cock.

"Anita's memorial service is on Friday," said Leslie Beck. "So many people loved her. St. Martin-in-the-Fields. At three o'clock. It would be a really nice gesture if you came. It will be dreadful for me, of course. I'll probably break down. But the Life Force—well, I think I possess it in great measure. I feel it already," he said, and spread his hands and looked at them, and I looked at them, too. His long thumbs arched away from his palm, bending and mobile even from the top joint. The memory of it made me all but gasp. He caught my eye. He smiled. And then finally he shut the door and went away.

Aphra had already begun to clear and fold the wrappings which had fallen from the painting. I was grateful for her. And, indeed, for Barbara, who, although she drifted and muddled, knew just what to say to the right client at the right time, and made the saying sound accidental—which I sometimes thought perhaps it was—and thereby genuine. She so disliked saying a disagreeable word about anything, was so eager to see the best in everything, she could scarcely avoid being enthusiastic about even the worst of our paintings—indeed, especially the worst—for fear words of distaste would somehow fly through the ether and upset the artist in his garret: Art, for Barbara, was sacred. Sometimes, all the same, I wanted to shake her. Just because it's Art, I wished her to understand, doesn't make it good. Just because it sells, doesn't make it bad.

"What a creep," said Aphra, of Leslie Beck. To this man, this creep, Anita had dedicated her life. When you're with a man, no one tells you he's a creep; they don't like to; they think, well, that's her choice, perhaps ours isn't up to much, either; how will we ever be sure in this polite world? In other words, as we all know, one woman's creep is another's true love, and just as well. I didn't want to believe Leslie Beck was a creep by any objective standard, for Jocelyn's and Anita's sakes, or Rosalie's, or Susan's, or Nora's, or my own.

Barbara had stuck the painting on a chair: she studied it. Aphra joined in.

"It oughtn't to work," Barbara said, "but it does. What's that comb doing? It seems to come out of another painting altogether. Rockwell detail in the middle, Monet magic all around."

"Monet mush," said Aphra, who liked to wind Barbara up. "Pity she's dead. I really like the bit in the middle."

"There aren't any hairs in the comb, I suppose?" I asked. I wasn't going to look too closely. There could have been four that I knew of—one of Anita's, reddish and limp; one of mine, perhaps, long and dark; one of Rosalie's, wiry and brown; one of Nora's, short and fair. And more, how many more? Leslie Beck's favorite bed was his wife's. Bloody Anita, always the innocent.

"No," said Barbara, and she sounded surprised. "No hairs, that I can see."

My voice had risen. I could hear it; it does when I'm stressed. That's what surprised Barbara. Creeps came in and out of the gallery all the time. They had a good deal to say and seldom parted with a penny. Nothing unusual.

"Put the painting in the stockroom," I said, "while I work out what to do," because I supposed something had to be done, and Aphra picked up the canvas and ran, her black-and-white legs, I suddenly saw, a rather welcome return to living op art; and my desk was clear again, but nothing was the same, or could be: what was done could be forgotten, but not undone. Twenty-three years, and at last I felt guilty.

NORA

*T*hat is enough out of Marion's eyes. I appointed myself her biographer, only temporarily, stirred on as I was by the return of Leslie Beck into our circle. I have the account of it only from Rosalie, mind you, to whom Marion related it over the phone, in some agitation: and the event has had to be filtered through first Marion's, then Rosalie's head, and the further distortion and exaggeration that I suppose must happen as I, Nora, commit it to paper. Though I don't want to believe that.

Marion Loos, spinster, art dealer, and gallery owner, is more Rosalie's friend than mine. She and I have of late rather lost touch, but then I don't buy paintings. Rosalie occasionally does, though she is mad to do so. She ought to save every penny she can.

I use the word "spinster" of Marion advisedly: the nature, I suspect, predating the event, or rather lack of it. "I am a spinster," Marion will exclaim, "and I am proud of it." Don't avoid the word, she suggests: better to concentrate on making the state desirable, and so render the word acceptable. Well, bully for her. She likes her life to be an uphill battle. I don't.

"Marion was trying to be bold and bright about it," said Rosalie, "but she was really upset. She even cried. I've never known Marion to cry, have you?"

"Not in public," I said, though I had always thought perhaps Marion did weep in private, or when she was alone with her two Persian cats, Monet and Manet, who were as well groomed, nervy, wide-eyed, and brave as she. When the guests were gone, and the apartment quiet, and the wide bed so steadily empty, did the paintings on the walls—those tributes to her taste, her judgment, her flair, not to mention her income—the books on the shelves, the flicker of the television, the expectation of another working day tomorrow, combine sufficiently to block off loneliness? Did Marion Loos live with the sense of a life wasted, or of a life well spent?

"I know what you're thinking, Nora," said Rosalie. "You think any woman who doesn't have a husband and children is to be pitied. You're nuts."

Rosalie has, or had, a husband who climbs mountains. Wallace Hayter went climbing one weekend in Switzerland, or said he did, and simply didn't come home again. No body was found; he was seen getting off a train at Zermatt; he had booked into a Gasthaus; he just didn't turn up there in the evening when expected. It was February and peak season, so they gave the room to someone else—an irrelevant detail, I expect, but it sticks in the mind. The courts have refused to declare Rosalie's husband dead before another two years have passed. In the meantime, by some miracle—or her husband's sensible contrivance—an insurance policy now keeps Rosalie and her two teenage children in modest comfort. Rosalie endures what to many would be an uneasy and distressing situation with an equanimity disturbing to myself, Marion, and Susan, her friends. Susan remains Rosalie's friend, although she is no longer mine.

"If he's dead," Rosalie says, "he can't suffer. If he isn't dead, he's with some woman, and happy."

She's let herself run to fat; she watches television and eats fish and chips with her children; she wears flowered shirts and elastic-waist skirts; she overflows her bra and is comfortable; she gossips with her friends.

One day, of course, as we the friends remind her, someone at the insurance company will query the necessity of continuing to pay out, and the source of her income will dry up; but Rosalie refuses to worry about the problem of outrageous future, let alone take arms against it. Marion, Susan, and myself saw her through the first tearful, agitated weeks after her husband went missing, fed her tranquilizers, then weaned her off them. Now Rosalie, even without diazepam, does nothing all day but sit around. This capacity of hers for idleness rather shocks us. If our houses are dusty in the corners, it's because we're busy, and other things are more important. Rosalie these days just doesn't care. Her panty hose sag around her ankles. If they are large enough at the hips, they are too big in the legs. You wouldn't look at her twice in the supermarket.

"Personally," says Rosalie, "I think the real reason Marion is upset with Leslie Beck is that he flirted with her staff and not her."

I didn't want to think that. I preferred to believe that Marion Loos was upset by news of Anita's death. The news had certainly disturbed me.

"Well," I said, "you have time to think about these things. Lucky old you," and I looked at my watch and went off down the hill to the office where I work part-time. I do general clerical work for a real estate agency by the name of Accord Realtors: "Accord" because that puts them toward the beginning of the yellow pages; "Realtors" because by thus describing themselves they acquire a transatlantic and go-getting air—or so they believe. Accord Realtors has its offices in the arcade of shops along from Richmond station, the busy terminus of the overland line which will take you swiftly, if not comfortably, into the very heart of London. Richmond is a pleasant place. The river Thames runs through it. It is far enough from the city to have its own character, near enough to borrow some of the

city's vitality. Look into any window at dusk, in the minutes after
the lights go on, and before curtains and shutters are closed, and
you will see stripped pine, blue-and-white china, bookcases, type-
writers, paintings on the wall; and if you are envious, you are meant
to be. Look at us, they announce, we belong to the gentle intelli-
gentsia of England: people with taste who appreciate the pleasures
of the mind, who are not plagued by too much money but one day,
one day, if there is justice in the world, will have it. Richmond is a
prosperous enough place. Its beggars are few, its homeless hostels
many; girl children can go unaccompanied to school. The public
library is well used; there is a shop that sells nothing but palms;
conservationists are active. There are enclaves like this all over the
world, where people like Rosalie and Wallace, Ed and myself, Susan
and Vinnie, shattered by the world, retreat to rear their growing
children.

My desk and computer are to the left of the door. If the receptionist
is out, and she often is, at the doctor or the dentist, life at Accord
Realtors is quiet—so quiet, reader, that I rather wonder if I will
have my job for long. But quiet enough to let me get on with writing
this unpublishable work for an hour or so every day. What I write
is bound to be libelous, and Leslie Beck loves going to law; and
who wants to hurt and upset their friends for the sake of a few
dollars, anyway? That, at least, is the kind of thing we like to say
in Richmond: we like to occupy the moral high ground, to our
certain disadvantage. It is the reader, therefore, who for once is the
invention, as the substance of this autobiographical work is not. But
I must say that the very thought of this nonexistent reader drives
me on, roots me to the page—both a hope and a fear that there
might eventually be someone out there reading, coming with me
through the journey of this narrative. But, reader, forget all that;
really, all I want is your company. I get lonely, here at Accord
Realtors. And a kind of sadness has fallen on the arcade, which no
amount of bright lighting can cure. No one seems to want the flighty

panties in the window of the lingerie shop, the Belgian chocolates in the patisserie; no one wants frivolity anymore; no one will *spend*. I am sure it has something to do with AIDS.

Sometimes I do still get chatted up by house-buying clients: not so often as I did, though I tell myself that's because there are fewer clients. I have "good bones" and always was too skinny for comfort, and I have short fair hair. Ed says I could be any age between thirty and fifty, but perhaps he's just being nice. Ed is thoughtful and kind; he works in publishing; he is thin, has bright eyes, wears glasses. He walks around the house with a book in his hand. I talk a great deal; he talks not very much. He likes to play jazz very loud. He has a gentle, disingenuous air. Sometimes he looks younger than his son Colin—they look very alike. But, then, Ed drinks very little alcohol, and Colin drinks quite a lot, and sometimes appears at breakfast quite raddled.

And this "Life Force" referred to by Leslie Beck, according to Rosalie, according to Marion Loos (who detected it in the tremble of Leslie Beck's hands), and taken seriously by myself, Nora, does, I swear, exist—runs through all our lives with enough energy to forge real and fictional characters into beings of the same nature, unites the reader both actual and figmental. In its glare, the novel you read and the life you live are not distinguishable. Leslie Beck's Life Force is the energy not so much of sexual desire as of sexual discontent: the urge to find someone better out in the world, and thereby something better in the self; the one energy working against the other, creating a fine and animating friction; or else racing along side by side, like the chariots in *Ben-Hur,* wheels colliding, touching, hellbent, sparking off happiness and unhappiness; creating in our excited heads wild notions of victory and defeat but, when it comes to it, mindless and about little else than accident and survival. For where are the chariots going but round and round the track, and how can the race ever end? Who is there to signal who's winner, who's loser? How difficult it is to reconcile the self of the night, the

dweller, as it were, in the mucous membrane, that creature of en-
gorged delight, with the organized and graceful self of the day? That
first self is irrational, uncontrolled, universal, shameful; the second,
the poor pitiful yet powerful thing, yearns for a moral shape to the
universe. Marion Loos so frightened herself early on with her own
first-self, Life Force behavior, she stunned herself into a half-life
with cats. So I believe, though Rosalie doesn't. Rosalie says Marion's
life is fuller than anyone's, since she sees it as an end in itself, not
just the tap through which other lives flow. Rosalie says that only
the childless command their own souls, are capable of hell and
heaven.

And Marion, until now, when she comes running to Rosalie
crying, complaining that Leslie Beck has turned up in our lives again,
and that Anita is dead, has said and thought precious little about
any of these matters at all. It always annoys me how for some
people day can succeed day and nothing happen; how can after can
of cat food can be opened and devoured, trash bag after trash bag
of cat litter be put weekly out the door while other people's children
get born and grow up; and how, while their life dribbles away, they
continue to act and chatter and behave as if everything were normal,
yet actually they are in a state of paralysis, and surely must know
it. People can die in that paralysis, that's the trouble, and only the
tears in their eyes as they dumbly depart this life indicate their final
awareness of it. Life has been wasted. The Life Force shot by just
out of orbit, disappointing, like an expected meteor passing so far
from the earth as to make no spectacle at all. If you don't do something, nothing happens, I keep saying to Marion Loos, and she says,
"Shut up, Nora, I don't want anything to happen. I am perfectly all
right as I am. You're talking about yourself."

At least one day Anita woke out of her slumber and started doing
something, started painting, even though she left it so late she was
interrupted by death itself.

Marion, Rosalie, Susan, and Nora, that's me. Among us we have eight children, now all in their teens, early and late. I will name them but not write about them much if I can help it: all that need be said is that these children provide endless anxiety and occasional gratification, that life has been organized around their existence for years—even Marion's, who acts as aunt, and says that's more than enough for her—and that we fondly and wrongly believe our worry about them acts as a kind of talisman. If you lie awake all night in a frenzy of despair waiting for the return of the feckless girl, the drug-taking son, they come home safe. On the whole. Sometimes they don't. If the despair is ambivalent—mixed with a half-conscious (at best) desire never to see them or think of them again—so much the worse. And if the sight of someone else's baby continues to fill you with instant, immediate, and genuine pleasure—the triumph of hope, as they say, over experience—so much the better. Their names are (Rosalie's) Catharine and Alan, (Susan's) Barney, Amanda, and David, (mine) Richard, Benjamin, and Colin. Marion—nil. The name of Rosalie's missing husband is Wallace; Catharine's father is Leslie Beck, as is Amanda's. Wallace never realized this about Catharine, nor has Vinnie ever wondered why Amanda has crinkly, orangy curls and needs to wear braces. Both Vinnie and Susan have wide jaws and strong, large, even teeth: the fact is that Amanda has Susan's teeth in Leslie Beck's foxy, nuzzling jaw; she has endless trouble with them, poor child, while the orthodontist struggles against an unkind genetic fate.

The things you know about your friends you must never, never disclose! In the States, people move a great deal, make new friends, learn the art of starting afresh: perhaps they're wise. Here in Richmond, England, we tend to stay rooted to the spot, aghast.

So let me take you back from the chaste safety of Richmond, and the nothingness of Accord Realtors, to the dramas and excitements of 1974, to Leslie Beck's tall town house, No. 12 Rothwell Gardens, London, NW1. It has just been painted white, after eight years of being coated in a rather startling sixties pink. The yellow drainpipes and guttering are now a sensible and prudent black. As does the rest of the nation, Leslie Beck is feeling cautious: a sobriety of vision reflects itself first in color schemes. IRA bombs have been going off in buses and trains; it is not safe to sit near the window in restaurants; worse, the price of oil is going up dramatically as the OPEC countries of the Gulf get together to form a cartel. Color may be brave, but ordinariness is safer. A rumor goes around that ration books are being printed; it is generally felt that the West is collapsing, somehow imploding, and that Marx was *right*. One up, in other words, to the Soviet Union. Little did we know.

It was a summer morning. It was coffee time. Rosalie maneuvered her stroller up the front steps of Leslie and Jocelyn Beck's house. Catharine, aged fifteen months, Leslie Beck's unacknowledged child, sat in a stroller rather too small for her. The elegant magnolia tree in the front garden was in bloom. It was a bright day. Rosalie expected everything within the house to be happy; the dramas and terrors of the outside world, back in 1974, having less effect on domestic life than they do now. In the nineties people will come to their front door weeping, and if you ask why, will reply, "I've been watching the news." Then, not so. Perhaps there were just fewer cameras about.

Rothwell Gardens is a row of twelve rather grand, late-Victorian houses, fronted by a pleasantly leafy private road, which sweeps off Rothwell Lane and back into it again, taking in a narrow strip of land as it does so, to nurture the trees which provide the leaves which put up the price of the houses no end. (Remember, I write this in a realtor's office; these details occupy my mind.) Rothwell Lane in the seventies provided excellent shopping facilities: a small grocer, a drugstore, a hardware store, a stationer, an antique shop, a shoe repairer, and so on. Now, of course, things have changed. The business tax has driven these useful and friendly shopkeepers out of business, and bathroom design and lingerie shops have taken their place. (Marion says they must be tax-loss enterprises—she sees no way they can make a decent living for anyone.) Now the dwellers of the Rothwells—the Lane, the Crescent, the Gardens— go up to the new Sainsbury's in Camden Town like anyone else, fighting their way through a maze of traffic and fumes to get there, waylaid and made to feel guilty by the new beggars and street dwellers of Camden.

The houses of Rothwell Gardens inspired loyalty and love. The rest of us moved out of the area as the horrors of the inner city pressed in upon us: Susan and Vinnie went first, to Richmond; Rosalie and Wallace, Ed and myself followed. But Leslie Beck stayed where he was, clung to the property through good times and bad —married for it and pimped for it, suffering, no doubt, as it suffered, from storms, blocked gutters, woodworm, and despair. (If the house fails, by some sympathetic magic, the owner fails, too. These things are known but seldom spoken of at Accord Realtors.) Twelve Rothwell Gardens is now worth a million pounds—if Leslie can find a buyer, that is. How much he would profit by selling it is another matter. It may be mortgaged above its current value, for all I know. Building societies and banks, at the time of the real estate boom in the eighties, often advanced money in excess of the value of the house, leaving borrowers who assumed, wrongly, that those who lent money would be meaner and more prudent than those who borrowed it, in the end, both sorry and astonished.

The Becks, being the grandest of us, and living in the biggest and best house, were well able to patronize the rest of us. No doubt we resented it. Rosalie and myself lived in Bramley Terrace, around the corner, a pleasant row of tall narrow houses built in the 1820s to the same classic design, like facing like, and still, I was pleased to see when I went retracing our old stamping grounds the other day, intact. These houses are now worth some half a million pounds (if you can find a buyer)—smaller by a third than the Rothwell Gardens property, but worth more proportionately, being cheaper to maintain and, if you can stand running up and down the stairs, easier to live in. Back in the sixties, a couple such as Ed and myself, the one a publisher's junior editor, the other on the editorial staff of the *Consumers Watchdog*, could comfortably afford to buy a house in Bramley Terrace, even when the other lost her job for attending too much to her children and too little to her work. Or so it was alleged.

I took Rosalie's Catharine with me on this outing into the past. I thought she might like to see the place where she'd spent her first few years, the streets in which she played. In the seventies, little girls could still play in the streets. Catharine said none of it seemed familiar at all. Then she went down on her knees.

"Are you praying?" I asked in alarm, but she was only shortening herself, to see if the street was recognizable from a different angle. And, yes, indeed it was, or so she claimed.

"Can you remember being happy?" I asked. What we want, after all, is for our children to remember happy childhoods, though many of them seem to have grizzled throughout, and it was none of our doing, I'll swear.

"Only if I don't think about it too carefully," she replied, and I wondered what in the world Rosalie and Wallace could have done to make it happier.

"I always felt like a cuckoo in the nest," she said.

Well, what are any of us except statistics? According to research on tissue typing, one in seven of us does not belong to the father we think we do. Add to this mere ordinary variations of temperament, intelligence, and rather aesthetic perception, and it is hardly surprising that so many of us feel like cuckoos, not fitting in the nest in which we find ourselves.

Rosalie and Wallace lived around the corner at No. 7 Bramley Terrace. The houses on their side of the Terrace were without gardens, they having been stolen by the big houses of Rothwell Gardens in the 1890s. The lower branches of the Bramley apple trees, which had originally been part of a large orchard, and had given the Terrace its name, were now used for the swings of the Rothwell Gardens' children. The kids of the rich can flourish anywhere: their parents have seen to that. Wallace climbed mountains and was away a lot. Rosalie looked after the kids and occasionally restored antique china. Bramleys are the large green sourish apples which fluff up when cooked and make excellent pies. Items of fact are easy to pluck out of the memory; affect—by which I mean feeling, response—is more of a problem.

Perhaps we were all cuckoos in nests to start with, which is why we ended up in our ancient apple orchard, like seeking out like, trying to puzzle out what was going on. The Bramleys, for all of us, was a new neighborhood, a step up toward where we felt our natural home to be. You could say, in relation to Leslie Beck, that once settled there, we set out compulsively to create as many new cuckoos as seemed feasible within the bounds of matrimony and accepted behavior. The life of the cuckoo, after all, is pretty good: uncomfortable in its nest to begin with, but rapidly and ruthlessly consuming all available nourishment until its maturity; and then it's off. It was hatched both greedy and ungrateful.

Rosalie came out of Scotland as a girl; her father was a baker; she rode down to England on the back of her boyfriend's bike, the works of Tennyson in her satchel; she ditched him, went to secretarial college, moderated her Glaswegian accent, got in bed with an antique dealer, learned furniture, ditched him, took up with a bookseller, learned the language and attitudes of the artistic middle classes, met Wallace outside a TV studio, and married him. (Her bookseller had just revealed a wife.) Wallace was tall and good-looking, difficult and remote. Nor was the marriage nearly as bad as it could have been. Rosalie admired him; she, too, was carried away, for a time, by the mystique of the mountain. She could, she once told me, enjoy sex with anyone. This could only be her good fortune.

I think Wallace treated sex with Rosalie as he treated mountains: something to be attacked with energy, but not too often; surmounted, finished, a flag planted to automatic applause, and then a nice long rest. He looked as craggy as one of his peaks, with bony knees and a prominent Adam's apple. He was alert and practical and considerate enough once problems were explained, but you could wear yourself out explaining. Silence and suffering might sometimes seem a preferable option, and I suppose along with those go, if only as alliteration, a propensity to secrets. Rosalie looked robust enough; she had a lot of dark hair which half hid her very pale face and grew so vigorously you thought she'd have had energy enough to look after herself, whatever happened, and so it proved. She would keep what you could see of her rather heavily hooded eyes downcast. Her mouth was almost lax. In the beginning she looked good in trousers, having a long, straight back and narrow hips, but she never seemed to know it, or, at any rate, to care enough to retain these assets after Wallace fell off his mountain. When Rosalie opened the door to you, you knew she would not judge you, or take offense. If you were her friend, you were part of her life, and that was that. She was generous; Wallace was not. Rosalie liked the fridge full. Wallace liked it empty. Rosalie poured wine to the rim of glasses while Wallace winced.

Since Wallace dictated the amount of housekeeping money available, Rosalie was unable to keep up with the Becks when it came to giving dinner parties, nor do I think she wanted to. The Becks liked to serve champagne, and begin the meal with smoked salmon, followed by something like boeuf Wellington—badly enough cooked by Jocelyn, Leslie's first wife. There would often also be a trifle, Leslie's favorite dessert, rich in cream and brandy. Leslie was both rich and lavish, and liked to be seen so. Susan and myself fought back with Elizabeth David's *Mediterranean Cookery,* putting our trust in good cooking and hard work rather than lavish ingredients: Rosalie would serve beef stew and dumplings and be done with it, and Wallace would say, "You see, you don't need to be rich to eat well," and would be the only one not to notice that Jocelyn was moving her feet under Rosalie's kitchen table to shift away the children's toys, and had the air of someone going slumming and not liking it. Leslie just ate with gusto and enjoyed himself.

Jocelyn served dinner on a shiny mahogany table set with the family silver and place mats with "Hunting at Redhen" upon them. Redhen was her uncle's estate. Leslie always drew attention to the mats. He had married above himself, and wanted everyone to know it. He had trained as a surveyor: competence and confidence had enabled him to rise to the top of the old established firm of chartered surveyors, once Agee and Rowlands, now Agee, Beck & Rowlands, and how he managed to sneak in there between Agee and Rowlands and become managing director was perhaps because Chas Rowlands was eighty and an Old Etonian who didn't understand the necessity for work, and Leslie Beck was young, vital, and offered clients glasses of champagne instead of cups of tea, and had friends in the Ministry of Works who, like himself, had passed through grammar school and gone on to Cambridge.

Jocelyn's father was a country doctor whose cousin was an earl; Jocelyn rode to hounds, and if she knew nothing else, knew how to behave, and how other people should. Leslie was vague about his own background—his father a civil servant in Lancaster? What did that mean? Train driver? Tax inspector? Whatever it was, Jocelyn, albeit not startlingly pretty, and without fortune, by virtue of her birth and breeding enabled Leslie Beck not just to live at No. 12 Rothwell Gardens, but to entertain, and feel at home among bankers, stockbrokers, and junior ministers of the Crown, the kind of people who could do a man in business a good turn or two. Leslie and Jocelyn Beck had two little girls, Hope and Serena, who were wide and stocky, as was Leslie, and who had inherited their mother's rather large nose and close-together eyes, but not his red, crinkly, and vigorous hair. It was, perhaps, not the most fortunate combination of parental looks, but Rosalie and Nora, Jocelyn's friends, supposed that when puberty overtook the girls, they would blossom. Something would have to happen.

At the time Leslie changed Jocelyn for Anita, Susan and Vinnie were living in Bramley Crescent, a street very similar to Bramley Terrace, only curved, following probably the original path of the river which marked the orchard boundaries and now ran underground, to well up in the basements of the big houses of Bramley Square, and give such a damp problem as to reduce their market value by at least a third—a state of affairs which went on for decades, until the housing boom of the eighties made such details as possible subsidence immaterial. Crescent prices were always twenty percent above Terrace prices; Crescent houses had managed to hang on to their back gardens and dated from ten years earlier, so they kept many original Georgian features, in the form of delicately railed balconies, ceiling roses, and marble fireplaces—rather too pretentious for the size of the house at the time of building, in fact, rather *nouveau,* I would have thought, but looking pretty good a hundred and fifty years on, and much sought after. The paper value of Vinnie and Susan's former house in the Crescent is some three-quarters of a million pounds; of Ed's and mine in the Terrace, under a half million. I don't know why this should make us feel inferior, but it does. Only Leslie Beck, of all of us, still lives round there. Anita died there.

This kind of property detail didn't occur to me until I started work at Accord Realtors. Please bear with me. I am reminded of the weaver bird, who spends his life building elaborate nests, picking up pieces of glass and silver foil, displaying them before his home. Look at me, look at me, what have I not achieved! How it sparkles! Come live with me and be my love—oh, glorious me!

Susan worked as a speech therapist for the local education authority, those being the days when such specialists were publicly funded; so she had not just the value of her house but the constant reassurance of her virtue to keep her warm, not to mention Vinnie, who had recently qualified as a doctor and was large, plump, fleshy, noisy, emotional, sensual, and animated. At that time they were seen as a foil for each other: Susan cool, critical, earnest, neat, humorless. But those were the days when Vinnie won every time, when society itself was on the side of the hedonist, the bon vivant, and Susan loved him and would take his views and his tastes, and not struggle for her own identity.

Vinnie worked part-time in the Bramley surgery and wrote *Help Yourself to Health* books, which sold well—well enough for Vinnie and Susan, when they felt the time had come to leave the central city for the suburbs, to buy a big house in the best part of Kew, still near enough to Richmond for us to meet up in the supermarket, when fate so decrees, but way, way beyond anything Ed and I could afford, let alone Rosalie, out of the proceeds from Wallace's insurance policy.

I do not think I should work at Accord Realtors for much longer; it makes me envious and materialistic. Better to do a stint at the housing charity and have shock treatment for the condition.

At the time Anita supplanted Jocelyn, Marion lived in the basement flat of Leslie Beck's house and had student status. She paid a reduced rent in return for helping with Jocelyn's children, and supplemented her income by babysitting and doing odd jobs for the others in our circle. Marion's father was a small-town builder, normally unemployed, her mother an idle housewife, and Marion—the cuckoo in their messy nest—a tall, slender, fastidious, wide-eyed girl. She had started her working life boringly in a bank, and been put, almost accidentally, in charge of a touring show of contemporary artists sponsored by that bank. Here she met my husband, Ed, and as a result, after taking a course in fine art at the Courtauld, had ended up owning a West End gallery, and richer than any of us. Potted histories.

The sad fact was that all of us, though we tried hard to be

egalitarian, and to tell ourselves that money didn't matter, took on the comparative status of the accommodation in which we lived. The Becks couldn't help but patronize; we in the middle jockeyed for precedence, and Marion was the poor relation. She sat at table with us, but spent more of her time helping clear dishes for whichever hostess it was in proportion to the relative status of whichever host, thus having it in her power to define that status. And we deferred to her judgment: she was the witness to the life.

Such was the group which Leslie and Jocelyn would gather round their dinner table from time to time. We were the second division, it is true. We would get to hear, via Marion, how the Becks had had the almost great and nearly famous—leading architects, writers, politicians—to other dinners; for these more formal events, we, apparently, were not fit guests. We consoled ourselves that we were couples he *liked,* not the ones he had to invite if his plans for the development of London's docklands and inner cities and so forth, in which Agee, Beck & Rowlands increasingly involved themselves, were to materialize.

But on with our story, reader, back to the convulsive day when Leslie Beck changed wives. As Rosalie knocked on the door she heard the sound of shrieking. Could it be Hope and Serena, usually so stolid, for some reason not at school? She wondered whether just to slip away, but she looked forward to the occasional morning cup of coffee with Jocelyn, who was always friendly and cheerful, if reserved, and Rosalie, especially if Wallace was away on an expedition, could often feel isolated, trapped at home and powerless with little Catharine. And besides, she did like to compare Catharine, a lively and handsome child, with her secret half-sisters, always to Catharine's—and thereby her own—advantage. Portraits of Leslie, Jocelyn, Hope, and Serena were hung side by side in the hallway, painted by a lady artist of some note, who, Rosalie and Nora agreed, seemed to like Leslie but loathe Jocelyn, Hope, and Serena. Their pallid faces, dumplinglike, rose on tiny necks from overbroad shoulders. Leslie at least seemed carved in solid rock, and was without a neck at all, which rather suited him. And art is art: Leslie Beck was known to understand it, and Jocelyn not. So the grisly cartoons—as Susan's husband, Vinnie, described them—hung on the wall and were much admired, and rose in value year by year, and ensured that no member of Beck's legitimate family could ever feel too well of themselves, or believe that if all else failed they could rely on their looks to get by.

Rosalie and Wallace would no more have had their portraits painted and hung on the wall than they would have robbed a bank: it was not their style; they did not live in the spirit of self-regard. Nor did Ed and I, at that time, have the sense of dynasty, let alone the time available, required for such an enterprise—forget the money.

Reader, I realize there are a great many people on the literary palette I have chosen; somehow I have to draw their portraits clearly in your head. It has the makings of a problem, I can see. Other people's lives are as full of detail as one's own, and in real time our own detail takes some sixteen waking hours to get through, and another eight sleeping—and heaven knows what adventures the mind has in sleep—so the problem of the setting up of characters on the page is daunting. I wonder, sitting here at Accord Realtors, how the convention has arisen by which you, the reader, who know Leslie Beck's exact height—one of our circle, one night, no doubt with many a muffled giggle of excitement, measured both Leslie's height and the length of his penis, respectively five feet ten and ten inches when erect (and now you know something else), one-seventh, exactly, of his height—are content not to know similar measurements for everyone else. Perhaps it is that the reader assumes a norm unless informed otherwise? If Rosalie has crossed eyes, you assume I will tell you. If Marion is four feet five, ditto. (Actually, she's five feet eleven, on the margin of exceptionality; now you know that, too.) I'm five feet three, which is pretty pathetic.

I, if you remember, am Nora, married to Ed, the publisher, and the one writing this book of an afternoon up at Accord Realtors.

Marion Loos is the one who describes herself as a spinster, runs the art gallery, and sold her baby to get it going. (I was going to break that to you later. It was, of course, Leslie's baby; I don't want you throwing the book aside, crying "This is ridiculous." Not my fault that what is true can also be ridiculous. Blame God, who invented Leslie of the active penis, not me. Me, I'm just filling in an idle afternoon as the recording angel, waiting for the property market to rise.)

Marion also has two indistinguishable cats, Monet and Manet.

Rosalie is the one who's gone to fat and seed, and whose husband, Wallace, fell off the mountain, or perhaps did not; her elder child, Catharine, was fathered by Leslie Beck and the two events may, of course, be connected. One day Rosalie may well tell me and I will tell you. I am pretty sure my son Colin is not Leslie Beck's; I am pretty sure Ed is Colin's father. If I am going very carefully through the past, it may be in the attempt to reassure myself on these two separate counts. But memory is so selective; wishful thinking presses it into service all the time.

Jocelyn Beck was Leslie Beck's first wife; Anita Beck was his second wife. I speak about Jocelyn in the past tense not because, like Anita, she is dead but because (a) she has moved out of our lives, and (b) by custom and practice, first wives are perceived to have existed in the past. Though to be fair, if Jocelyn married again, from her point of view Leslie Beck would also be considered unentitled to the luxury of the present tense.

Susan, married to Vinnie, was our friend until a couple of years ago, when she did something so terrible, she, too, gets to be put into the past tense, but she still lives near us all in Richmond, and I have an idea we will soon be forgiving her, or she us. It takes an illness, or a death, or just the passage of time, at least among women, for the power of shared experience to overcome the transitory nature of affront. I know it is not proper to say, "Oh, women are like this" and "Men are like that," because the more we emphasize gender differences, the more they are used against women, and to men's benefit; but nevertheless, I think it is safe to say, cautiously, that men cling to their hatreds, their taking of offense, more than do women. That may well be because men are more likely to come rushing at each other, with their axes raised, than are women, who might like to but would have to drop the babies so to do. Just as when estrogen levels sink in a woman, it is safe for society to give her hormone-replacement therapy, which keeps a female female, soft, sweet, and smiling, but antisocial to give the aging man testosterone injections, for if you do he runs round raping women and hitting other men on the head. What a bummer!

While we contemplate this problem, and come to terms with it, the temporary solution is, of course, for women just to hand the babies over to the men. Susan tried this with Vinnie for a time; she went out to save the world and he looked after Amanda. But perhaps she chose the wrong baby: it looked so like Leslie.

Susan now just nods politely and says hello should she run into one of us at the supermarket or the station, and we'll even say a word or so about the weather and political events, but she is no longer trusted with feelings or enthusiasms or woes, the very stuff of friendship. All the same we miss her, and I expect she misses us. One of us will go rushing at her with arms outstretched, and the business of reconciliation, which takes nations decades, will be done in a trice. Just I'm not going to be the one to do it. But more of that later. We were recapping.

The children are Catharine and Alan (Rosalie's), Richard, Benjamin, and Colin (mine; *I'm Nora*), and Barney, Amanda, and David (Susan's lot; they get mentioned because the animosity of the adults has not been allowed to infect the children). Marion's baby wasn't around long enough to be named. I feel peculiar even mentioning it; we swooshed the episode out of our minds so fast, and yet I suppose this particular child was the key to the Leslie Beck Story.

Leslie Beck, whose penis was exactly one seventh of his height. I know; it was I who measured both.

True confessions!

I've never told anyone about that, either, until now. If only the recession would end, and the property market look up again, I wouldn't have time to contemplate my life in this way; there'd be no time to so much as consider the state of my navel, out of which, like scarves from some magician's very deep and personal hat, I seem able to draw events and memories, like bloody entrails. . . .

My fear is this: Supposing I were to draw out too many, or they started spilling out of their own accord, uncontrolled; how could I continue to digest? I might just die from loss of undisclosed material. We bury memories out of consideration for our mental health.

Myself and Leslie Beck, dancing naked around a room! And where was my husband, Ed, at the time? Safely at home, believing I had gone to see my mother in the hospital. She was in a coma, and so couldn't report back whether or not I'd sat by her bedside as a good daughter should. And what house were we in, Leslie and I, dancing and measuring? Why, No. 12 Rothwell Gardens. And what room were we in? Anita's bedroom? Of course!

When Leslie Beck came to Marion's gallery with a painting by poor dead Anita of that very same bedroom, and Marion went round to Rosalie's and wept, and Rosalie handed the event on to me, and I wrote it down, doing my best to stand in Marion's perfect (I won't say polished; they would be too new to need polishing) shoes, and speak out of her persona—Marion's "I"—as reported to Rosalie, who is closer to her than I am, as interpreted by me, Nora, in a piece of writing I polished and polished, and am proud of, I suggested that the source of Marion's disturbance was guilt. But I don't think Marion ever feels guilt, nor is Rosalie much given to it. I am the one whom it disturbs.

So here we are, back at the beginning, in the 1970s. Leslie Beck

is still married to Jocelyn (just), and Rosalie has maneuvered her
stroller up the steps of 12 Rothwell Gardens, the better to sustain
her secret, wobble it like a loose tooth with the tongue, to find out
if it's still hurting, and found Jocelyn in crisis. Or such is Rosalie's
account of it.

Jocelyn Beck, so says Rosalie, flung open the door. She was
wearing a silk dressing gown with nothing underneath; it fell open,
and Rosalie could see the pink-nippled breasts—larger than she'd
imagined—and a glimpse of black pubic hair. Jocelyn's normally
well-ordered hair was wild, her eyes pink and smeary. She sobbed;
she was hysterical; she pulled Rosalie to her and clasped her, which
relieved Rosalie, who had thought that perhaps Jocelyn had somehow discovered that Leslie was Catharine's father. Little Catharine,
startled, began to cry. Hope and Serena stood at the back of the
hall, silent and distressed. "I phoned Leslie's office," wept Jocelyn,
"and someone left the receiver off the hook. I overheard what was
going on. Leslie is having an affair with someone he works with."

"How could you tell," asked Rosalie, "from just something
overheard?"

"It's too terrible for me to say it," said Jocelyn, mouth puckering
again. "How did I end up being married to such an awful person?"

"It may all be a mistake," ventured Rosalie. "Has he said
anything?"

"Of course he hasn't," snapped Jocelyn, bad temper beginning to
replace distress. "I know who it is now, at least, and he can't talk
himself out of it. She's a boring, ugly, and common woman. Her
name's Anita Alterwood. I never paid her any more attention than
I did the daily help. She whines when she answers the phone."

"I don't suppose it's anything very serious," said Rosalie. "You
know what Leslie is," and she quieted Catharine, persuaded Jocelyn
to get dressed and wash her face, and ruthlessly sent Hope and
Serena out into the garden to play. Rosalie always enjoyed taking
charge in a crisis. She gave Jocelyn two of the tranquilizers her

doctor had given her because when Wallace was away she couldn't sleep properly for worry, and if she did, she only had nightmares of him lying dead and broken at the foot of a crevasse. ·

Days similar to this one, in which Jocelyn discovered Anita's place in her husband's life, are lived through by wives all over the world. That they happen is not so unusual. Remarkable and awful days, all the same, and memorable, when the very foundation of existence shifts and alters, and all the love, the nurturing care, and the self-sacrifice which marriage to a man entails is revealed in a flash as folly, thereby making the self a fool. Within a second the future shifts into uncertain gear, and the prospect of domestic redundancy looms, and self-esteem takes a swift dive down into the bottomless pit—perhaps that very same deep magician's hat I spoke of earlier—and it's all she can do to steady it, prevent it being lost forever. And the fact that it happens every day to so many doesn't make it any better when it happens to you. Insecurity dogs the life of the dependent woman, yapping at her heels. And most women, wages being what they are, remain dependent, no matter how hard they work. Takes two wages, these days, to keep up one home.

I daresay it happens to men, too; of course it does, on discovering the infidelity of a wife, the coming home to a note on the mantelpiece and an empty bed. But the shock for men seems more sustainable; the abandoned woman has far lower a status in society than the abandoned male. "You're so old-fashioned, Nora," I hear Rosalie complain, even as I say it. "Because you think something, you assume the thought is universal. It isn't. Who do you think is thought better of by the world, Marion or Leslie Beck? Marion, of course." I'm not sure Rosalie's right. If Leslie Beck wants to remarry, he'll be able to. But Marion will have a problem finding someone to take her on, even if she goes about it the right way, which she won't. "Oh, Nora" (Rosalie again), "please get it out of your head that it's sad to be single."

Back to the day that is seared into Rosalie's memory: the day she helped Jocelyn come to terms with the truth about Leslie Beck. She ran down to the basement in the hope of finding Marion, but Marion was out at a lecture on cubism, or whatever. So Rosalie ran up again to find Jocelyn beating the scrubbed pine kitchen table with her rather large and competent fists; she was washed but not dressed. Hope and Serena were outside swinging on the swings that hung from the apple trees which by rights belonged to Bramley Terrace.

"I could understand," said Jocelyn, "if he had an affair with someone better than me, but why does he have to choose my inferior? What does that make me in the eyes of the world?"

"The world doesn't have to see it," said Rosalie, rather put out to find Jocelyn now more concerned with her public image than with personal grief. In those days we were all, being younger, a good deal more censorious than we are now. We thought there were certain ways in which people ought to behave, in order to conform to the norm of the good and the nice, the orthodoxy of the civilized classes. You must not be materialistic; you must not be elitist; you must stifle anger; you must pursue consensus, not force confrontation; and so forth. Only when the lights were out, or faces turned the other way, did we behave with a depravity we felt to be singular to us, though of course it was not; only when really pushed did we scream and shout, report the au pair to the immigration authorities, sleep with our friends' husbands, cheat the butcher, smack our children, run out into the street in our nighties, hope our husbands would swim out to sea and never come back. We hated and despised ourselves, and others, when we did it. These days we are less likely to condemn others, because we can no longer avoid the notion that others are no different from "us." Condemn your sister, condemn yourself. Condemn your brother, live lonely forever! A hard lesson, but we learned it. Presently I will forgive Susan. I can feel it coming on.

And it is true enough that Rosalie would have felt better if news had come of Leslie Beck's infatuation, not with his typist, but with, say, a film star. To be rejected in favor of someone of higher status makes it easier to maintain one's self-esteem as fate buffets it about. When a man takes a girl twenty years his wife's junior as sexual partner, it is certainly painful, but the passage of years is not the wife's fault. If he prefers a working girl, a mere subordinate, and she is the same age as his wife, and plainer than his wife, and her merits observable only to her husband and not the world, what can that make of his wife? Except she must have done something terrible. Cast out, rejected, sent home to her parents, no good in any society in the world.

Rosalie was upset, too. She conceded to Jocelyn the rights of the wife—prior use, and so forth—but felt, as you would, reader (should you be female, which I can't take for granted), that if Leslie Beck was going venturing outside his marriage, it ought to be back into her, Rosalie's, arms. She was willing enough.

Rosalie remembered saying to Jocelyn on that Day of Dread, "Jocelyn, perhaps you've misinterpreted some casual conversation? Perhaps it was a crossed line? Whole lives can't change because someone leaves a phone off the hook."

Oh no?

"I'll tell you what I heard," said Jocelyn. "If Leslie says, 'Shut the door, Anita, I want to fuck you sitting on my knee,' and the other one says, 'But Leslie, you wanted this letter to Austin's typed in order to catch the mail,' and Leslie replies, 'Okay, then we'll do both at the same time,' I reckon there is no mistaking what is going on."

And Rosalie thought a little and said, "Jocelyn, these may have been voices heard in your head. Fantasies," but remembering the way Leslie Beck had once crept up on her from behind while she was making sandwiches in her own kitchen, remembering the feel of sand and surf on the skin, Rosalie supposed the voices to be real enough.

Rosalie stopped feeling jealous quite suddenly and felt instead that she was on Leslie Beck and Anita's side and wished them every good luck in the world: Jocelyn was the kind of woman on whom a man could never creep up. He would have to wash well first and ask permission, which would be grudgingly given. No doubt many of the women at the Becks' first-division dinner parties, the ones who wore real diamond brooches, carefully placed, not hasty ethnic ornamentation slung around necks and arms, were of that particular nature. We second-division types don't bargain with our bodies; it isn't done. We tend to offer ourselves freely, perhaps too freely, for a little excitement and the preservation of our marriages, for our children's—and, indeed, our husbands'—sake. I suspect Rosalie, Susan, and myself all married men with a little less sexual energy than ourselves—that is to say, truly *nice* men. We were always on the wooing side of the male-female divide, not that of those consenting, and then only just, to be wooed. The former seldom get given furs and diamonds; the latter do. But, then, we don't want them. We would rather have the soul of a man than his money.

Marion watched it all from her flat down below and never got married at all. It was dark and damp down there in the early seventies, before the builders were brought in to turn the premises into something rather more like a rentable garden flat than a mere basement for storage and servants. It was from those earlier days that Marion dates her asthma.

But back to the day of dread. Jocelyn rose from the table, threw off her wrap, and stalked naked from the room. Rosalie admired the pink and solid perfection of her body, her bold high breasts, the muscular buttocks, the general sense of unavailability. But Jocelyn wasn't waiting for admiration; she just wanted to get dressed as quickly as possible. Rosalie picked up the wrap and folded it. Leslie Beck never liked to see women's clothes thus discarded. He liked them properly hanging in the cupboard. He would fold his own clothes even while his penis grew to its full ten inches, one-seventh of his height.

Jocelyn came back smartly dressed in a white blouse and a navy skirt.

"Where are you going?" asked Rosalie. "Don't do anything silly. Remember you've been munching tranquilizers." She had taken the opportunity of giving Catharine some milk from the Beck fridge and a biscuit from the Beck tin; she felt the little girl was entitled to it. But Jocelyn was on the phone. She called the man at Rothwell Hardware and asked him to come over at once to change the locks. Then she called her mother.

"Mummy," said Jocelyn, "I'm so upset. Leslie is leaving me. He's going to live with his secretary. Daddy must cut off his allowance at once, and I think he should ask for the car back."

Hope, or was it Serena, out in the garden, began to scream. She'd fallen off the swing, or, rather, the branch that had supported it had snapped. Apple is a soft wood and not suitable for swings, but try telling that to the cuckoo dwellers of Rothwell Gardens, rejoicing in their stolen orchard, home at last. Rosalie ran outside at once to help. Hope lay winded and stunned on the ground; Serena heaved with an asthma attack. They were hopeless children, thought Rosalie. They would reflect little glory on Leslie Beck, who loved glory. Jocelyn stayed on the phone for some time; now she was talking to her lawyer. She wished for a divorce from Leslie on the grounds of mental cruelty, and a court injunction to keep him out of the house in the meanwhile. "Jocelyn," begged Rosalie, returning with Hope in her arms, "please don't be hasty. At least talk to Leslie." But Jocelyn would not listen.

Whereupon Marion, thank God, came home from her lecture and volunteered to take Hope to the emergency room for an X-ray in case she had a concussion, and took Serena along as well because she was turning blue about the lips. It was, as Marion later said, that kind of day. Either nothing happens for ages and ages, or everything happens at once.

Marion took the children to the hospital in Jocelyn's car. "Shouldn't you go to the hospital, too?" asked Rosalie of Jocelyn. "You are their mother."

"Hope's perfectly all right," said Jocelyn. "I was falling off horses onto my head all through my childhood, and there's nothing wrong with me. What's a swing? And as for Serena, she's just demanding attention. She can't bear Hope getting it all. If Marion's so fussy, let her do it. I expect she only wants an excuse to borrow the car."

She went up into the bedroom and Rosalie followed, since Jocelyn had with her the garden shears. Jocelyn took Leslie's beautiful, if rather stodgy, suits from the filled wardrobe and flung them into a pile on the bed; then, picking out the trousers, she started cutting them up, slicing first from crotch to waist. Catharine had fallen asleep in her stroller and remained in the kitchen. Rosalie again begged Jocelyn to consider that she had been taking tranquilizers, which can have the side effect of turning the taker violent, and pleaded with her just to stop and sit down, or Rosalie would feel it was all her own fault. She pointed out that perhaps if Jocelyn simply did nothing, waited for Leslie to return and then talked quietly to him, perhaps suggested family therapy, the matter might resolve itself and the marriage end up stronger than ever. Wasn't it a pity—the house, the children, the friends, everything, so much at stake . . . ? But still Jocelyn slashed and ripped.

"The man's sex-mad," she said. "He's an animal. He's disgusting. My father paid for the suits. They're mine to do with as I please."

Leslie had told Susan, and Susan had told Rosalie, and Rosalie had told me, that Jocelyn thought sex once every six weeks was generous. Jocelyn's father, it seemed, had told her when she was little that once every two months was the norm, and Jocelyn had this frequency of "intercourse," as she called it, imprinted somewhere in her psyche. Her father was a doctor, so how could she doubt him? And we all knew about Leslie's predicament, though we never talked about it among ourselves, thinking it was restricted information, as indeed it was. But we thought less of Jocelyn for what we saw as meanness.

One of the most noticeable ways in which 12 Rothwell Gardens differed from the rest of our houses, apart from the size and the number of rooms and the width of the stairs, was that it was without bookshelves. It seemed that Leslie and Jocelyn seldom read anything except the newspapers, and Jocelyn subscribed to *Vogue*, though to what end was not apparent. The rest of us read novels and so had some idea of what went on in other people's heads; even Wallace would carry a thriller in his backpack, to read in his tent in a snowstorm. Jocelyn would sometimes read historical biography, but very few biographers carry details as to frequency of intercourse in their subjects' lives, so once the idea of every two months had been put into Jocelyn's head, how was she to replace it by any other? Jocelyn exemplified the sad life of the rich, which we liked to believe in. It stopped us from feeling jealous, and not feeling jealous made us think better of ourselves.

"Why not go down to Leslie's office," suggested Rosalie, "and have it out with him? You might feel better."

"Bloody Marion's got the car," said Jocelyn, snipping and tearing, "to take the bloody children to the hospital."

"I'll call a taxi," said Rosalie, and did. When it came, Jocelyn, having finished her task of cutting up trousers, but still tearing socks to pieces with her teeth for good measure, got in without protest.

Agee, Beck & Rowlands had its offices in one of those rather pleasant squarish houses in a staid road behind Fitzroy Square, where well-established firms of architects, surveyors, and structural engineers have their offices.

Picture the scene. (In the days when we still dined out, Rosalie often dined out on it.) Rosalie pays off the taxi. The front door of Agee, Beck & Rowlands is closed. There is an intercom attached to the side of the door, a button you press and a panel into which you speak, and are heard if you are lucky. The ground-floor window is open; this fine spring day offers the first sun and warmth of the season. Standing in the window, looking out and stretching even as Jocelyn and Rosalie watch, is Leslie Beck. He looks handsome, satisfied, and well entertained, as no doubt he is: stocky, cheerful, vigorous. Can that be Anita at the electric typewriter behind him? A rather plain and dowdy girl, with a large nose, a dull complexion, and her hair in an elaborate and old-fashioned beehive? Is it the same letter she is engaged in—the one to Austin's? Perhaps she has been obliged to retype it, inasmuch as she failed to get it perfect the first time round? This is before the days of the word processor, remember; there was a lot of retyping to be done, a great deal of giving up and starting afresh. Or perhaps that was just Rosalie's fancy, and the Austin letter was already in its envelope and six more done since. Though if Anita's typing was anything like her cooking proved to be, that was unlikely.

Be that as it may, Leslie saw Jocelyn and Rosalie, and first he blanched, according to Rosalie, and then he smiled.

"Darling," he cried from the window, "how wonderful to see you. And Rosalie. And Catharine, your new baby! The more little girls in the world, the better. Just push the door and come on in."

Catharine was fifteen months old, but Rosalie could see that this was no time to remind him.

"Bastard!" Jocelyn was shrieking, for all the street to hear. "Fornicating pig! Adulterous swine! I'm going to chop it off and feed it to my father's dogs. It's unnatural, it's fiendish, it's monstrous."

Somehow she had managed to bring the garden shears with her; now she brandished them. Leslie Beck, with surprisingly quick reflexes, slammed down the window and vanished from view. Passersby turned. A startled face, that of Mr. Roger Agee—Rosalie had once been privileged enough to dine with him at the Becks'—looked out of the top window. Anita Alterwood, for it was indeed she, rose from her typewriter and for a moment took Leslie's place at the window. She half smiled; she seemed both displeased and yet gratified.

"Jocelyn," pleaded Rosalie, "you're playing into her hands. Can't you see?"

"Bitch!" yelled Jocelyn. "Whore, slut. What do you use for hair spray? Leslie Beck's semen? Cupfuls of it?"

"Jocelyn," begged Rosalie. "Please don't. Not like this. Not a public scene. He won't put up with it."

"Good," said Jocelyn savagely, giving Rosalie an ungrateful shove, so that Catharine began to cry. Small children hate it when those allegedly in charge raise their voices and prove themselves not fit for the task.

"Just come home," begged Rosalie, and Jocelyn hesitated for a second, and then tried to push the front door open, hearing the sound of locks on the other side of the grating, but was too late by half a second. The door was now securely bolted. Jocelyn kicked it savagely. Then she crouched down and yelled more insults through the entry-phone panel.

"You're all curs and bitches! You're animals; you're all in heat night and day."

The ground-floor window opened. It was Mr. Roger Agee.

"Jocelyn," he said, "I don't know what's happened, but you're clearly upset. Please just be quiet and I'll come out and we'll talk about it. Probably better if you don't see Leslie just at this very moment."

"Why? Is he having it off with her in the broom closet? You're in on it, too. If you don't fire that woman immediately, I'm reporting you to the director of public prosecution. You and your Berkeley Square development. My lawyer says it stinks! The lot of you stink! I've read the files, and you're all rottener than rotten fish, so don't you tell me what to do, Mr. Roger stinking Agee."

Passersby were gathering now, and in some number. A couple

of gray-suited men, who might well have been senior officials from the Ministry of Works, emerged from a taxi and approached Agee, Beck & Rowlands, and would have come up the steps, but Jocelyn turned on them, too, brandishing the shears.

"My husband is Leslie Beck," she said, "of Agee, Beck & Rowlands, and he's fucking his secretary and I'm his wife, and if you do business with him you're as corrupt and evil as he is. The whole lot of you stink around the crotch!"

Roger Agee apologized to them from his window and said they were being besieged by a madwoman, he was sorry, the police were on their way. They hailed a taxi and departed.

"I'm not mad," shrieked Jocelyn, "the world has gone mad. The whole lot of you are in collusion with that evil bitch."

And Rosalie told me that in her opinion Jocelyn was quite right, everyone was indeed in collusion, if not particularly with Anita, at least with the principle of doing away with everything familiar and whoring after the new and the fresh. Older women are meant to grin and bear it, not rant and protest; rejected wives are no fun. People pay them lip service, but they'd rather, really, they just went away. Besides which, word had got round that Jocelyn would only let Leslie into her bed once every two months, and what sort of wife was that? No one was on her side.

Rosalie took Jocelyn home, because Catharine's wailing began to drown out even Jocelyn's shrieks, and the windows of Agee, Beck & Rowlands were now silent, and the police were on their way. Blinds were pulled; shutters were closed all the way down the street. The place reminded Rosalie of the Chinese embassy in Portland Place, which has looked like that for twenty years: its windows boarded up, blank, and silent, albeit in multi-occupation. Faceless and brooding: does it plan attack or expect it, who can ever tell? I suppose to plan one is inevitably to expect the other. Susan maintains that insomnia is a symptom of repressed anger: you are back in your cave, adrenaline flowing, both planning the tiger's death and expecting it to pounce. Susan can't even let you lie awake at night without construing it as your fault, not your misfortune.

Once they were home, Rosalie left Jocelyn in Marion's charge. Serena had had an injection and was breathing freely. Hope had had her X-ray and nothing amiss had been found, though she was still crying, having been traumatized, Marion explained, by the X-ray machine—in those days a great hefty piece of equipment which swung on angled arms over the patient, like some slow metal monster planning how best to devour its victim.

"I told you not to bother, Marion," said Jocelyn, and then loudly to Rosalie, "Why is it that people you employ to help only ever make matters worse?"

"I should go to bed," said Rosalie, leaving Jocelyn with another couple of Valium.

"I don't think she should take those," said Marion. "They seem to make her very aggressive," but it was too late—Jocelyn had taken them, swilling them down with whiskey, and more whiskey.

"Now I suppose I'll be left to put the children to bed," said Marion. "I was hoping to do my essay."

Rosalie and little Catharine went home to make Wallace's tea. He would be back soon from the TV studios. Jocelyn wept and raved at the kitchen table in Rothwell Gardens. Then she went into Leslie Beck's bookless study and emptied the filing cabinet and got a bottle of olive oil from the kitchen and sloshed it over everything. She pulled down a painting he said was a Watteau and kicked it; she got a Swiss army knife from somewhere—Marion having locked the kitchen door so Jocelyn couldn't get at the knives—and slashed what Leslie Beck said was an undiscovered Stubbs, but which Marion said was only some old horse by some rightly undiscovered amateur; then Jocelyn sat on her chintz sofa in her pretty room, which had the most expensive curtains in all Rothwell Gardens, and wept.

It was Marion, by the way, who usually reported on everything that went on in No. 12 Rothwell Gardens, from the price of the curtains to the absence of books, who confirmed what Leslie had said to Susan, who told Rosalie, who told everyone, about what Jocelyn's father the doctor had led her to expect of married life. Marion would babysit for us as well: news from one house carried fast to the next.

"You can give your life to someone," Marion said to Jocelyn that evening, "and all that someone is, is someone who gets a typist from the pool to sit on his knee with bits of him inside her to type a letter. Perhaps none of it is very important."

Jocelyn said to Marion, "What do you know about anything? You're just some trumped-up bank clerk living rent-free, eyeing my husband, neglecting my children, and traumatizing them at whim."

Marion was affronted and did not help Jocelyn later that evening, when perhaps she should have done.

By eight o'clock in the evening Jocelyn was beginning, in the manner of wives, to miss her husband's return. Dogs do it, too; it is not only wives. If the master fails to return at the expected time, no matter if all he can be expected to do when he arrives is kick and shout, they begin to get restless and wonder what they've done wrong; habit and guilt make them fawn and lick in the instant between his return and his getting the boot in. "I might have imagined it," Jocelyn was saying to Marion by half past eight. "Or perhaps I got a crossed line, as that boring woman Rosalie said. What have I done? Will he ever forgive me? Why did Rosalie make me go round to his office? It's her fault. Poor Leslie; I hope he doesn't go into his study. I'll clean up tomorrow. I'm too exhausted now. I'll wait up till he comes home, and then I'll kiss the hem of his garment and anything else he likes. If he wants me to be an animal, I'll be an animal. Who cares? I give up!" and she called and called Leslie's office, but of course all she got was the busy signal. No doubt, wisely, everyone in the office had taken everything off the hook.

Jocelyn was too drunk and maudlin to hear the telephone ringing in Marion's basement flat. Marion went down to answer it. It was Leslie.

"Is she still there, or has she gone to her mother?" he asked.

"Still here," said Marion.

"Is she quiet?"

Marion, still smarting, told him Jocelyn was quiet now but had done some damage.

"What?"

"She kicked the Watteau to bits and slashed the Stubbs and poured olive oil over the kilims and the prayer rugs. Oil is the worst thing to get out of silk carpets. I think you should come home as soon as possible, Mr. Beck. It isn't fair to leave me responsible for a woman in this condition. I'm too young, and I've got an essay to write."

There was silence for a little. Then Leslie Beck said, "Okay, Marion, I'll see to it," and put down the receiver. Marion checked Hope and Serena, who were safely playing checkers in their bedroom with the television on, and went back to Jocelyn. Jocelyn had taken off all her clothes and finished the whiskey, and was trying to race wood lice across the table. They kept curling up in terror when Jocelyn banged her fist and made the surface they walked on tremble and shake.

The bell rang, and Marion, expecting Leslie Beck, went thankfully to open it. Two men and a woman stood there: one man was a doctor from the practice Vinnie worked for; the other described himself as a psychiatrist, and the young woman as the duty Social Welfare officer. Jocelyn came to the door with no clothes on, took one look at the visitors, darted past them, and would have run down the street had they not caught and gently restrained her. They drew her inside with expert hands, settled her on the sofa, and sat soothingly around her. Jocelyn remembered she had no clothes on

and looked round for them, but Marion, mindful of Leslie, had
already hung them in the wardrobe upstairs, so she gave up. Marion
found her a blanket. Jocelyn said she didn't like wool next to the
skin, so Marion found her a silk bedspread.

"Well, now," they said to Jocelyn when all that was arranged,
"what seems to be the trouble? We hear you've been a naughty
girl."

"Me!" said Jocelyn, rising to her feet, "me! I'm not the one who's
a tart from the typing pool! I'm the wife!"

They tried to ease her down again; Jocelyn declined and jabbed
the duty officer in the eye with her elbow in so doing.

"Sorry," Jocelyn said, not meaning it. "This is my house, bought
with my father's money, and if I want to stand or sit that's my
business, and if you come here uninvited and I happen to have no
clothes on that's your bad luck—or good luck, depending on how
it grabs you."

"Yes," they said, "but we gather there was a little trouble in the
street today."

"Who told you?"

"Your husband. He's very concerned about you."

Jocelyn screamed.

"Now, now," they said, "try not to wake the children," and the
matter of the Watteau and the Stubbs came up, and the fact that
their value was more than half a million pounds was mentioned.

"They're no more Watteau and Stubbs," said Jocelyn, "than I'm
a copulating dog," and she went woof, woof quite sharply at the
lady duty officer.

The three asked Marion for confirmation that Mrs. Beck was acting
out of character, to which Marion, after some hesitation, agreed.
They asked Mrs. Beck if she would agree to admitting herself as a
voluntary patient at Colney Hatch psychiatric hospital, and when
she indignantly said she would do no such thing and asked them

to leave her house, adding that if there was a Rembrandt in the house she'd take an ax to it if she felt so inclined, they nodded to one another and told her in that case she would be compulsorily admitted under section 136 of the Mental Health Act. The duty officer and the psychiatrist held Jocelyn's arms while the doctor administered a sedative, and presently they led her away wrapped in a blanket.

Some twenty minutes after the ambulance left, Leslie Beck let himself into the house. He had Anita with him.

"Thank you for coping," said Leslie to Marion. "I hope you'll be able to see to the children until we can sort things out a little?"

"I can't tomorrow," said Marion. "I've got a lecture."

"I'm sure if you explain the situation," said Leslie Beck, "they'll make allowances."

Anita wandered through the house picking over Jocelyn's satin cushions, shaking her head at the presence of wallpaper, the wall-to-wall carpets in the bedrooms, the fact that she cooked with electricity. Clearly there were changes on the way.

"You mean you have that great big flat down there practically rent-free?" she asked Marion.

"It may be big," said Marion, "but it's damp and there's no proper heating."

"All the same," said Anita, "you've got a bargain there. Leslie's very generous. But someone's got to look after the children, I suppose. I mean to go on working. So you might as well stay."

Leslie reported the destruction of his suits to his insurers over the emergency line, and Anita and he spent the night in the marital bedroom among piles of shredded fabric and teeth-torn socks, and Marion went downstairs and slept like a log, she was so exhausted. She moved out very soon afterward, and our special entree into the ins and outs of the Beck household was gone. As I say, the Becks were never exactly friends: they were from the Rothwells, not the humbler Bramleys. We did not feel for their distress, though I think we should have.

So that was how Anita replaced Jocelyn in Leslie Beck's life, and how Jocelyn lost house, marriage, and children. Women, when the breakup of a marriage appears imminent, should never on any account leave the matrimonial home, as any lawyer will affirm. It leads to all kinds of trouble. Possession, they will add, is nine-tenths of the law, and so it is.

And if you try arguing your case from the nuthouse, which you can be forcibly prevented from leaving, and your family has provided you with the old family lawyers, and Leslie Beck has access to the most expensive ones in town, as Agee, Beck & Rowlands naturally did, why then you don't stand a snowball's chance in hell. Judges don't like the idea of women standing in the street in a respectable part of town shouting abuse at their husbands while those husbands try to get on with their work, especially if respected firms thereby lose clients and business. The more so if you, the shouting woman, claim you were perfectly sane at the time, merely provoked—you having to say that in order eventually to get custody of your children—because not only, they fear, might you make a habit of it, but other women might begin to do the same. It might all end up in rank upon rank of wives of the judiciary making noisy scenes outside the Law Courts. If Jocelyn was sane it looked bad, and if she was insane, worse.

"Framed!" shrieked Jocelyn at the court. "Stitched up!" And they led her back to Colney Hatch, and thereafter a friend of the accused represented her in court and made a pretty bad and drunken job of it, too. But that was Leslie Beck's luck, not his devising.

It does no one any good, in the public or the legal eye, to have carved up the cultural heritage of Europe, and it was difficult, by the time the paintings were produced in court, to affirm that they were not Watteau, not Stubbs, merely Leslie Beck's affectation, his desperate need to be one up on Rothwell Lane Antiques—more of that later—and the family lawyers couldn't see that it would affect the case one way or another whether the paintings were worthless (actually six pounds the one, seven pounds the other, at Rothwell Lane Antiques, as Marion could have affirmed; but no one asked her) or worth half a million between them.

So it went. Leslie divorced his wife and retained possession of the marital home and, for a time, custody of the children. It took Jocelyn some nine months to persuade Colney Hatch that she was no longer insane (she had given up the argument that she'd never been insane in the first place, merely drunk, provoked, and having a low tolerance for Valium; what was her account of herself as sane worth, in the face of a declaration that she was not, on the part of the doctor, the psychiatrist, and the duty officer?). That finally managed, it was another year before she could persuade the court that she was now fit to look after her own children, if she lived with her parents and remained in their care. Leslie undertook not to contest the new custody arrangements if Jocelyn made no claim against 12 Rothwell Gardens. Accordingly, she transferred the property to him by deed of gift, in token of her natural trust and affection for him.

This document, thus worded, was drawn up by the family lawyers. Their offices were in the Berkeley Square area and presently became part of a big new development, in the course of which a whole and perfect row of early-Victorian London town houses were pulled down and a glass-faced office building erected in their place. Agee, Beck & Rowlands played a major part in this development. I only mention this in passing. The value of 12 Rothwell Gardens—especially at that time, when it had a good fewer zeroes on the end of it than it does now—was, of course, minuscule by comparison to the sums of money spent on the Berkeley Square development, and I am not suggesting anyone was bribing anyone. Of course not; it's just that people like to do one another favors. Down here at

Accord Realtors it's very often only drinks in the Black Lion or a good lunch at the Bear, and I've known waiting lists for desired but scarce new cars suddenly to disappear, and for surgical operations likewise, and minor committees to let through rather tricky decisions on the nod after these little social events, and that's only what I know about and not what I don't. Me, I'm just an assistant clerical hand round here. Anyway, what's life without favors? And Rosalie doesn't forget being called "that boring woman" (as reported by Marion), any more than Marion liked it being suggested that she wasn't giving value for money in return for her low rent, and I never liked the way Ed and I were relegated to second dining division, and I suppose the fact is none of us could forgive her for living in the big house with the fabulous Leslie and then allowing him to go to waste, and Jocelyn, frankly, was just never really *likable*.

So here I am, reader, many years later, sitting in Accord Realtors, writing, marveling at the past, when in comes Rosalie herself. She's wearing a kind of maroon velveteen track suit, which I daresay is comfortable, and the thick hair has been grabbed up and wound in a bunch on top of her head and secured with a pleated purple elastic hairband, probably Catharine's, and she seems at ease and happy. She's carrying a Marks & Spencer shopping bag overfull of frozen meals. It's a branch where they pack for you. They must be cutting down on bags, or someone just couldn't be bothered. That's what happens when you wear maroon velveteen track suits out shopping. She has the appearance of neither a vendor nor a purchaser of property, but someone come in to waste time and put possible clients off, and I look round nervously, but neither Mr. Collier nor Mr. Render seems bothered. The property market is so bad that normal misfortune can seem good by comparison.

"Hi," she says, and she smiles and sits on the edge of the desk, and her broad rump squashes right up to my little pot of spring flowers so I have to move it over, and her face lights up and in spite of everything she's pretty.

"I've been thinking about Leslie Beck and Jocelyn," I say, "and all that business."

"She was always half nuts," said Rosalie. "In fact, if a court says you can only have your children if you live with your mother, you might even be three-quarters nuts."

"That doesn't excuse the way Leslie Beck behaved," I say. "At the time it was just something that happened step by step, as you obviously didn't notice, and because no one else seemed to see it as appalling we didn't register it as such, but when you think about it, it was. And he's still about; and God hasn't even punished him."

"He's got older," volunteered Rosalie.

"We all get punished that way," I say.

Mr. Collier is looking over at Rosalie. Rosalie says she doesn't think Leslie Beck behaved worse than another man would in a similar situation. If men can't have sex with wives, and the wives are bad cooks, men seldom understand why they should be expected to hand over to them any proportion at all of their worldly goods.

"I don't remember Jocelyn as such a really bad cook," I say, but Rosalie remembers clearly a certain beef Wellington which Jocelyn once presented: dense, tough, gray meat inside and a thick pastry case outside so solid Rosalie lost a crown.

"If she cooked for Leslie's important clients like that, and we must suppose she did, it wouldn't have done Leslie Beck much good. No," says Rosalie, "women must keep to their side of the domestic bargain. If men pay, women must deliver: sex, home comforts, and kids. Look at the number of men," says Rosalie, "who default on maintenance or argue through the courts till the cows come home that they shouldn't have to pay it, who falsify accounts, bribe witnesses, refuse to buy absent kids socks and shoes, but can manage expensive toys and holidays. They're not nasty men, they're just fighting in the cause of what they see as natural justice. It is unnatural, they think, if the wife isn't in the bed or at the sink, and the kids aren't under their nose, to be expected to pay for them. Why?"

Mr. Collier looks as if he might come over any minute. He is a gray kind of man with a double chin and owl glasses.

"Rosalie," I say, "you only defend Leslie Beck because he's Catharine's father—"

"Don't *say* that—"

"And you have somehow to justify your adulterous relationship with him."

"It's not a question of justifying. Jocelyn wouldn't sleep with him, therefore it wasn't a marriage—"

"Then how come she had those children?"

Our voices were rising. Mr. Collier came over with some property descriptions for me to type. "Sun-drenched patio" had been changed to "agreeable walled yard" in response to rising consumer protest concerning misleading information from the realtor profession. They were cleaning up their own act before the government was tempted to interfere in matters it knew nothing about.

"Isn't it Mrs. Hayter?" Mr. Collier asked. "Wallace Hayter's wife?" Rosalie said yes. Mr. Collier said what a tragedy, what a mystery; her plight had always preyed on his mind. (I was surprised that Mr. Collier had the kind of mind on which things preyed, but then was ashamed of being so easily dismissive of another human being. I find that as I grow older, I have to train myself not to cast other people out of my sphere of inclusion, as it were; it is appropriate to young women, and, to a rather lesser extent, young men, engaged in the full ferocity of their mating behavior, to deride and dismiss those they do not see as appropriate sexual partners, but it ill becomes them when they get older. There!)

Rosalie said it preyed somewhat on hers, too, and Mr. Collier stammered and apologized, and said, since it was lunchtime, why didn't they both go round to the pub. Rosalie said before they left why didn't I come round that evening; Marion had been on the phone to her for hours. I said very well. She dimpled, yes, she did, at Mr. Collier, and at least straightened the elastic waistband before she left.

I got back to "Life Force." Mr. Render dozed.

Now I will allow Marion to take up the story again—that is to say, my version of the events of the following Friday as seen through Marion's eyes, or as I suppose her to have seen them, having only Rosalie's word to go by. In order to transfer the "I" from myself back to Marion, I have had, as it were, to subtract Rosalie's addition to the tales in order to get back to what we so wistfully call "the truth." We writers have a hard task, thus mixing biography and autobiography. I suppose I could just call Marion on the phone and say "What happened, what happened?" and tape the answer and transcribe it, but where would be the fun in that? And would she tell the truth anyway? I'm sure she'd try, but would she manage? I can see I am gracefully and gently edging over into fiction, in thus letting Marion speak, but never mind.

*L*eslie Beck came into the gallery around five o'clock on Friday night. Saturday is the best day for off-the-street sales, and Barbara, Aphra, and myself were busy taking down the MacIntyre and arranging the spring group show, which was to have a flower-and-fish theme. Not necessarily in the same painting, of course. Such a show was Aphra's idea, not mine; but recession makes cowards of us all. Next to pigs, fish sell best, and flowers are always safe. But a group show is not as good a long-term investment as is a one-man show: you may achieve more red dots at the opening, but the real money is in the large, slow-to-move, idiosyncratic canvas by the artist with a known name, which can end up in a Tokyo boardroom or as some palace folly in Sydney, making money every step of the way. Pigs, fish, and flowers end up swiftly—and there is no money in swift—above mantelpieces in the smaller reception rooms, up the stairs, or even in the kitchen of ordinary domestic houses, and this is neither Bond Street style nor appropriate marketing strategy for an ambitious gallery such as the Marion Loos. But the show would hang for three weeks only, would ease the cash-flow problem, and if we were sufficiently lighthearted about it, jokey even, I reckoned we could get away with it and not lose reputation. And it pleased Aphra. MacIntyre had acquired only seven red dots out of twenty possible, but there had been an interesting long-term nibble or two, even one from the Metropolitan in New York. Which you'd never get for fish, flowers, or pigs.

Aphra and Barbara looked up, interested, as Leslie Beck came in. That capacity had not worn itself out, then: to activate at least some response in women, if not one of actual liking. Leslie still comes across as male: men these days, especially young men, tend to register themselves on women as merely more human beings. I had thought this was something to do with my generation, but Barbara and Aphra's response to Leslie made me change my mind: it is men who have altered, softened, who see themselves as people first and of a certain gender second. It is an improvement, I daresay, but it does nothing to cheer me up.

"You didn't come to the memorial service," said Leslie Beck, reproachfully. "You were missed. Serena and Hope were there. They've grown up into fine young women. They were so very fond of their stepmother. Serena's about to make me a grandfather. Hope's a social worker, too dedicated to her work to take the plunge into matrimony."

I said I was indeed sorry to have missed the service, but couldn't afford to leave the gallery at such a critical time. I was glad Hope and Serena were doing well; I had only really known them for a few months when they were little, in my student days. As he could see, we were busy and would be working late into the night as it was.

"Late into the night!" he repeated. "How romantic. Can I be of any help to you ladies? Perhaps I could buy you all dinner afterward? It would cheer me up if I did. Life must go on."

"There's this amazing Japanese around the corner," said Aphra, to my astonishment.

"I'm sure Ben wouldn't mind looking after Holly an extra couple of hours," said Barbara.

What could I say?

"Let me take one end of this," said Leslie to Barbara, of a rather heavily framed MacIntyre. "Don't worry, I'm used to paintings. I know how tender they are. We have a Stubbs at home—you see how hard it is for me to grasp that it's no longer 'we,' but 'I'—so, correction, I have a Stubbs at home. Anita really adored that horse."

"You're still living in Rothwell Gardens?" I asked.

"Of course."

"And Hope and Serena come to stay, I expect, sometimes?"

"They're busy young women," said Leslie, "like you, Aphra, and don't have all that time to spare for their old father. You wait till your little one grows up, Barbara. Take my advice, look after yourself; children can look after themselves. No woman should sacrifice herself for a child. Deny herself pleasures. Life's short."

He looked younger today. His blue eyes were lively; his muscles moved beneath the fabric of his fine cotton shirt. Barbara had belted her dress more tightly, I noticed. I refrained from pointing out that Hope and Serena would be more Barbara's age than Aphra's. I asked instead what had happened to the Watteau. He said briefly he'd sold the painting at the top of the market for thirty-two thousand pounds. It had been much restored, or it would have fetched more. I couldn't resist asking if he'd given a percentage to Mr. Tallow at Rothwell Lane Antiques.

"It was way back in 1970 something," I explained to Aphra and Barbara, "when I was a student at the Courtauld and living in Mr. Beck's basement and helping him look after his two little girls by his first wife."

"Is that one still alive?" asked Aphra, without, I thought, much sensitivity; but I told myself that so far as Aphra was concerned, the seventies were history, and no one grieves for people in history—when would one ever stop?—or refrains from mentioning their demise out of respect to the living who do not want to be reminded.

"So far as I know," replied Leslie. He was wandering in and out of my office, reading my memos, looking over my correspondence, moving Anita's painting into a more favorable position—taking it out into the gallery proper and placing it against a wall in a good light.

"Then," I continued, "one day, when we were all out walking together—that was unusual, but I think it was an election day and Mr. Beck had had to come home early from his office before the polls closed—we passed the window of Rothwell Lane Antiques." I did not care if Leslie overheard. He had invited himself to my gallery. He could not expect much courtesy.

In the window had been two particularly dark and dingy paintings—one a rather sentimental portrait of a girl in a whitish dress, the other a childish version of a horse.

"What do you think those are, Marion?" Leslie Beck asked. "All that time off work up at the Courtauld; you ought to know." I was not, of course, taking time off work to go to the Courtauld; I was taking time off from my studies to see to the Becks' plain and boring little girls, in exchange for a damp and dingy half-underground couple of unheated rooms for which they had no other use—but forget that. Leslie was, and I knew it (in Aphra's language), "winding me up."

"You could say these were a very bad Watteau and a rather less bad Stubbs," I replied, "or you could say someone's favorite uncle painted them and no one had the heart to burn them."

So we all crowded into Rothwell Lane Antiques, with Jocelyn complaining that we couldn't take the time, the polling station was about to close, it was more important to vote than to fill up the house with yet more junk, and Mr. Tallow took the two paintings out of the window for us to examine.

"They've only just come in," he said. "I haven't looked them up in Bénézit."

The shop was filled with the musty smell of damp bindings and woodwormed furniture, but Mr. Tallow, for his stock in trade, also liked the excessive and the exotic: painted ships' figureheads, stuffed birds in cages, and glass eyes vied for space with the more ordinary stripped pine.

Mr. Tallow wanted twenty pounds each for the paintings. Leslie Beck beat him down to six and seven pounds, and would have got the seven down to five had not Hope been keening and Jocelyn lamenting and Serena putting the glass eyes in her mouth.

"If they turn out to be anything," said Mr. Tallow, "I expect you to see me right."

Leslie laughed and said, "Of course," and clinched the deal, and as we left he added, "Of course, Marion here says those paintings are a Watteau and a Stubbs! And she's up at the Courtauld," thus making Mr. Tallow blanch and Leslie laugh.

"Don't be stupid," said Jocelyn as we ran to the polling station. "They're just rubbishy old paintings."

"I'm not so sure," said Leslie. "Marion has a good eye," and he pinched my bottom and I squealed and Jocelyn took offense and we arrived at the polling station with half a minute to spare.

"Who did they vote for?" was all Aphra asked, but I didn't know, and wouldn't have told her if I did. That was Leslie's and Jocelyn's affair.

Leslie called me over, from the other side of the room, and I went, as if it were still all those years ago and myself the drudge again, despising myself for doing it.

"I see the exact place for Anita's painting," he said, and he indicated that prime patch of wall that catches the customer's eye when he enters the Marion Loos Gallery for an opening: facing the door, just to the right.

"I hadn't intended to hang it at all," I said. "It's not in keeping with the rest of the show."

"Really, Marion," said Leslie, "stop sulking. It's the least you can do. You should have come to the memorial service. It hurts me that you didn't."

His face fell sad and silent; his hands trembled—not, I thought, for once, with the Life Force coursing through them, planning some new mischief, but as the effect of real and barely contained sorrow, the desperation of the bereaved, who know that life has to continue, or there'd be no point in lamenting the loss of it for the departed, but can hardly find the will to keep going. "Marion," said Leslie Beck, "we are all getting older. Shouldn't we just forgive and forget? Isn't it time?"

The problem was rather, I thought, that we had all forgotten long ago and were only just now beginning to realize that there was a great deal to forgive: a whole great indigestible lump of it. All the same, he was persuasive.

"And it isn't fair to take it out on Anita," he said. "She doesn't deserve it."

His hand stretched out to touch mine, and I didn't want that.

"Let me think about it," I said, and found something else to do on the other side of the gallery.

Leslie Beck's pinches and pats, in the days of my employment by him, had been quite frequent, but normally happened when Jocelyn was in the room, so I did not take much notice of them, and could, in any case, hardly afford to take offense. But I began to dream of him: alarmingly graphic dreams, in which I could feel the weight of his body, the texture of his skin—a kind of virgin's dream of idealized sex. I think I was a desolate kind of person in those days. Perhaps I still am, or am seen to be by others. I was born strange to my parents, as if I inherited from my mother and father genes which lay undisclosed even to themselves. My mother's mother painted, my father's grandfather played violin in a church orchestra; but the creative urge had bypassed Ida and Eric, who saw only what was under their noses, and could not understand the artist's desire both to interpret what was there and to set up alternatives.

"Do take your nose out of that book," my mother would say, "and go for a healthy walk," and my father would add, only half joking, "That girl will educate herself out of the marriage market if she's not careful." And I would bring home prints from the library, as well as books, and hang them on my bedroom wall, and my mother would say of Picasso, "I could do as well as that standing on my head," and so on, but I don't want to knock them or disparage them. They were kind, even loving, and if the joke during my childhood was, when I pushed away some massive piece of half-cold battered fish, with its limp pile of greasy potato sticks beside, and the red dollop of tomato ketchup (for color), "I reckon that child was switched at birth; she's none of ours," they spoke not so much out of malice as confusion. Other girls had boyfriends; I did not. I daresay I looked down my nose at them.

In storybooks, teachers discover girls like me and ease them out of the cultural desert, but I suppose I was just unlucky. I never encountered teachers who weren't bored, cranky, and in a cultural desert themselves. It was only when I came across Vinnie and Susan, Rosalie and Wallace, and Nora and Ed, and they allowed me into their lively, chattering, responsive circle, and I went into homes where there were books on the shelves and wine to drink, and a kind of cultural hedonism pervaded everything—even, I imagined, the bedroom—and laughter and tears came and went unashamed, that I began to take my first breaths of real life. Susan got me the place at the Courtauld, and Ed and Nora the use of Leslie Beck's basement, and now here I was, in my midtwenties, dreaming of Leslie Beck and wondering how to lose my virginity (though I had a feeling that celibacy and a proper and meticulous response to art history—indeed, to anything—went hand in hand). At that time, mind you, I was making a special study of illuminated manuscripts, and the essay I was trying to write the day Jocelyn was sectioned under the Mental Health Act was on the connection between the monastic life style and the pursuit of excellence. These things can render you impatient with the untidy mess people make of their lives.

It had certainly shocked me to come home from the Courtauld one day and discover Jocelyn hysterical and about to be replaced by Leslie's secretary Anita, Rosalie flapping, little Hope lying in the garden semiconcussed, and Serena gasping for life itself. This was the bad side of cultural hedonism: days such as this one just did not happen back home in Ida and Eric's domain.

And I was upset and a little jealous, I daresay, to discover the existence of Anita. I had thought that if Leslie Beck's eye was to stray anywhere, it would surely be toward me.

Later, of course, when he had lost interest in Anita, she having served her purpose, it finally did; and that is an episode I am not quite strong enough to reassess, but I suppose I had better try, since the reappearance of Leslie Beck in my gallery has made some evaluation of the past inevitable, as if fate intended it, gave us these sets of experiences in the first place the better that we may, later on in life, make some retrospective sense of them. At the time we're glad just to survive them, meeting each wave of chaos as it comes; forget dissecting them.

I hope Leslie does not attempt to pinch or pat Aphra. She's of the new school. She'll bite his fingers off.

"Marion," says Aphra, "Leslie's right. It looks really good just inside the door. We always get red dots there."

(Leslie! So soon the creep has ceased to be a creep, has gained personal and familiar identity in Aphra's eyes. How did he do it? By taking off his jacket and hauling weights about, I supposed, while fresh from a memorial service; and the offer of a real dinner after, of course. Never forget the free dinner.)

"First thing you see when you come in the door."

"See how the light catches the curtains," said Barbara, not apparently to be outdone in treachery. "Your wife was a very accomplished painter, Mr. Beck. And now I've begun to adjust to the hard edges of the comb, I can just about reconcile it with the rest. . . ."

Lucky old you, I thought.

"As to price," said Leslie Beck, "what do you think, Marion? Six and a half thou?"

"You're out of your mind," I said. "A total unknown? In a show where everything's between three and five, with the odd bargain drawing in the six hundreds?"

And Aphra said, "Well, it's going to have pride of place, the first thing you see, perhaps we could risk it. . . ."

And Barbara said, "It has a kind of real quality—you can tell, everything else begins to fade into insignificance. It really is the *pièce de résistance*!"

I wished Aphra would get back to her dingy squat and Barbara back to her baby and the kitchen sink, where she belonged—why did I employ such imbeciles? Leslie Beck smiled at me, and just as a scent can bring with it total recall, so the smile brought with it what I believe is called the feeling tone of those early virginal dreams, more powerful than the memory of anything that came later. I sat down.

"Tired, Marion?" he asked.

"Yes," I said. "It's been a hard week."

"Harder for me," he said, and I knew it was true.

"I take sixty percent commission," I said, still fidgeting.

"You sometimes do thirty percent for friends," said Barbara.

"I didn't really know Anita," I said.

"But you know Leslie," said Barbara.

"As well as a woman can know a man," said Leslie, coy and corny both, sitting down beside me on the little upholstered gilded bench with the curving-away arms I'd picked up at Christie's—a bin end, as it were, from the contents of some middle-of-the-road Renaissance Italian palace. I felt quite ill. "Good lord," he said, "I think we're sitting on a love seat. It belongs in a brothel."

Aphra and Barbara looked at it with interest.

"How does it work?" Aphra asked. "I suppose if the woman hitched her legs over the arm and the man was behind . . ."

"Or if she were on her elbows, crouched . . ." said Barbara.

It was beyond endurance. I asked them to finish hanging the show without me, since I seemed superfluous, wished them well with their Japanese dinner, called a taxi, which fortunately arrived promptly, and went home.

"Thirty percent, then?" inquired Leslie, as I left.

"Take the lot," I said. "Who cares?"

I fed Monet and Manet, soothed myself by stroking them into ecstasy, and listened to a little Vivaldi, which always helps. Then I called Rosalie and talked at her for half an hour.

"Why am I so upset?" I asked her.

"Because you're guilty," Rosalie replied.

"About Anita?" I asked. "So I slept with Leslie Beck. So did a lot of others. What's so special?"

"Guilty about Anita and Leslie Beck, too," she said. "You did him a dreadful injury and he doesn't even know it, and you can't face it."

What injury? I'd spent a lifetime asking Rosalie to explain me to myself; now I began to think I'd rather listen to my own, less facile interpretation. I was Leslie's victim, not he mine. It's always the man's fault, everyone knows.

I went to bed and dreamed about Leslie Beck: not the dreams of innocence, as once they were, but those of experience, of the piercing and halving and pinning of the body through its center, where the legs meet the trunk. At first everything was rusty and creaky, like some oil drill that has been unused so long it seizes up, but little by little the plunging and plucking became easier and quicker and faster, as if the machinery were at last fulfilling its proper purpose.

I woke up midstroke with the conviction that Leslie Beck was at that moment having it off with either Aphra or Barbara, or both, and resolved to fire the pair of them forthwith. They'd taken more than enough advantage of me as it was. And this was the end: an absolute liberty.

I took two sleeping pills, fell asleep, and woke up quite sane.

So much for the quiet lives of those who live alone, with only cats for company, in flight from Leslie Beck.

*S*o much for Marion on Friday night. It is with some relief that I leave her consciousness and return to my own, which flows more easily. Marion is hard work. I feel *being* Marion must be hard work. All that responsibility, and so little trust in anyone, and really nobody to turn to. I think I'd rather be me, peacefully pecking away at my word processor, day after day.

Be that as it may, reader, or putative reader, that Friday night, I, Nora, went round to Rosalie's to follow up our abortive lunchtime conversation, so surprisingly interrupted by her departure with Mr. Collier for lunch. Why, I wondered, did I bother with face creams, low-fat diet, scalp massage, the exact length of my skirt, and so on, when all Rosalie seemed to have to do was slop around and exist? But then again, why, since I had never given Mr. Collier a second glance, and presumably Rosalie had, out of some secret corner of her eye, should I be put out about it?

And Ed (my husband, if you remember; the one who reads while he walks about the house) was never going to fall off a mountain, as had Rosalie's. Ed would always come home to me, was reluctant, indeed, to set forth from the house without me. In the mornings he would kiss me goodbye, once, twice, fondly, no matter how fine it meant he had to cut the catching of his train. "The run down the hill," he'd say, "will do me good. And the faster the run, the more good it will do me." Once Ed had seemed set to be one of those grand London publishers who talk in lofty tones about the nature of culture, eat status-conscious lunches with notable writers, take their vacations in Italian villas with contessas, and are amusing about what Umberto Eco said to Melina Mercouri on the Concorde; but his life (and thereby mine) had, thank God, turned out other than my parents had hoped. Ed was now a senior editor at a publishing house, with a few shares in the company, and had survived unscathed a decade of takeover bids and mass firings. We lived modestly but cheerfully. Ed's enthusiasm and knowledge of the literary end of the fiction market remained undiminished; his belief that everyone was as dedicated, honest, and well-intentioned as himself had been a little shaken by the decades, but not miserably so. My parents between them had left me a house, a car, and thirty thousand pounds. Otherwise I don't know how we would have managed. Accord Realtors paid peanuts—as, when it came to it, did the House of Arbuss, the publishing conglomerate for which Ed, simply by sitting at the same desk and doing the work under his nose, now worked. Teenagers are expensive and take up a lot of room. Ed does his job and believes the world will all fit into place around him if he does; I do the worrying.

Occasionally I worried that in some mysterious way my existence defused him; had he married someone less practical, less whatever it is I am, with my short fair sensible hair, my precise features, my skirts at their proper length, someone more likely to take to drink or to shoplift, he might have allowed himself more temperament, be more inclined to write inflammatory articles in *Publishers Weekly* than steady and informative pieces defending the status quo in *Book World,* as he regularly did. He was respected in his profession.

When I said I was going round the corner to see Rosalie, instead of watching a documentary on the slums of Argentina, he looked a

little wistful but said nothing to dissuade me. Please do not mistake
me. Ed is not a boring man; or only so far as he is *good,* for there
is an area where these qualities in a person do seem to coincide.

Rosalie was speaking to Marion on the phone when I arrived. I
made myself coffee. Catharine was away at college and Alan out
for the evening. Two TVs were on in different rooms, unwatched.
I switched them off, including the documentary on the slums of
Argentina, which I felt both glad and guilty to miss. Ed's tastes are
superior to mine. We live with a certain formality, well aware that
the bad coin ousts the good, that if children read comics today, they
won't read the classics tomorrow; TV programs are carefully selected
for their cultural and political correctness; and Ed is right—it's just
that sometimes I long for the energy and brashness of what is random
and to the common taste. Lights at home are switched off so as not
to waste electricity; meals are taken at the table, not on the knee
watching TV; the cat is wormed regularly; the children take their
turn washing up. Left to myself, I think I would live like Rosalie
without Wallace: not bent on self-improvement, forever conscious
that discipline and effort are required if everything isn't simply going
to fall to pieces, degenerate into chaos, and thence, losing energy,
deliquesce altogether into basic sludge, but rather thinking, well,
life is short; if eating chocolates while watching a horror video is
your fancy, then face the fact and do it!

I even put sugar in both our coffees, not just Rosalie's.

"Now Leslie Beck is back," said Rosalie when finally she put the
phone down, "he means to stay. That was Marion. Leslie Beck has
beaten her down to a thirty-percent gallery commission, and possibly
no commission at all. She must be in a state!" and she gave me
Marion's account of the second Beck encounter, which I, Nora, have
already given to you. And then I asked Rosalie about lunch with
Mr. Collier. What had they talked about? Had they mentioned me?
Who paid? What would happen next?

Rosalie laughed and said, "I know what you're thinking, Nora.

You wonder how desperate I can be, to go out with a creep like Collier. Take off his glasses, take off his suit"—*Had* she? Surely not!—"he's a man like any other. Your trouble is you're too discriminating. You're too picky. Like Marion, just luckier, because you and Ed got together early on, when the urge was strong, and you grew together. You don't even know what you're like on your own, or what kind of person you'd be, not married to Ed."

"I'd manage fine on my own," I said. "It was the same for you, and you're okay."

"It wasn't the same," she said. "Wallace and I were always more separate. We never understood each other, or tried to. I don't think you could exist without Ed, and you know it, or else when you found Susan in bed with him you wouldn't have got into such a panic."

"Almost in bed," I said, "and certainly not inside the bed, just rolling around on top of the spare bed among the coats, and only then because she'd put hash in the chocolate mousse. All the same, it was unforgivable of her."

"I don't think it was Susan who added it to the mousse," said Rosalie. "It's hardly likely. I think it was more probably Vinnie, still not recovered from the sixties. Perhaps she was as much a victim as Ed; perhaps it's time you forgave Susan."

But I wouldn't talk about it. The incident of Susan and Ed, the last of the great events, the great obstacles, seven full years into our Richmond life, when great events, great obstacles, should have been behind us and all of us allowed to live in peace and fidelity, not divorcing or thinking of divorcing, not swept off our feet by emotions we couldn't control, driven by motives we didn't understand, had shattered my peace of mind; and though I knew Ed was indeed part of me, and me part of Ed, the whole of us, the oneness of us, was sullied. I said as much to Rosalie. I could not forgive. Not yet.

"You are so hypocritical," said Rosalie. "One rule for you, another for Ed," and I rather wished I hadn't come round to see her, even though the slums of Argentina was the alternative. But she was right; of course she was right. I must have looked as if I had taken offense, though I hadn't, because she started talking about her affair with Leslie Beck, way back when, as a kind of peace offering. And this is what she told me.

For the beginning of Rosalie's affair with Leslie Beck, reader, I am grateful to be allowed to take you out-of-doors, to the Dorset coast, where the waves pound themselves to bits against cliffs, like a frantic woman pounding her fists against the chest of some un-moved lover—if you'll excuse a rather strained metaphor, but it came to mind—and the sky arches high, windswept, and mindless above. A relief for me, and perhaps you, to be away from domestic interior plus TV set, real estate offices, art galleries, and those prem-ises in general which mankind has devised for its safety and comfort, its diversion and the individual manifestation of status. I have, I grant you, given a description of a street or so, and of how Jocelyn stood outside Leslie's offices and shouted her ire (while trying to get in, out of outside, as it were, as quickly as possible), but even these scenes have related back to house prices; I wasn't content to let just you and them *be*. I like you to think, not just to see.

So how about, for light if painful relief, looking at these two, Rosalie and Leslie, walking along a deserted beach. Rather a short beach, as it happens, high headlands curving round on either side of it. They have walked around one of them to reach where they are, and are making for the next one. Their car has broken down; they are going for help. Leslie is at the time married to Jocelyn. Rosalie is married to Wallace. Wallace is on an expedition up Ev-erest. He should have radioed back to base camp two days previously but failed to do so. This may well be because radio conditions are bad, but it could be because the party of three have all been killed; Wallace has an engraving of Whimper's party falling off the Mat-terhorn over the mantelpiece in the Bramley Terrace house, and Rosalie does not forget it. Rosalie has been married for only a few months and is hurt because Wallace prefers the Himalayas to her. She finds it hard to forgive him for both making her so anxious about his safety and yet making her want him never to return, to vanish from her life as quickly as he entered it, talking of love and integrity—and how better and more simply than by death?

Leslie strides along. He is not very tall but he is stocky, strong, and energetic; Rosalie has to all but run to keep up with him, and this makes her feel childlike and curiously dependent. He is wearing jeans and a shirt open to the waist; he has tightly curled reddish hair on his chest and wears in it, against the wishes of his wife, a gold medallion given to him by that wife on the occasion of their wedding, a celebration which was a cause for the exchange of many valuable gifts. This medallion is an antiquity and of the highest value, or was, and depicts Europa riding into the sea on a bull's back. Leslie took it to a jeweler, who made a hole in it, strung it on a chain, and sharpened up the embossing so you could see what was going on, which was when it lost its value. His hair reaches his collar and curls up like a child's. Rosalie is wearing a sloppy dress with a long skirt made of purple crushed velvet, which is much too hot, and her shoes are too tight. She has never known what to wear when, but just likes purple.

Jocelyn called her that morning and said, "Leslie and I are taking Hope and Serena to the seaside; we hear Wallace is away. Why don't you come, too?"

So Rosalie put on whatever was to hand, without thinking, or only enough to wonder why Jocelyn had asked her.

It became apparent presently. The au pair, Helga, had irresponsibly taken the Sunday off, seeing it as a holiday and not the day when she was obviously needed most, and Jocelyn was left without anyone to help with the children. Hope was still in diapers and sat damply on Rosalie's lap all the way.

Picture the shore as they walk along. Behind them, Jocelyn sits with Serena and Hope in a car which won't start. Rosalie is accompanying Leslie because Jocelyn wanted her to, since Serena and Hope, amazingly, have fallen asleep in the car, and Jocelyn doesn't want Rosalie's chatter to wake them. Rosalie is a little offended because Jocelyn isn't in the least jealous of her, thinking herself so superior as to make worry unnecessary, or so Rosalie construes it.

The walk along the beach is without incident. Leslie talks about his bid to become a director of Agee & Rowlands. He is tired of working on a small scale; he wants to embark upon great schemes. It is dangerously ambitious to wish to move mountains, to reroute rivers, to build dams, in general to interfere with God's plan for the human race; but it is impressive, and Rosalie is impressed. She walks with her head bowed so as to appear shorter; her shoes can hardly get any flatter. She feels docile. "Is the tide coming in or going out?" asks Rosalie, and the crumpled purple velvet glints in the sun. Her eyes are very blue. So are Leslie Beck's. She has narrow sloping shoulders and, in those days, a soulful pre-Raphaelite look. Her hair is frizzy and halolike as she stands with her back to the sea and looks at Leslie Beck and the high cliffs behind him. And the sea creeps up and up, to the foot of a headland. They are taking their time.

"Out," says Leslie.

"That's strange," says Rosalie, "because the last wave made my shoes wet and the one before didn't."

"Then take off your shoes," says Leslie, and she kicks them off over her bare shoulder into the sea.

"Rosalie," I said to her, "you're not being totally accurate about this."

"It's accurate in essence," she said. "The essence has sustained me all my life."

Thus, while Jocelyn, out of sight on the other side of the headland, unsuspectedly soothed Hope and Serena. (They were bottle-fed; Jocelyn did not fancy breast-feeding, and who could blame her? Not I, for all it's fashionable. Little goats tugging at the teat! Yuk!) Leslie and Rosalie romped and cavorted, counting the waves to see if every seventh was biggest, as alleged, chasing her shoes in and out of the sea. Leslie kicked off his as well, and took off his shirt, and the hair on his chest was tightly curled, gingery and plentiful, like the hair on Wallace's red setter, which he had insisted on bringing into the marriage and now expected Rosalie to look after in his absence. And was Wallace ever coming back, or was he frozen and stiff in some crevasse, penis limp and swollen and blue for good?

"I'm so hot," cried Rosalie, and, indeed, the sun was hot and strong overhead, and the sea, now driving round the headland, astonishingly fierce and swift.

"Then take off your dress," he said. "It's for winter wear, not summer. Even I, a man, can tell you that."

"I couldn't possibly," she said.

"Don't be coy," he said. "I can't abide a coy woman. And you'll have more on underneath it, I bet, than most women do on top."

"Now how did you know a thing like that?" she asked, and took off her dress, long thin arms stretched high, softly fringed with fine fair hairs, and stood in a white Terylene half-slip over staunch white panties, and a substantial bra from Marks & Spencer, not so white, having been washed along with one of Wallace's blue mountain-eering shirts long ago. A memento of Wallace. And they rounded the next headland, waist-deep.

And there they were on another little deserted beach, with the sea gulls calling and the sun in their eyes. Leslie Beck laughed, and Rosalie wasn't sure she liked the laugh or the thought behind it.

"We can't just leave Jocelyn stranded there in the car," said Rosalie. "It isn't fair."

Leslie Beck raised an eyebrow.

"You needn't have come with me," he said.

"She didn't want me to stay," said Rosalie sadly. "She wanted me to go away."

"I know the feeling well," said Leslie Beck, with equal or even greater sadness.

And, sobered, they set off apace, the better to gratify Jocelyn, who would not gratify them.

They traversed this headland more easily than the last, debating the while whether it was that the tide was coming in, as Leslie had suggested, or the rocks they clambered over made the difference.

"You were trained as a structural engineer," said Rosalie. "I expect you would know."

"Did you really say that?" I asked.

"Something like that," said Rosalie. "Leslie's foot slipped into the sea and he had to take off his jeans."

"If the sun was so hot," I said, "they would have dried quickly enough if he'd left them on."

"Oh, you're so practical, Nora," Rosalie complained.

Be that as it may, Leslie and Rosalie rounded the headland to find themselves on the next beach, a charming little cove with white, steep, smooth sands up which the foam surged and fell back rapidly.

"If we're not careful," suggested Rosalie, "we'll be cut off by the tide."

"Good Lord," said Leslie Beck, "I think you may be right." And they inspected the next set of rocks, but, alas, the sea had covered them and surged in and back in a most tumultuous and dangerous manner.

"I can't swim," said Rosalie.

"Nor can I," said Leslie Beck.

"That is not true," I said. "That simply is not true!"

"I learned to swim later," said Rosalie. "I could see the importance of it."

So what could they do but wait, inspecting the high-water mark to see whether they could expect to live, and finding that it ran some four and a half feet from the foot of the cliff—just about as wide, Leslie Beck said, as a double bed.

They sat at the foot of the cliff and waited for the tide to advance. Rosalie took off her M&S bra and lay on her face and sunbathed while Leslie Beck paced the ever-narrowing strip of land, now the width of a king-size bed. Then he said, "I might as well sunbathe, too," and took off the rest of his clothes and lay down beside her, on his front for modesty's sake, but not before she'd had a glimpse of what he referred to as his dong, his magnificent dong, enormous even at rest, in its nest of reddish hair. Now, she already knew about the size of it. One morning, pushing open the bathroom door, which he had neglected to lock, Marion had seen it, and she had passed the word along. There was no doubt the fact of it preyed on all minds, though we would have hated to admit it at the time.

"How vulgar," I said, "how unspeakably vulgar he was, Leslie Beck the magnificent."

"How magnificent he was," said Rosalie, "Leslie Beck the vulgar."

"Women are too kind to men," I said. "Forever telling them that size makes no difference."

Rosalie felt the first cold touch of foam along one flank and squealed and rolled over into Leslie Beck's arms and felt a long hard touch along the other.

"But I might get pregnant," said Rosalie.

"I'll look after that," said Leslie Beck, famous last words, "and besides, the tide is now well over the high-water mark, and if you ask me it's a leap tide, and we might as well die happy." And still she demurred; she even talked of Wallace.

"Protect my magnificent dong," he begged, "from damage by sun and sea and salt. Shade it, shelter it, enclose it, take pity on it. You have no idea how this thing hurts if thwarted. It is women's blessing, but my curse."

So Rosalie did, and nearer and nearer they rolled to the foot of the cliff, hooked together, hot, damp, sandy, and shrieking, while the tide slipped under them and over them, warm, thin, and foamy beneath, cold and clear above; and death seemed not too terrible a thing, or only the stairway to heaven, up which they labored. Or so Rosalie claimed, though I can hardly believe a thing like that.

And then there was no cold water above or foam beneath, for the tide had turned, and receded as swiftly as it had crept in. Rosalie's shoe by some miracle—

"Rosalie, you are making this *up*!"

"No, no."

—was left washed up on the shore, and Leslie Beck's jeans, besides. His gold medallion, the wedding present from Jocelyn, which swung above her eyes, went chunk into his chest and bounced away, and chunk, chunk, chunk, chunk again—

"It wouldn't be like that with Mr. Collier," I said.

"How do you know?" she asked. "How could you know?"

And we both fell silent. We both knew well enough. Nothing's fair. Those were the days of the extraordinary; these, of the ordinary.

And then, Rosalie said, Leslie Dong—a slip of the tongue, I'm sorry, Leslie Beck—just so happened to discover a path up the cliff both of them had overlooked, and when they had made their way to the village they found Jocelyn, Hope, and Serena waiting for them outside the post office. When Jocelyn had tried to start the car the engine had taken—

"I must have flooded the choke," said Leslie Beck. "I'm not a mechanical man!"

At which Jocelyn looked surprised as well as hot and indignant, and said but she thought Leslie had a certificate in mechanical engineering, or was he making that up, too? She was impossible.

"And I suppose you found a table of tides in the glove compartment," I said to Rosalie, and she looked surprised and said, "Yes, as it happens, I did! But he can't have planned it, can he? I don't seriously believe he said to Jocelyn that morning, what, no au pair? Let's take poor Rosalie, she'll help, and her husband's away, she'll be glad of something to do. And then managed to stall the

car at one fifty-eight, and timed the tides, and only got them a little
bit wrong; so it was rather more watery than he'd planned. Don't
be absurd, Nora. It was all perfectly spontaneous, and therefore
forgivable."

"And that," I said, "was how Catharine was begotten."

"Yes," said Rosalie, at last. "You only have to look at her. Leslie's
child. Nice straight teeth in a nice wide jaw."

"I'm surprised you didn't call her Nereid, or something watery.
'Catharine' seems such an ordinary name, in the circumstances."

And I wished that one of my children were Leslie Beck's, not
Ed's at all, and tried to remember back if it could possibly be the
case. It is so easy to disremember these things. What is inconvenient
gets forgotten.

"Wallace liked ordinary names," said Rosalie. "He said there was
enough in life to overcome without adding your name to the
obstacles."

We contemplated this.

"Nora," Rosalie added, "I was very young; I didn't have children
at the time. I didn't understand how serious things can get. If I'd
known, I wouldn't have done what I did to Jocelyn."

"I don't think," she said, after a while. We discussed further the
nature of the male organ and agreed that though length and breadth
could certainly incite to lust, they hadn't much to do with love in
marriage. But our heart wasn't in the discussion. I think we were
both affected by the melancholy of nostalgia; we did not have the
courage or energy, that Friday night, to come to a bolder conclusion.

Rosalie had sat in the back of the car on the way home with
Serena on her lap. Jocelyn held Hope on her knee in the front
passenger seat. In those days it was not unusual for children to be
so carried, and, of course, seat belts were seldom worn. People were
more prepared to trust to luck. Leslie Beck drove rather jerkily,
Rosalie thought, and she derived comfort from that, feeling it implied

that Leslie would rather have Rosalie sitting next to him than Jocelyn.

Serena, in the back of the car, stretched out her little hand to stroke her mother's short and practical hair, and Rosalie was moved and felt ashamed of herself again, at least for a little—only until they were back in the Rothwells, and Leslie was turning into the Bramleys, and Jocelyn said, "Oh, no, Leslie, we'd better go straight home. The children are exhausted. It's only a couple of minutes for Rosalie to walk back," and Leslie put the car on course again for Rothwell Gardens.

"They'd love you to read them a good-night story," said Leslie to Rosalie, as they disbursed the paraphernalia of a Sunday outing with the kids to the coast, but Rosalie said no, she ought to get back, and when she did, found a telegram from the Everest expedition to say Wallace was on his way home, with slight frostbite to his nose but nothing serious; she was to meet him at the airport that night. She had to set off at once.

"The dong with the luminous nose," I said. She didn't laugh. "Over the mountains and hills he goes." Edward Lear, whom some call a poet and humorist, but whom I call frankly nuts, has a fine wild subtext, for those who know what they're looking for.

"I didn't love Leslie," said Rosalie. "Not the kind of terrible, awful, besotted, glorious love you can feel for men who treat you badly. The size of the cock does not dictate the depth of the emotion it creates. The pebble, shale, and medallion bruises all over my body didn't show through for a couple of days, so I was able to attribute them to Wallace.

"He was very pleased to see me; he had had some dreadful brush with death and said he was never going up a mountain again. He now valued life itself, which I represented; he had lost his appetite for death. We were very happy, until Mount Annapurna gave a little tug to his heartstrings one day, and he was off. As he said, it was how he earned his living; it was how he kept his little family fed.

It wasn't now because he wanted to go, but because he had to go.

"That certainly felt better. But I hated it when Wallace referred to us as 'his little family.' It didn't ring true; it was as if we existed as snapshots in his pocket. It was sentimental."

"If Catharine wasn't his, that's what you would feel."

"But he didn't know that. How could he?"

"Supposing Leslie had told Jocelyn, supposing he turned out to be the kind of man who always tells—and supposing Jocelyn told Wallace?"

"I'd have denied it. I'd have said it was a typical male fantasy on Leslie Beck's part. I had it all worked out in my head. I remember going over the medallion bruises with a nail file, in order to fudge the imprint of the bull, but it hurt too much, so I had to stop. I used a lot of makeup base instead. I had to buy it especially. I wasn't in the habit of buying cosmetics. I was desperate for Wallace not to know. I didn't regret it for one moment; I just didn't want Wallace to know."

"And no guilt about Jocelyn? Not even when you went on eating her dinners, going round for coffee?"

"I just thought she was a fool. Going on a family outing with someone like me and letting yourself get separated from your husband."

"It makes her sound rather nice," I observed.

"But she wasn't, was she?"

"No." I had to agree.

"I was sorry for her. That's why I kept going round for coffee. She seemed lonely."

We both contemplated this statement. We both knew it didn't ring true.

"You just went round to gloat," I said, finally.

"Yes," said Rosalie. "I'd stolen something from her from under her nose, and I loved it."

"Horrid old you," I said.

"Horrid old me," she said. "Horrid all most of us."

The phone rang. It was Ed, wondering how I was, suggesting I watch an interesting program on glaciers. Rosalie might like to see it, too. I thanked him for the suggestion. Home tugged, but I resisted it. Colin was not yet back, said Ed. Shouldn't he be? Did I think he had a girlfriend? He seemed alarmed at the thought.

"May the Life Force be with him!" I said. "I hope so. See you later," and I put down the phone, and then felt guilty. I had joined with Rosalie against Ed. It is what husbands fear will happen, and what does happen, and why they resist their wives' friends, even the best of them.

"The trouble is," said Rosalie, "these scenes, these events, sear themselves into the inner vision. I didn't love Leslie Beck, but even so, I began to dream of him, and the dreams unsettled me, and whenever Wallace and I had a row, I soon realized, it would be after one of these dreams. So I had to accept what I never had before, that I was at least partly to blame for our rows, and by the end we were scarcely having rows at all. I suppose Leslie Beck should be given the credit for that."

"You can't say 'by the end,'" I said, "because it may not have ended. Wallace may walk in through the door at any moment, frostbitten nose or worse; then what?"

Rosalie shrugged. She didn't want to think about any of that.

"I want to hear more," I said. "I need to know about you and Leslie Beck, and I don't want to know, because it hurts."

"There isn't any more," she said, "except Catharine. After the episode on the beach I didn't hear from Leslie for another ten days or so. I was so busy with Wallace coming home and doctors and the media asking questions, I hadn't the time to hurt and brood. That saved me. That space of empty time in which, while she waits for the telephone to ring, the assignation to be made, the woman

gets to fall in love quite passed me by. It's out of that terrible cycle
of self-destruction and rebirth, I daresay, that Leslie's Life Force is
born. Thank God none of that happened. I escaped. Within a couple
of days the memory was taking pride of place in my life narrative,
as it were, and I didn't particularly want it disturbed by reality, let
alone a ten-inch cock, which was so real it had practically cracked
me asunder. And when he did call, the following Saturday—

" 'Hi, Rosalie,' he said, 'this is Leslie.'

"And I thought, Christ, Wallace is sitting here at my elbow, how
am I going to manage this? But all Leslie Beck had to say was this:

" 'Jocelyn and I wondered if you were both by any chance free
for Sunday lunch tomorrow? I know it's short notice, but we're
dying to hear Wallace's exploits . . . ,' and I understood the course
that this was going to take, and was relieved. It was to be as if it
had never happened—or, at any rate, left just as a source of secret
pleasure for when Leslie and I, flanked by our spouses, faced each
other across the dining table. And our social relations with the Becks
hotted up no end, though I think mostly, to be honest, because
Wallace got his own monthly TV show, *Mountains and Me,* after
that, and Jocelyn loved a celebrity. Once a fortnight! Such a terrible
waste of Leslie Beck, don't you think, to lie beside him in bed and
thwart his natural and legitimate desires? It doesn't bear thinking
of. She deserved what she got."

I said I had to get back to Ed; he would be going to bed soon. I
wanted the consolation of his warm and friendly body beside mine.
Alan had come in and was in the kitchen with the radio turned on
very loud to the pop channel. He was a tall, gangly boy who took
after his father and was Richmond's junior pole-vaulting champion.
Catharine had turned out to be the more rewarding of her two
children, but that was just my opinion. I am not a sportive person;
neither was Catharine, by nature, but she tried. She wanted her
official father's approval, poor girl.

Rosalie walked me to the gate.

"Jocelyn came to visit me in hospital when Catharine was born," she told me, "and I was nervous when she bent over Catharine's crib and turned back the coverlet to see her better. Wallace was there, too. 'Just like Wallace,' Jocelyn said. 'The spitting image. Isn't it amazing how babies look so like their fathers for the first few days?' And after that it was just accepted that Catharine looked like Wallace; people kept telling me so, even my own mother, though I could never see it."

"I certainly never said it," I observed.

"Leslie even came to see me in hospital, too. I was so surprised! He just sat in a chair and looked at me and looked at the baby, and held up his hands and counted off nine fingers, one for each month. I said nothing. He smiled. Then he kissed me on the forehead and bent over the baby and kissed her. He was wearing the medallion outside his denim shirt and it went clunk against the crib, and I felt faint. You know how hot these maternity wards can be. 'Well,' Leslie Beck said to me, mother of his child, 'what can you do in the face of the Life Force?' Then he went away."

"You're making that bit up," I said.

"Yes," said Rosalie. "I just wish it had happened. You know what it's like when you've just had a baby and are no longer center-stage. Some row over paternity would have landed me back in the middle; but fortunately, I resisted the temptation to confess. And now there is no reason to do so."

"If Catharine ever wants a mortgage," I said, "it would be useful for her to claim Leslie Beck for a father. Still alive, active and healthy at sixty, looks better on a form than lost down a mountain at fifty-two."

"You're insane," said Rosalie. "And the sooner you stop working at Accord Realtors, the better."

The author as God. If only it were so. I would like to be God. I rolled quietly out of bed after Ed was asleep and wrote the following by hand. I folded the paper and put it in my bag. I do not want Ed to know I am writing an autobiography. He would want to read it, naturally. And naturally, I would want him not to. Writer-as-wife turns out rather different stuff from writer-as-underemployed-clerical-assistant.

Dinner-partying groups of young marrieds and middle marrieds form and re-form in the suburbs: in and out of each other's lives, each other's front doors; a sign of vigor and contentment; demonstration that the parental home has been efficiently and finally left, the new and better unit formed than the parents had ever managed. Just see, Mother, Father! Look here! Witnesses to the life! People who take me as seriously as you ever did, close enough to worry with me about the cat being ill, yet distant enough to make a judgment about the job I should or shouldn't take. While you, parents, only ever had your own ax to grind. You thought I'd just taken a husband; but see, here's a whole new life unfolding, a whole gracious world. . . .

The group serves as the anvil against which social skills are sharpened and political attitudes refined, sparks of discord occasionally flying off, quickly extinguished. Through the group you learn how to behave, how best to seat people at the table, what to expect from children, how to cope with obscene telephone calls, how not to make coq au vin, how not to serve chocolate mousse after boeuf en daube, how not to be caught rolling around with other people's husbands on piles of party coats. A few singles are invited into the group, drift around; are welcome so long as they know their place, don't upstage. Pace Marion.

The problem with the group is that it tends to intertwine erotically as well as socially. Something happens—a telephone call overheard on the extension, a look intercepted—tensions build, and suddenly the group's no more. Who knew what and didn't say; who didn't know and said too much? Treachery is too deep, trust too shaken, to heal the break. If you're a friend of this one, you can't be a friend to that one—it's too much.

The group that centered for a time, and never with a full commitment, on the Becks collapsed in on itself quite suddenly and neatly and without undue anguish when Anita replaced Jocelyn. When we moved out to Richmond, leaving Leslie and Anita behind, we managed to reconvene, but only for a time, until I discovered Susan with Ed, together on the bed among the coats. An isolated incident, Ed assured me, and I think I believed him, had to believe him; we had been together too long, were too kind to each other, to fall into nonbelief and all that might lead to. But that was the time we stopped giving dinner parties for one another: they were too expensive, or we were too tired, or the new dietary laws of the eighties stymied us. Fiber, low fat, and little alcohol failed to inspire us to entertaining. We felt the loss, but not enough to issue invitations.

That is enough from writer-as-wife—or, at any rate, all she could manage before sleep overtook her. It has been entered on a floppy disc under "Gutters," where the autobiography is filed.

When I came home from Rosalie's that night, Ed was already in bed. It occurred to me that I could wake him and confess what had happened once between Leslie Beck and me, and indeed between Vinnie and me, and be back center-stage. (Remember Vinnie? Susan's doctor husband—the fleshy, energetic, exuberant doctor, so very different from Ed?) And after that I'd be free to talk about it with Rosalie and not be afraid she'd gossip; because who by now could possibly care, except Ed? Or, I supposed, perhaps, Leslie?

But even as I thought it, I knew I wouldn't confess. I still wanted the world to go right, not wrong. You leap into the world, if you're someone like me, with amazing ambition. You flail your red lanky infant limbs about and mean to put the whole thing right. You yell and protest your woes, you gurgle your contentment, concerned not so much with notions of hunger, thirst, pain, and pleasure as with justice withheld or gratified. It is the infant's indignation that always impresses me: how we are born with the sense that everything should be supremely okay, how furious and puzzled we are to discover it isn't. And how we give up too early.

"You were a crier," my mother would tell me. "You were the eldest, you roared night and day, and nearly put me off children for life. But by the time you were six or seven you'd cheered up. You turned into a great little helper."

Well, thank you, Mother. You rocked me and lulled me into acceptance. So, okay, I couldn't have you to myself; so you littered my world with other little greedy sucking mouths—it was tear you to bits, or give in and be a good little girl. I gave in, and I passed my exams, cleaned my shoes, helped my little sisters and brothers to cross roads instead of hurling them into the traffic, got to college, terrified myself witless by setting myself up for a near-rape by a lorry driver, and fled into the arms of lovely Ed, who was suitable if poor, when I was twenty. Everyone came to the wedding and rejoiced, and said how lucky my mum and dad were that I'd given no one any trouble ever. "Or only in the first five years," said Mum, and I think she felt I'd somehow failed to live up to that early willful, riotous, complaining promise of nothing but trouble ahead. You can get to be my age and still know nothing about yourself.

And Ed had his First in English when I was only halfway through a language degree course I was likely not to do well in, so it made sense for me to forget the degree and come south with him and do a secretarial course, which is always practical for a young married woman to do. And now I work part-time at Accord Realtors, or would if there were any work to do; the outside world has its realities.

What I am leading up to, as you may have guessed, is a really good justification for my affair with Leslie Beck. I do feel it needs justification. Rosalie hadn't had children, hadn't been married for long enough to identify sufficiently with either mothers or wives, to understand that these roles are held in common by all women, and that copulating with other women's husbands in secret, no matter how the self-esteem rises, no matter how exciting secrets are, is also in some way to lower the self. Rosalie will be forgiven; she just didn't know. Ignorance of the lore is every excuse.

But I, Nora, knew what I was doing. And all I can offer in my defense is to say, look, I am capable of more than being good Ed's good wife; in other words, I bore myself; I feel I creep around at less than my potential, and it's painful, and I don't want to die like that.

When I was alone with Leslie Beck one day in his office, he suddenly looked at me and said, "Tell me all about it, Nora," and I was taken aback and flustered.

"All about what?" I asked.

"Why you're unhappy," he said, and that was the end of the dinner-party relationship, the general helping-out-at-the-office. Leslie and I were into something different.

Now what, you may ask, was I doing in Leslie Beck's office, back of Fitzroy Square? Sitting at the desk where once the new Mrs. Beck had sat, where the vibes of bad, mad Jocelyn (or poor, sane Jocelyn, depending on your point of view) still somehow hung so strongly in the air that Chloe (the stunning black girl in reception, who was clearly so much a sex object in the eyes of the almost entirely male clientele of Agee, Beck & Rowlands as to outweigh any possible equal opportunities credibility) would still, a year later, jump nervously at sudden noises in the street, sudden buzzes from the doorbell, or the initial crackle as the entry phone was activated. Chloe was six foot three and made me feel both small and pallid to the point of invisibility; but, then, as wife and mother, I had been feeling my invisibility lately.

It was Ed's idea that I work for Agee, Beck & Rowlands. I think I was offended that he was so sure of my common sense and reliability that he would suggest such a thing. That he did not believe

Leslie Beck the businessman could be any kind of rival, present any kind of threat, no matter what the size of his dong or dick, was, I told myself, the ordinary reaction of the academic man—the kind who has achieved a First and then grandly renounced academia—who has a sense of intellectual self-worth so great that for all his self-depreciating ways, it can never really be dented. No wife of mine, he says to himself—and, by implication, to her—will put up with a man less intelligent than me, will find philistinism attractive, could possibly be seduced by the merely physical. We live in a world where the intellect counts. My wife can share an office with Leslie Beck the magnificent, and her imagination will not race out of control.

Yet what are all those incestuous dinner-partying group cavortings about except the pleasures of imagination? Leslie and Jocelyn Beck, Ed and me, Susan and Vinnie, Rosalie and Wallace, and Marion thrown in for good measure, promoted to guest from babysitter, all round the one dinner table, picking over the moules marinière, okay, but an exercise as well in see-what-I've-got, wouldn't-you-like-it-too? Wallace's steady mountain hands, the curve of Susan's neck, Ed's kind and mischievous glance, Rosalie's rounded breasts—what would they be like in bed? How did it ever occur, the half of this couple can only wonder, that I ended up in this pairing, when it could so easily have been that? And wouldn't perhaps that one over there be preferable to this? And, looking up, meet and keep an eye a fraction of a second longer than required? The wonder is that couples stay friends, that discretion gets the better of desire. And, of course, it is not only about sex; it is about the whole business of spousing as well. That one standing barefoot at the kitchen sink, that one at the desk answering letters from the bank—what would it be like?

As I say, after Leslie divorced Jocelyn and installed Anita in her place to look after Hope and Serena, dinner invitations from Rothwell Gardens seldom came our way, and were less and less frequently reciprocated. The real problem was not with Leslie's behavior, I am sorry to say, but that Anita was so hopelessly dull. She'd wear the kind of shapeless brown dress that only the flamboyant can get away with, and she was not flamboyant, with a string of long beads that looked like her grandmother's, no matter how fashionable they were; and she picked over her food as if there were something wrong with it and only spoke when spoken to, or, in an attempt to be interesting, say things like, as we gratefully received our poulet rôti à l'estragon, "I read in the papers that eighty percent of all chickens die of cancer," or, as we talked about South Africa and sanctions, "I don't think if people haven't been to a place they've got any right to pass an opinion on it." And Leslie, who now speaks of her death as a tragedy, scarcely so much as addressed a word to her if he could help it, and we all noticed and did nothing, worse than nothing. We shouldn't have mocked her; we should have drawn her out, helped her, reformed and refined her spirit, taught her the error of her ways, counseled her about the necessity of at least providing hot plates if you're serving lukewarm food; but we never took the time or trouble. At ten forty-five precisely Anita would look at her watch and say something to Leslie in her nasal voice about babysitters and he'd pretend not to hear, and she'd get agitated in a pink and sullen and upset way, and by eleven thirty he'd finally give up and they'd go, and those left behind would exhale with relief and mirth, and then feel guilty about it.

When I think of Anita, I think of the wringing of work-worn hands. I think of Leslie saying to me, as I lay in his and Anita's bed, "And on top of everything else, she's paranoid. She goes through my diaries to check up on me. She's convinced I'm cheating on her, though I give her not the slightest cause to suspect me," and I even remember thinking how sad for Leslie, to be married to so dull, boring, and paranoid a woman, and why ever had he done it? And why had I married Ed, when if I'd waited around a bit I might have married a man more quixotic, more sexually active, more individual, and, let's face it, less self-satisfied. Someone who would leave me so exhausted, so worn out after sex, it was all I could do to get to the shower to dress, to be out of the house before Anita returned. In Anita and Leslie's shower, the soap, in the form of a Mickey Mouse, hung from a rope. I'd never seen anything like it. In our circles white soap lay plainly in a white dish, unperfumed and unscented, in accordance with Vinnie's belief that the functional was beautiful, the beautiful functional. Though these days, I noticed, Rosalie preferred her soap bright pink and smelling of roses.

The children it was who called me home at that time, not Ed. Little helpless voices calling in my head. Mother, Mother, we want you. We are not fully grown; we need you to feed us, notice us, comfort us, stand between us and the outside world, until the day we want to leave, when we'll make such a dash for the door, knocking you aside! Mother, Mother, leave your lover's bed, come back to lay the table. We need you here in the mornings, rolling out of the parental bed as the alarm goes, warm and satisfied, but not so satisfied you'll burn the toast. Mother, we didn't ask to be born. You brought us into existence, now see it through!

Reader, I can't face it. I keep putting the actual facts of the matter off. The run-up to how it happened that Leslie and I came to be alone in a room, on a summer's afternoon, when his secretary was on holiday, and girls from the temping agency too inefficient or too expensive or both for Leslie's taste, and he was saying, "Tell me about it, Nora." I suppose I want myself to be there by some kind of magic, propelled by destiny, not knowing in advance, perfectly well, what was going to happen.

But the truth is, it wasn't like that. It was at one of our few dinners at the Becks' (new-style), when Anita was jumping up and down trying to organize the lamb and apricots, which was hopelessly undercooked, pink to the point of raw (Jocelyn overcooked, Anita undercooked), and I had already caught Leslie's eye and held it just a second too long. And thus it went:

LESLIE: The letters pile up, the phone goes unanswered. We're busier than ever, but I might as well close up shop now the holiday season's started. It's a nightmare.

ED: Why don't you ask Nora to come and temp for you? She's looking for a job through July.

ANITA: Leslie, do you think the lamb's done?

ED: In fact, she's got to have a job through July, if we're to put the car on the train to Bordeaux and not have to drive it down through France.

ANITA: Why don't you hire a car when you're there?

LESLIE: I warn you, Nora; Agee, Beck & Rowlands overworks and underpays. They're famous for it. And I'm a monster, as everyone knows. But if you're game, Nora, so am I.

ED: What do you say, Nora? The children can manage without you for a few weeks.

ANITA: Why don't you ask *me* to do it, Leslie? I'm the obvious person.

LESLIE: You're too busy with the house, dear.

ANITA: And Nora isn't?

LESLIE: I think the lamb should go back in the oven, Anita.

ANITA: Oh, dear.

LESLIE: Now don't spill all that pink juice down your nice brown dress. Go carefully.

But she did spill it, and dissolved in tears on the grounds that the gravy had burned her, which was highly unlikely, in the circumstances. I think it was because she was just miserable. She was pregnant.

It might be that I took the job because I was inquisitive, in order to find out why Leslie married Anita. But if you'll believe that, you'll believe anything; I was just trying it out for size. "Nora," said Leslie

Beck finally, and after two whole disappointing weeks of formal secretarial work, in which Leslie was often away at site meetings, and I was setting up appointments with clients, and paying his bills when they came in for the third time, and sending out invoices and the occasional letter to the local authorities and planning committees, and typing up transcripts of the tapes on which he recorded all his telephone calls. "Tell me all about it, Nora."

"All about what?"

"Why you're unhappy."

"I'm not."

"Yes you are. I can tell by your eyes."

And then there was a phone call from Mr. Agee, and off he went, leaving me to contemplate my unhappiness and my discontent.

I went to the washroom and stared into the mirror, to see if it was possible to read emotions in the eyes. If we smiled and smiled, as I did, could people ever tell? Chloe came in and asked me what I was doing. I said I was searching my face for signs of unhappiness. She laughed and said, "That old line. Leslie tried it on me." How was I to know it was a line? I realized I was a woman of little experience. That disconcerted me even more. Who wants to end up a woman of little experience?

The next day, Leslie Beck said to me, "So, have you thought about it, Nora? Why you're unhappy?" And I replied once again, "I'm not." And again he want away, and left a kind of vacuum behind him, man-shaped.

On the third day, Leslie Beck said, "Nora, your problem is with the Life Force. It batters away at you and you won't let it flow. You're a good little girl, you're inhibited, and you're married to Ed."

"I love Ed," I said.

"Sure you do," he said, "and I love Anita." A comparison which shocked me. "And how are you getting on with the letter to West-minster Planners?"

It was in my typewriter. He looked over my shoulder; I could feel his breath on my bare shoulder.

"You've reworded it," he said.

"It was ungrammatical," I said.

He bit my shoulder. Now, I can work at Accord Realtors with Mr. Collier and Mr. Render, without their maleness intruding upon me. They can instruct me and reproach me, dictate my comings and goings, reward me and fire me, stick-and-carrot me, and I can manage not to feel like a concubine. When I worked for Leslie Beck, I came to understand why when women first started working in offices they were seen as little better than whores. The basic situation is intolerable. Man powerful, woman powerless. What can you do, in the end, but enjoy it? Marriage (if you're lucky) takes place between equals. Sex happens between men who earn more and women who earn less. I should have walked out of the office when Leslie bit my shoulder, but I had corrected his grammar and felt bad about it, and it seemed to me I deserved the sudden sharp pain.

"It's a terrible life for a woman," said Leslie Beck, "when the best thing she can do for a man is correct his grammar. I'll tell you what, Nora, we're not going to discuss a thing; what you feel, what I feel. None of that boring old stuff. We'll just do what we do, and find out what happens when it comes along."

"Shall I go with you to tomorrow's site meeting?" I asked. "You'll need someone to take proper notes. I do what I can with the backs of your envelopes, but it's not good enough."

"Well done," said Leslie Beck. "Let the Life Force in through a pinhole, and the next thing you know it's sweeping everything along with it, like water through a crumbling dam in one of those old films. I hope you have a head for heights."

That night, I dreamed of Leslie Beck. Nothing to do with crumbling dams. Each to her, his, own image. We were in a hot-air balloon, and up, up, up we were swept, into the navy-blue ether, where clouds formed into waves and beat upon us. I was so restless that Ed woke up, he who slept the sound and dreamless sleep of the innocent, and we made love, and he even got out of bed to turn on the light, so stirred was he by some new liveliness in me, that is to say, in the hovering, jeering presence of Leslie Beck, into whose arms he had pushed me. Sometimes I wonder about men, and their alleged desire to keep women to themselves. The urge to hand them round seems pretty strong.

But really, I had no cause to complain about Ed, and to want Leslie as well was greedy—as greedy as the infant wailing me had ever been. By coincidence, I got a letter from Alison the next morning; I have twin sisters, Alison and Aileen, younger than me by less than a year. Both are in Sydney. They spend a lot of time with their families sailing round the harbor, drinking white wine in the hot sun under grapevines. Philistines. I despise them and envy them, love them and hate them. Alison was coming home for the summer. She proposed staying with me. I put off thinking about it; I did not even speak to Ed about it. He kissed me three times before he left for work. Why?

That morning I wore jeans and flat shoes to go into work at Agee, Beck & Rowlands. Colin, who had just passed his driving test, drove me to the station, which both terrified and pacified me —but I resolved, did I not, to speak as little of the children as possible?—and at eleven I went by taxi with Leslie to the site conference, where I stood around in a hard hat taking notes. Over the last few months, the old buildings which had once housed Jocelyn Beck's solicitors had been reduced to rubble, and behind improvised fences composed of assembled front doors of elegant proportion, many still with brass door fittings attached, dealers were groaning as they picked over shattered chandeliers and ceiling moldings, ebony floors, cracked Italian firebacks, and Dutch tiles, which in those days demolition engineers loved to destroy, not understanding that therein their greater future lay.

Of the two glass-and-steel slabs that were to replace the solid, low-slung elegance of early-Victorian London, one had already risen, to some twenty-eight skeletal stories; building work on both was behind schedule. Leslie had been called in as a troubleshooter, oil-fire fighter of the development world. Entire floors had been rented in advance to conglomerates who needed a good London address and needed it fast. Their lean, hungry, and manicured representatives were present at the meeting; they, too, brought with them young women whose function it was to record decisions on tape and in notebooks. With our bosses, we presently rose, in a kind of miner's cage especially devised for just such use, to a wooden platform on the fourth floor, and felt for some reason privileged so to do. From here we could get a better view of the entire site. To the east, St. Paul's tower glittered; over in the near west, the flag on Buckingham Palace fluttered to announce that the queen was actually at home today; by some trick of sound travel at this level, you could hear the lions in Regent's Park zoo to the north. Fully blocking off the south was Leslie Beck, in his element up here: Tarzan to my Jane.

I could not see that this cluster of intent and powerful men was unduly wicked, although Ed, Vinnie, and Susan, and, to a lesser extent, Rosalie and Wallace, were united in the belief that everything to do with the removal of the old and its replacement by the new was of itself bad. The general supposition had been that if I worked at Agee, Beck & Rowlands, I would be associating with people both worldly and wicked, but that a few weeks of it wouldn't do me any harm. Perhaps I had already been there too long, and my standards had already fallen, for those I encountered seemed civil, polite, and friendly; and this particular group, albeit in hard hats on top of a half-built building, seemed mainly concerned with car-parking facilities, traffic flow, population density, and glare factor. Leslie carried sets of figures in his head and stood as some kind of infallible human computer of the south, the one to whom they turned.

"Leslie, would you say . . . ?"

"Leslie, in your experience . . . ?"

"Mr. Beck, what are your views on . . . ?"

Whereupon Leslie, with a kind of adroit and confidence-creating lightheartedness, would oblige with an instant and definite opinion. I felt proud of him. Wind whistled through the open girders beneath us. Whatever we were doing seemed to me good, as construction always does to those who engage in it. That it might be the wrong building in the wrong place, that what stood there before might have been okay—never mind. Putting up a building is as satisfactory to the human spirit as cooking a dinner. Cavemen hollow out the cave and scratch a drawing upon its walls; wild men of the trees build houses in their branches; swamp men put their dwellings on stilts; Eskimos carve ice into blocks and live inside them: building is as natural to men as cooking is to women. (Having uttered this swingeing piece of discriminatory gender disinformation, could I bring to your attention the fact that if you look around you in primitive parts of the world, you will see it's women carrying bricks, chopping trees, and erecting makeshift dwellings in the street, while the men just sit and stare, zonked out by drink, drugs, or depression; but I daresay this is due to the breakdown of rural society and the oppressive nature of capitalism rather than any basic flaw in man, as opposed to woman, so forget it.) Let me just say that one-seventh of the way up that building, I had the strong impression that these gray-suited men were decent guys doing a man's job, and the semi-naked, tattooed men who swung on the girders likewise, and it was right and proper for me to be there as a tender woman taking notes.

A wind got up; the meeting took to the workmen's lifts and reconvened in the site office. A girl served coffee from a vending machine. I got mine last, I noticed. The man I took to be a senior planning official from the Ministry of Works and was down on my "in attendance" list as Mr. D. Alterwood, dropped his official manner and said to my boss, "Well, Leslie, and how's Anita?"

And Leslie replied, "Anita? Living the life of Riley. A house to

run, a man to love, a party to go to, a baby on the way, what else
can a girl want? You'll be a grandfather soon," and I remembered
that Anita's maiden name was Alterwood, and now understood the
marriage rather better than I had, and, moreover, thought I would
keep it to myself. Poor Anita! In return for her husband's favors I
would forgo even the pleasure of going home and saying to Ed,
Rosalie, Susan, et al., "Leslie married Anita to get on in the world.
All that stuff about the love of his life is nonsense," so that when
thereafter Leslie poured the wine and Anita brought on her tureen,
we, her guests, would silently contemplate the manner of her existence, and pity her the more. Married to Leslie Beck because her
father, risen by fouler means than fair from the back street where
he was born, was on some planning committee somewhere, could
pull a string or two and make a local authority dance nicely to his
vulgar tune! Once the route to riches was the merchant's ship, or
the camel on the silk route, or the cartful of slaves, or the iron
foundry belching smoke into the air; for the last fifty years, as the
cities of the world have redefined themselves, sent their steel spires
and glass façades shooting up into the sky, instead of huddling
low against weather and the god of battles, the secret has been
"permission to build," and women are married for it, and men die
for it.

I did not think worse of Leslie Beck because he had married Anita
for her dowry. I merely felt less guilty about what he and I were
clearly going to do.

I had always marveled at his ruthlessness, the ease with which
he had disposed of Jocelyn. And, seeing no way in which I could
be useful to him, assumed in him a selfless passion for me.

I was quite insane: out of context, in my little yellow hard hat
and reporter's spiral notebook, my husband out of mind, my children
thrust into some corner of it where their little piping voices could
not be heard.

Leslie Beck the magnificent. How could any of us ever forget what Marion Loos had told us, in the days when she was skittish, when she lived in Jocelyn Beck's basement with the cockroaches and the spore of the dry-rot fungus, and babysat for Hope and Serena, and went daily to the Courtauld the better to appreciate and assess the creative history of mankind, and went from house to house of a weekend, to Rosalie's and Susan's and mine, cleaning, washing up, walking children, earning the small sums which kept her fed and clothed, part friend, part companion, part servant, how she brought us a tale of Leslie Beck's cock, or dong, or dick, or willy, or whatever awed, affectionate, familiar, or derisory word you choose to call it by: the thing which goes ahead, in any case, and stops men and women from being all spirit, all idea, all art appreciation, rooted and thwarted as they are in the entrancements and necessities of the flesh.

In other words, Marion opened the bathroom door one day and saw Leslie Beck erect and alone, his thing mottled and, to her mind, enormous, like the giant carved into the chalk hills of Cerne Abbas in Dorset. She closed the door quickly, but the sight was seared into her eyeballs and put her (she said) off sex forever. "If that thing inside you, in and out, in and out," said Marion Loos, of the large eyes, slender legs, and fastidious nature, "is what it's all about, I'd rather do without." She was just too picky, we all said, at the time and often since, for her own good.

And as for Marion, even while she worked for us, she felt superior to us. We were all flesh and hot dinners, baby poppers, nest builders. Our men had dongs of conventional size, and lived within the rather wide norm of conventional existence; but still were not to Marion's taste; and just as well. Our beds were filled with a familiar, smelly warmth; we swelled up and turned over and gave birth and sank down again, and leapt out of bed to nurture, nourish, and keep the dirt at bay, and fell in again gratefully—while Marion gazed at some medieval Virgin plus Child, and picked up a notion that a visitation by the Holy Ghost would be okay, and that you'd know it was Him because of the one dozen red roses He'd offer you first. I think she told us this to trouble us, and so it did.

"Come with me, Nora," said Leslie Beck to me that very day. "I have a few more notes to make," and we ascended once more by the workman's lift to the fourth floor, one-seventh of the way up a skeletal building.

Mr. Collier has just been over to my desk. He said, "What are you writing, Nora?" and I replied, "A fictionalized biographical sketch, Mr. Collier," rather hoping he would suggest this was no way to spend the time he paid me to spend, but all he said was, "Well, be kind to yourself," which I thought was an interesting thing to say, and went away. He is, apparently, taking Rosalie out to dinner. I hope he does not see marriage to Rosalie as some kind of meal ticket when his business fails, as it must surely do; if so, he will be disappointed. Rosalie's future is insecure; it is she who needs the meal ticket. And, besides, Wallace might turn up at the wedding.

I know that it is leaping ahead to envisage marriage between them: one pub lunch and one dinner invitation don't add up to a wedding, but it is the kind of thing that happens. Rosalie was not meant to live happily and fatly alone; she was born to sudden events, and as you are born, so you continue. I am proposing no faith in astrology here, merely observing that certain natures do seem to be predisposed to certain patterns of life. The way it goes when you're a child, that way it continues. If you're the kind of person who is rescued in the nick of time, you can expect it at fifty as well as at twelve. We play the cards of life a certain way, albeit unconsciously; we can acquire skill in handling them, of course we can, but mostly it just comes naturally, and the most important factor is the hand we are originally dealt: it is our fate pattern, like it or not.

So it seems safe for me to say that Rosalie is not the kind of person who lives alone. Sudden rescue comes, but often with a sting in its tail. Rosalie's mother, widowed, finds and marries the perfect stepfather, but he dies of a heart attack on moving day. Wallace comes home from Everest but has frostbite. Jocelyn turns up to say Catharine looks like Wallace, but Leslie never acknowledges his child. Wallace doesn't return; the insurance pays up—but there's a time limit somewhere to spoil it. I think Rosalie can expect to marry Mr. Collier, and quite precipitately, but I also think there will be a sting in the tail. We'll see. I hope this time it's just a little one. A life of strange events, separated by long stretches of peaceful boredom, that's how I see Rosalie's life.

Leslie Beck was the kind of person, you could also safely say, who tended to land on his feet.

Why is it that neither Rosalie nor myself, on hearing that Leslie Beck is a widower, has displayed any apparent desire to reestablish a relationship with him, find out how his dong is doing? Perhaps he's now too old to be interesting. Perhaps the only point to him was that he was married to someone else—that the one-seventh of him that we found so important was forbidden.

Okay, there I was with Leslie on the wooden lookout platform on the fourth floor of what is now Broadcaster House. The rest of the party had gone. Ropes and pulleys all around us; a crane moving high above; buckets of wet, slopping concrete being hauled up and down on either side of us; tattooed men with bare muscled chests passing in and out of our field of vision, walking deftly on girders overheard, swarming like monkeys on scaffolding, vanishing again. The wind was strong and noisy; the day, hot and dusty; the wooden floor of the platform, splintery. It seemed both the brightest and the most unprivate place. I said as much to Leslie.

"Unlike the grave," he said. "The grave's a fine and private place, but none, I think, do there embrace."

Well, even electrical engineers occasionally get to hear a little poetry. He spoke it awkwardly. I was touched.

"My favorite place," he said. "You'll remember it fondly."

"I suffer from vertigo," I said. "I can't bear to look down. I get dizzy."

"Then don't look down," he said, taking off my clothes, piece by piece, until I stood naked except for my hard hat, conscious of space around, below, above, the sound of hammering, metal on metal, and the rise and fall of sirens below, and the sting of wind and dust against my skin.

He weighted my clothes down with a stray scaffolding pole. "In case the wind tries to steal them," he said. I was reassured. He meant me to survive. He had red curly hair thick on his chest; his shoulders and arms were muscled and glossy. He stood in his natural state in his natural place: he was meant to poise between heaven and earth; he had elevated me and I was honored. The dimension of his prick was neither here nor there—as tall as a tree, as thick as a pole; who cares. I only ever told you its measurements to confine him in my mind, define him, and so lessen him, because I am a practical person and don't like to suffer from loss any more than anyone else; and I need to stand up to the Life Force and confine it in inches, give it a practical, conceivable measurement. Leslie Beck's laughable Life Force. If I laugh, it's only to get through my days with Ed.

He leaned me against the scaffold barrier that untrustworthily ringed the platform.

"Supposing it gives?" I asked.

"It won't," he said. "Men trust their lives to these every day."

And it didn't give, and I wouldn't have cared if it did. Little Nora, married to Ed. Happily, too. Who'd have wanted to be married to Leslie, falling from heights and not caring? But I think Leslie Beck was a very different man to his wives. Jocelyn refused to respond to him—though this may have been mere insanity. And Anita, once married, seemed to find little pleasure in him, or in anything. Or perhaps he married them because they took no pleasure in him: sex and marriage, in some men's heads, simply don't go together.

I will have to make friends again with Susan; we will have to make some common sense of the past. It seems important.

I got splinters in my back, my knees. He wore no medallion; perhaps Anita had made him take it off. A sea gull landed on the barrier and flew away, shrieking with what sounded like mirth, as the master species took its pleasure.

"Suppose someone comes," I remember me saying, and I remember him laughing. "All the better," he said. "Better luck for a building, this, than anything else. Luckier than dead cats in the foundations, or bishops' blessings—better than anything."

I asked him how buildings could have luck. He said they were as prone to it as any human being. Some were lucky, some weren't. Yes, he thought on the whole he was lucky, but hard work went into it. If you didn't look after yourself, who else would. He asked me kindly to stop talking now.

I didn't think through to the future at all; nor, I think, did he. The Life Force is not about futures; it is all here and now. Leslie Beck could plan a building, plan a marriage, plan a site for a seduction, and achieve his plan simply because he didn't worry about the consequences. He looked ahead, but never too far ahead. Got as far as his blue heaven, never to the blackness of outer space beyond. He'd forget that if he married Anita he'd get planning permission, okay, but would have to put up with her cooking forever; he'd get into my panties now and forget he'd have to face me in the office, at the dinner table, rely on my discretion, put himself in my power. Leslie Beck schemed, but Leslie Beck was rash.

"Get into my panties," I said, but I was trying to diminish him. It wasn't like that. It was something more. I'll swear it was.

When at last he helped me to my feet, he went on his knees and embraced me, his head lying against my crotch. I don't forget that. I thought then that Leslie Beck the magnificent, Leslie Beck the wicked, Leslie Beck the life liar understood the nature of the universe, and what is important in it, more than any other man I'd ever known. And do not think my knowledge of men is confined to Ed and Leslie Beck. It is not.

Leslie Beck felt it was his duty to get on in the world. His aspiration was to be ruthless: he would cheat and stamp upon and ruin others to do it. He was a fool, he had no taste, he would swim around out of his depth and be laughed at; but his one great attribute he used, and used it well. God will forgive him.

Mr. Render came toward me with our standard specification sheet relating to redecoration clauses in leasing contracts. Three coats of paint was becoming two coats of paint. By such thin, grudging margins did the balance swing in favor of the emptor rather than the vendor. So many wanted to sell; so few wanted to buy. No one wanted to develop anything. Everyone wanted just to go back home and hide. Pull down an old building—a great howl of protest arose. Put up a new one—it stood empty. Leslie Beck must be having a hard time of it. Poor Leslie Beck. Less magnificent than before, no doubt; obliged to sell off his dead wife's paintings, scrape together a few thousand somehow. I'd heard of property developers lately who'd gone bankrupt—had to sell the family home, the Porsche, the lawn mower for a knockdown price; distribute wife and children among relatives and take jobs as waiters or bus drivers. (I didn't hear tell that they now lived off the state, mind you. An energetic man remains energetic, even in myth.) Others who were made ordinarily and more painfully redundant, as small firms, hitherto considered safe, went out of business, who had no Porsche to sell, no rich relatives to pick up the pieces, seemed to get less attention than those who suddenly moved from riches to rags; but that's the way of the world. Even in adversity, those who had most continue to get most, if only in terms of attention.

I said to Mr. Render that I would attend to it. I remarked on how, at least these days, Accord Realtors didn't have to stay open late, to cope with the flood of business after other offices had closed, or open early to cater to the commuters, and were eager either to profit by a hysterically rising property market or to get into the market quick. Those were the days when no sooner did we erect a For Sale sign outside a property than we had to send someone out to slap a Sold sign on it. But in those days I got no writing done. I do now.

"At least," I said, "nowadays you and Mr. Collier can get to see something of your families."

I wished to check out whether Mr. Collier was married. He had told Rosalie he was not, but you never knew. I did it clumsily.

"Don't worry," said Mr. Render. "Your charming friend is quite safe. Mr. Collier's wife died two years ago. Didn't you read about it in the papers?"

"No," I replied, rather startled. What manner of wife gets her name into the papers simply by dying?

"It's why we still have trouble getting staff," said Mr. Render, "or the kind of staff we need. At any rate, he is free to marry again, and I am sure he is anxious to. He and Sonia had no children, but he has a Pekingese who is lonely and needs a proper home."

I searched his face for irony and found none, and was, as so often nowadays, ashamed of myself, this time for assuming that Mr. Render—walking swiftly and desperately on soft carpets between filing cabinet, computer monitor, desk, and telephone, dealing politely both with desperate vendor and teasing, flirting, possible prospective purchaser—was a gray man with a gray spirit. He was not.

"My friend has a red setter her husband left behind," I said. "I am not sure the two breeds will get on," and it was his turn to search my face for irony and find none.

I sent out a circular offering bargain deals in newly built houses, at a fixed mortgage rate, complete with custom-built kitchens—twenty-percent discount if purchased within three months. I knew there would be no takers.

Sonia Collier, I thought. Sonia Collier? And I remembered Ed saying once at breakfast, "Why is it that in that particular stratum of society, racehorse owners and real estate agents, and smart restaurateurs, people who live off froth and other people's gullibility, the sippers of gin and tonic by swimming pools, are always conspiring to do one another in?" And I looked over his shoulder at the headline in the newspaper, and it said, in twenty-point bold, "Husband in Bath Case Goes Free," and beneath it, in fourteen-point, "Sonia Collier reaped what she sowed, says coroner," and he read the passage aloud to me.

Of course. That Sonia Collier. The very Sonia Collier who had conspired with her lawyer lover to murder her husband. The lover, naked, had crept up upon the husband in the bath and plunged into the water a live power cable rigged up to the electric mains. But the bath was of old-fashioned cast iron, not molded in plastic, and hadn't been grounded as it should have been; a massive electric surge found its way through the wet tiled floor and back up through the lover's bare wet feet and burned out his already racing heart. He fell jerking and shuddering to the ground; Sonia Collier, screaming, trying to embrace him, caught the end of the power cable, still vibrantly alive, and met her death as well. Mr. Collier received nasty burns but quickly recovered. Or such, at least, was Mr. Collier's story. Three naked people, two male, one female, one of each dead, and a live electric cable in a bathroom in the middle of the afternoon could have many explanations, not necessarily the one Mr. Collier gave. The coroner's jury deliberated for some hours but eventually seemed to accept his version and passed a verdict of accidental death. Sonia Collier was an adulterous wife, and a childless one; her motive for murder was her desire to lay possessive hands on her husband's beautiful mock-Tudor house; her lover was under her thumb. No one liked her—only, it seemed, her husband. Ed had quoted him over breakfast: "Poor Sonia. I blame the property boom. I was too busy to pay her the attention she deserved." As a statement, it made Ed laugh, but I thought it was rather a nice thing to say, in the circumstances.

Following my conversation with Mr. Render, I'd wondered

whether I ought to call Rosalie and suggest at the very least that she take no baths with Mr. Collier. I decided against it. Their wooing was their business, not mine. I wish I could not so easily construct a perfectly adequate alternative scenario, in which Mr. Collier had electrocuted both wife and lover. The latter had been bathing together midafternoon, and Mr. Collier had rigged up the electric cable, shoved the raw end into the bathwater and so electrocuted them, dragged them out of the bath (getting a shock burn or two himself), then taken off his clothes and called the police. But if a jury hadn't come to that conclusion, why should I?

I would give Mr. Collier the benefit of the doubt, unless it began to look as if he and Rosalie were indeed to be seriously involved, were overcoming obstacles such as how red setter would get on with Pekingese. Then I supposed it would be my duty as a friend to put the matter to her, though I didn't look forward to it. One hates to be a wet blanket. My mind spins forward to jokes about wet electric blankets, but I suppose Rosalie would have to take it seriously.

So when I called Rosalie, I didn't even mention Mr. Collier. In any case, Marion had been on the phone to Rosalie again, complaining about Leslie Beck's interference with the group show, an episode which I herewith give you through Marion's eyes.

"*M*arion," said Aphra to me the morning after I slammed out of my own gallery, which is not the way anyone should treat his own property, leaving my staff to discuss love seats with Leslie Beck the egregious, Leslie Beck the creep. "Marion, I'm sorry."

"In future," I said, "call me Miss Loos," but I knew she wouldn't. She humored me, in the way the young these days humor those who are more settled in the world than they, who like to have furniture polished and a steady disposable income and their clothes taken to the cleaners. "What are you sorry about?" I asked, curiosity overcoming dignity.

The opening of the group show was to open its doors at five thirty. A couple of the artists had phoned to say they would be dropping in to see how their works were hung. Barbara was already rehanging these to advantage to save argument. Sometimes we stood firm, but today no one seemed to have the energy to do so. Let them have their own way. The painters who worried most were the ones who needed to worry; the others were sitting in the Italian sun or snoozing in their penthouse garrets—a couple of paintings in a group show wouldn't affect their income or their reputation one way or another. A couple of leading newspapers were sending critics; this did not please me particularly. Why hadn't they turned up at the MacIntyre? And, of course, thanks to the Life Force, Anita Beck's painting had pride of place, and was the most expensive in the show by twenty percent, and made me extremely nervous. But I didn't have the heart to move it. And it wasn't any worse than Halliday's comical goose or clumsier than Beldock's boring fish-on-slab: let it be where Leslie thought it ought to be.

"We went to the Japanese with Leslie Beck," said Aphra, "and he discovered he'd left his wallet at home. So I came back and took seventy quid from the petty cash. Barbara said it would be all right."

Oh, did she?

"It must have been a good dinner," I said. "I'm sorry I missed it."

"Just bits of slimy pieces, as usual," said Aphra, "but hardly any calories, and he was okay company."

"I thought you said he was a creep."

"Okay for a oldie," she said. "And I didn't know all that stuff about how you began in the world. I'd like to have my own gallery one day."

"I bet you would," I said. "So, when is he going to replace the seventy pounds? Or did he say I could take it out of the sale of the painting?"

Aphra laughed. "I was right the first time," she said. "He is a creep. That's exactly what he said."

The wine for the opening turned up. I don't try to save money on it. I see good wine as an investment. The more you spend on frills, the richer people think you are; the richer they think you are, the more likely they are to give you their money. When I lived in Leslie Beck's basement on nothing but dribs, drabs, and handouts, cleaning up the mess of other people's lives, I put up with second best and received second best. I was tired of it. It was like Eric and Ida switching forever to the game shows on TV, the unfunny comics, the Sunday hymn program, while the wisdom of ages flickered through on other channels. They felt at home with the shoddy. I never did.

Sometimes I wonder if I'm hard, without feeling. But I feel for Monet and Manet: I cried when Monet got ulcers over her eyes and had pads put on them by the vet and was blind for a whole ten days. It's not that I'm incapable of emotional pain; it's just that I prefer not to seek it out. I like to have money in the bank. I never, ever want to be in the state I was when I got pregnant by Leslie Beck.

A delivery boy carried in a couple of cases of Australian Chardonnay. I asked him to carry them downstairs to the basement, where it's so cold you don't have to use the fridge, and he didn't look too pleased, but that's what he's paid for. While he was downstairs, his van was ticketed.

"I hope you're pleased," he said.

I said I wasn't pleased at all; with any luck, at least a couple of chauffeurs would be dropping rich clients off in front of the gallery that evening, and I didn't want some boring ticketed van cramping their style. Chauffeurs have as much right to display their skills as anyone.

"I take your point," he said, though I was sure he did not.

He was an attractive lad—dark, fleshy, and quite witty—but I had no time for any of that today. I handed the whole problem over to Barbara.

And then Leslie Beck stood in the door.

"I'm very busy, Leslie," I said. He handed me a wedge of ten-pound notes. They were crisp and pleasant to feel, and still slightly warm from the cash machine.

"Seven of them," he said. "You'd better count them, you're so full of doubt."

What did he mean? I was full of doubt? I remembered that was Leslie's stock-in-trade. He would make a remark about your essential nature, and in the moment when your mind stood still, wondering what he meant, feeling grateful that somebody cared, somebody noticed, in he would come for the kill. The transition from the grateful to the physical is easily made.

If I had bothered to make the delivery boy grateful (rung up his boss, said it wasn't his fault he was ticketed, offered to pay), then pleaded some sad female necessity of my own (a sink to unblock, a lonely evening), he would have been over at my place in a trice, if only to get back at the difficult, beautiful bitch and then dump her, and talk about it; but who wants such adventures? Sometimes I do; not often. It's just good to know you can have them if you want.

Leslie Beck was staring at me.

"I know what you're thinking," he said. "You could if you wanted, but you don't. You were always like that. The things you've missed in life."

I had the strong impression he was here to make trouble, to stir things up, and I was almost afraid.

"You should have come out to dinner with us," he said.

"I was tired."

"Barbara didn't get home till three," he said. "And she seems okay. She came back to Rothwell Gardens to look at Anita's paintings. Has she talked to you about them?"

"She hasn't had time," I said. "Leslie, I have to get on," and I walked off into the stockroom before he could read any more of my thoughts, which were, as he well knew, in the language of the cheap novels Ida used to read very occasionally, in turmoil.

*A*nd there, in turmoil, reader, we will leave Marion's ego, and get back to mine.

To tell or not to tell? This is the stuff of which the advice columns are made, and just because it is the advice column of a lowbrow women's magazine is no reason to believe the problem does not exist. Why, we could even elevate the problem a little—transpose it to the masculine realm. Just suppose I'm Mark (Did you notice that, reader? Now I'm some young guy called Mark), and I'm married to Sue, and our best friends are Alan, married to Ellen, and our other friends are Helen and Peter, and Sue tells me Ellen is having an affair with Peter. So I say to Sue, Wife, I don't want to know any of that, don't tell me, it's just rumor, and if we all look the other way it will simply fade away; Alan will be none the wiser, or Helen. But then I hear the scandal from another source, from mere acquaintances, and merer colleagues, and it appears that everyone knows except Alan, who is my good friend, and now all men pity him and in their hearts even deride him. And it's obvious that sooner or later Alan must find out—for someone's bound to tell Helen, and Helen will be on the phone to Alan, and Alan will feel the shock of his wife's deception, and, worse, the way his friends have betrayed him by not telling him. What do I do? Tell Alan now? Betray Ellen, whom I like? Who is my wife's best friend? In theory I am supposed to have a word with Ellen, or persuade Sue to do so—she has, anyway, and it's made no difference—and ask her to desist for Alan's sake. Of course, Ellen won't do any such thing. She'll be outraged. Her business; what's it to do with me? But it has everything to do with me. Marriages are held in common. You can't get away with such bad behavior and upset no one.

Illicit lovers always believe that they are invisible, but of course they are not, nor truly want to be. They are seen (like Mrs. Sonia Collier and her lover) together in parked cars, or holding hands in unlikely restaurants, or in corners of public gardens, or coming out of hotels in their own neighborhood, and word gets round, even in big cities, where everyone likes to think they are anonymous but actually, within the wider context, have created villages of their own. Look at the zip codes of the Christmas cards you send out—after a year or two in a certain district, the great majority will be going only so far as just around the corner.

Mostly we do nothing, for who wants to be the bearer of bad news, the wrecker of domestic peace, the stirrer up of unnecessary strife? We the friends stay silent, and the marriage splits, the couple part. We the friends then take sides, go with one or the other—not necessarily the innocent, because it's the innocent who weep and are dreary; the guilty have a bright new life, a new energy to bring home. Even so, if you ask one, you can't ask the other, for fear of embarrassment. And presently the group begins to feel bad, and blame gets apportioned, and there's too much tension about who said what to whom, and before you know it, the group's split apart. Individual friendships within the group seldom stand the strain. And Alan, the innocent victim for whom you suffered in silence, says to you, "Mark, you bastard, you knew and you didn't tell me. What kind of friend are you?" And he's right.

That's enough of being Mark, who has no real way out of his

predicament, and must suffer insult and contumely for no fault of his own. I'll return to my own, female assessment of the situation.

Ellen slept with Peter one night and got a taste for it, and so that particular valuable, life-enhancing little nexus of friendship which surrounds the two of them gets unknotted, and the frayed strands lie around in disarray until some vigorous, undaunted couple spies the wreckage, and picks up the choicest pieces, and knits them into some other basic exercise in group social intercourse; and in the end, the Marks and Sues, Ellens and Peters, Alans—and who? Shall we give him someone exotic? Adeline!—Alans and Adelines are sitting round other people's dinner tables, communing with a new set of familiar faces. But something's lost. I don't think, statistically speaking, Helen will find a new partner for some time: whom one man rejects, another rejects, too, especially if the slur is fresh—

"Are you insane?" asks Rosalie, incensed. I was on the phone to her again, quite carried away. "You're back somewhere in the past. The world is not arranged in couples anymore. Giving dinner parties is not the center of life, nor is going off with other couples to share some chalet in the sun. People have friends; they get by one way or another. The loss of a husband is personal, not social. Life without Wallace is freer and wider than life with Wallace, no offense to him."

"Anyway, he'll be back," I say, automatically. But it's been eighteen months, without even knowing whether to grieve or not. And I suppose it has indeed been "terrible" for everyone, but Wallace was away a lot before hauling out for good, and there was a sense in which for months every year anyway Rosalie was married in name only, and now we just have a lengthy extension of those months. Besides, I don't feel Wallace is dead. I am not sensible of it. When I think of people who have died I am conscious of a kind of space in the air their shape, a blanking out in existence, a hollow through which they vanished; I don't feel that with Wallace, no matter what reason says. His thin, angular body, his Adam's apple, his craggy face, the greenish pullovers he wore, always slightly too tight (did he buy them that way, or was it Rosalie's habit to use too hot a wash?), still seem to me to have his rightful corporeal existence. And how, of all people, could Wallace cease? The way he would turn his eager, concentrated face if anyone said anything interesting, the bright abstraction of his gaze—he seemed so much less rooted in his physical being than did, say, Leslie Beck, as to be all air and fire, and, being so little rooted in the flesh, by rights should be immortal. The sensualists of the world deserve to die young—and, of course, often do, they being the smokers, the drinkers, the fornicators. The Wallace Hayters ought to outlast us. The older I get, the more I appreciate Wallace.

And what am I going to say to Rosalie about Mr. Collier? Because I begin to see something must be said. Simply, "Guess what I found out about my boss the other day?" Well, that would do. But it will sound as if I want to spoil something—chomp up happiness and spew it out; wreck her world with tales of murder and mayhem; bring the brides-in-the-bath syndrome lapping at her front door. Step out of line, sister, and the ghouls will get you! Stop being Penelope to Wallace's Ulysses, and see what happens. Cease your weaving, leave the loom; see, the mirror cracks from side to side, and you lie jerking and dying from the current on the bathroom floor.

"I wish you wouldn't keep saying Wallace will be back," said Rosalie briskly. "There was a time when it helped, but that time is past. And why these long silences? What are you trying to tell me, Nora?"

"Nothing," I said.

"Good," said Rosalie, "because I've just had Marion on the phone yet again, and I think she is falling in love with Leslie Beck."

"That is insane," I said.

"She's jealous of her own staff."

"Leslie Beck was good at that," I said. "Always, if only by implication, holding the existence of other women over the head. If you don't, such was the undercurrent message of the Life Force, others will. Others are after the magnificent dong; they'll race you to it. There are more of you than there are of me, says Leslie Beck. What a privilege to have the light of my attention turn upon you. But Marion's too sensible to fall for it."

"Look," said Rosalie, "we were all too sensible to fall for whatever it was, but we did. I want to know more about your affair with Leslie Beck; come round this evening and tell me about it."

"It's a secret," I reply, quite shocked.

"Don't make me laugh," said Rosalie, "we all knew and we never told."

"I thought you only half knew. How could you possibly really know?"

"You looked so pretty," my friend said. "Kind of wild-eyed and excitable. And you overcooked everything, which wasn't like you —sloppy pasta and watery vegetables. You were mooning about, for once, instead of trying to be like Susan, and doing everything perfectly and precisely."

"But Ed never knew?" I was terrified.

"I don't think so," said Rosalie. "He just thought having a job was good for you."

"I never said anything," I defended myself.

"Perhaps Leslie did," said Rosalie. "Didn't you think of that?"

Outrage! I was eaten up with anger, and yet I was pleased. When you're with a man like Leslie Beck, who, however he complains about his marriage, has yet a wife and chose her and sticks by her, and you acknowledge that and with it your status as concubine, there are unwritten rules. The powerful—the married man who does not care what his wife feels—should not betray the powerless: that is to say, me, the hopelessly in love who yet, for her children's, and, indeed, her husband's, sake, must keep the marriage going.

Can you imagine me, Nora, the neat, clean, competent, straight little thoughtful sun-sign Virgo, married to sinister, vulgar, businessman, con man, sting-in-the-tail, sun-sign Scorpio? It was out of the question. I didn't want to be married to him. I just wanted to be forever on a wooden platform with Leslie Beck, poised halfway between heaven and hell, drawing down blessings into a half-built multistory office building.

I went round and told Rosalie all about it. I left Ed watching a documentary on chimpanzees.

"It's very interesting," he tempted me, and usually it is the most pleasurable part of the day, and I'm not knocking it, to sit quietly with a husband by the fire, together on a sofa, just watching television. It is a wonderful thing to have (I will not say a husband, pace Rosalie) someone who wishes to share an experience with you, a sofa, and television, and peace to watch it in. But it isn't enough. More! More! We are greedy for more. What we have is of no importance. What we don't have consumes our attention.

"Poor Rosalie," I said. "She's feeling low. Of course, she could come round here—"

"I'd have to find my shoes," said Ed, though he's fond enough of Rosalie, "and do up my belt, and there's not enough wine for all of us. You go."

And I went. Rosalie has one of those gas fires that look like a real log fire if you haven't been round to the gas showrooms and seen them and know how much they are and how expensive to run. Since Wallace went, she has it on most of the time. She leaves lights on. Her fridge is so full of food the bits at the back grow stale and hard and jammed together unnoticed and have to be thrown out. She is wasteful. She has taken down from the wall Wallace's many photographs of mountain crags and has put up painted mirrors instead, and moved out the sensible filing cabinets and put squashy chairs in their place, and changed the carpets from patterned red to totally impractical cream, as if with Wallace she had a surfeit of practicality and frugality, lived too long in a perpetual cold bath of

English common sense, and now, finally, had turned the hot tap on. And I paced and talked and told.

"I suppose the truth was," I said, "Leslie had nothing to lose. He liked to possess women, he liked to have a hold over them, he laid claim to you at the foot of a cliff; but he didn't want to upset his marriage, or at least not until it suited him, so once he had you, that was that. And he gave as much pleasure as he got."

"Yes," said Rosalie.

"And he kept me going for months, not because he loved me but so I'd go on working for him all through the summer—August and September as well as July."

"You underrate yourself," said Rosalie.

"It was a wonderful summer," I said. "I don't care what his motives were. I just don't delude myself he had no motives, and I want you to know that. I don't want to claim any great love between us."

"You never claim anything," said Rosalie. "That's your trouble. That's why you've reached the age you have and you're living down a suburban back street, watching telly with your husband, working part-time for a failing estate agent. But the market will pick up."

"Who says? Mr. Collier?"

"Sandy. He's got a lovely home, Nora, if you like that kind of thing, which I think I do. It's detached, in half an acre, with a drive, Tudor beams, carriage lights and a porch, and inglenooks and a custom kitchen."

"Tiled bathroom floor?" I asked.

She looked surprised.

"We didn't get as far as the bathroom," she said. "That's upstairs. There's a downstairs loo, so why would I? We're only at drinks-before-the-show stage. He behaves very correctly."

"I'm glad," I said.

"He's civilized and pleasant. Apart from saying I bring uncon-ventionality into his life, and he feels a terrific sense of liberation with me, I have as yet no indication whether he just wants companionship, or companionship leading to something deeper, as they say in the lonely-hearts ads. He's a widower."

"How did his wife die?"

"He'll tell me in his own good time. You're changing the subject, Nora. We were talking about the summer you screwed Leslie Beck and cheated on Ed and went on talking to Anita Beck over the dinner table, and getting a kick from it."

"I'm ashamed of myself," I said.

Well, I was and I wasn't. In these circumstances you build up a set of defenses, which enable you to live with yourself. Ed not caring enough, the peculiar idea that if you're discovered it will somehow improve your marriage—a notion encouraged by articles in women's magazines headed "How the Affair Enriched Our Lives," in which the deceived husbands or wives, discovering the existence of a rival, wonder what they've done wrong and set about remedying it forthwith. What, not romantic enough for you? Why, then, dearest, here's a dozen red roses. Neglected you? My darling, let's take a holiday! In this scenario Ed would realize he'd hurt me by not caring, not understanding that I was still attractive to other men. A likely tale!

And so on and so forth. Boring, boring. And Anita was wrong for Leslie. Poor Leslie! What a narrowing of life's possibilities, an insult to the cosmic principle, to doom Leslie to only Anita. Boring, boring. What it was really about was trouble, destructiveness, self-pity; the vengeance I longed to take against my mother, creator of the hated siblings, by stealing my father from her; and in my mind, Leslie Beck, the vast-penised one, stood for my father, and Anita, the boring pregnant one, my mother. Of course. How does that version grab you? Meanwhile, the real world went on.

Anita was pregnant with Polly, who turned out as dreary as Hope and Serena. How horrible and dismissive I am to Leslie's children —had you noticed?—except the illicit ones, whom I deign to appreciate. Catharine and Amanda. Why do you think that is, reader? It has to do with my mother's children (other than me) by my father: my perfectly pleasant twin sisters, my amiable brother, whom I also despise for no reason at all. I went to a Kleinian therapist for a time, but she told me to leave Ed, or that's what I heard her say, so I left. Her, that is, not Ed. But some of it seemed valid enough and stuck.

Female reader, I warn you, do not take into your home as your friend the kind of woman who hates her mother and loves her father: she'll be after your husband in a trice. Male reader, reverse the sexes in the above. I'm a mild case of mother-hate. When it came to it, I accepted the role of Leslie's concubine; I didn't fight and struggle to oust the original wife, or try to get pregnant. I wasn't the kind who calls up on the phone and listens to the voice, his or hers, and hangs up.

And don't you believe those wrong-number calls when you pick up the phone and it goes dead. They're not wrong numbers. It's the passions and envies of the outside world, battering ghosts at the domestic door, shocking the phone into life—bringg, bring-g-g, bring-g-g—trying to get in, and what's the betting you've brought it on yourself?

"Insane," says Rosalie. "Insane!"

Leslie Beck cornered me on stairs and under them, after office hours and before them, in muddy rivulets at the bottom of deep, deep excavations, in on-site Portakabins tottering halfway up hillsides, in my home while Ed was taking Richard to have his wisdom teeth out, in the marital bedroom while Anita was in hospital with a threatened miscarriage. And I allowed myself to be cornered—in fact, put myself in the way of his cornerings. I cannot see a hard hat or pass a building site to this day without a lurch of the heart, although my feelings for Leslie Beck were, when it came to it, so little to do with the heart. It is merely in recollection that I have so promoted them.

True to Leslie Beck's original confining of our relationship, we discussed neither our past nor our future, nor what I might feel toward him or he toward me. It had the effect of focusing the present quite miraculously, so that every coupling became a new and sudden beginning. I daresay he knew what he was doing.

"Did Anita lose the baby?" asks Rosalie.

"Who cares?" I say.

"I expect she cared," says Rosalie, snottily.

"What about you, then?" I ask. "Poor Jocelyn. What a family outing you gave her to treasure up in memory. A fine beach trip you gave her, oh yes."

"She never knew."

"What makes you think Leslie didn't tell her?"

That silences her. I continue.

Once I said to Leslie, Leslie I said, wouldn't it be nice to do this somewhere ordinary and proper, somewhere comfortable, both physically and emotionally, somewhere we're not going to fall off a ledge, smother in mud, or be disturbed by our spouses? Somewhere which doesn't have danger and uncertainty as a built-in punishment factor? Somewhere tranquil?

And all he said was, "If you don't like it, say so. We don't have to do this at all," so I shut up.

"What did you talk about?" Rosalie asks.

"Nothing in particular," I say. "The same kind of silly conversation you had with him on the beach. For example, does the moon always rise in the same place; when the clocks go back do you gain an hour or lose an hour of life; is the tide coming in or going out? Ed talked about ideas, concepts. Ed would pause in the middle of lovemaking to consider Socrates on the conflict between love and duty; Leslie applied himself with silent concentration to the task of sex. Leslie and I exchanged information about the material world and occasionally reflected on its ironies, but that was all. Speech did not play a large part in his life."

"Had it occurred to you," says Rosalie, "that screwing you was his revenge on Ed the intellectual? That Leslie Beck felt inadequate when we talked about political details he couldn't follow, books he hadn't read, plays he'd never heard of? So what, he'd say; so I don't run my own telly program like Wallace, so I don't publish books like Ed, or write them like Vinnie, so I'm a philistine. But I can have your wives at will and make money. Sneer at me if you dare."

"I don't want to think it was because of anything," I say. "I think it was for itself; just for his body and my body, between us acting out the urge to make the perfect baby—my competence, his energy—except I was on the pill, so it didn't happen, so nature got bored and suggested to both of us to 'try again.' Leslie split first— that is to say, so offended me that I never wanted to speak to him again."

It was a Thursday evening at the end of August. We were at 12 Rothwell Gardens. Anita was out of hospital, the baby saved; she had gone to her parents' house to be looked after properly. She'd been home for one day between hospital and family. During that day she'd washed our dirty glasses and emptied the ashtrays —I smoked in those days; so did Leslie, but not Anita—and changed our sheets. Not knowing that they were "ours." They could just as well have been "theirs." Did she know of my existence? I don't think so. I hope not.

"Perhaps she went to her mother so as not to be upset?" says Rosalie. "Perhaps being upset was what made her almost miscarry. Perhaps she had to make a judgment: Do I go home from hospital and suffer the misery of knowing Leslie's with Nora? Do I go home and endure the lesser suffering of just letting him get on with it, knowing the baby's life depends on my not allowing myself to be upset?"

"I hope not," I say. "I hope not," and begin to cry.

"That's better," says Rosalie.

"Hypocrite," I say.

Anita had dressed the marital bed with her best white cotton

sheets with frills, the kind you have to iron, the kind no sensible
person has. The pillows were the square French kind. The bed itself
was brass, high off the ground, the metal smoothly and gracefully
worked. There were tall windows with kind of beige velvet curtains,
and a rather elegant yellow button-backed chair, and that kind of
smudgy dun-colored wallpaper that was fashionable at the time, and
a very pretty dressing table with one of those awful Victorian silver-
backed brush, comb, and mirror sets that had probably been her
great-grandmother's most valuable possession—they used to serve
as popular silver wedding presents, once upon a time. The room
would make a good painting—yes, I can see that: textures, fabrics,
and colors all alive and united. Anita's bedroom was surprising. She
was so plain and unexotic in herself, I wondered if she had copied
it from a painting seen in some gallery on a school trip, or reproduced
in a magazine. I had no idea at the time, of course, that she could
paint herself, or had any interest in it. Leslie mentioned once to me
that she'd been to art school before being sent off to secretarial
college; her father could not abide fancy ways. Of the coming baby
all Leslie had to say was this: "What's the betting it's another girl.
My wives are incapable of begetting boys." In those days everyone
thought the mother dictated the sex of the baby; I thought so myself,
and despised Anita for not having the gumption to give Leslie Beck
the boy he deserved, since that was the gender he wanted. Personally, as the mother of boys, I always longed for a girl.

"His wives had daughters; his mistresses had boys," says Rosalie.
"What do we make of that?"

Married to Leslie Beck. Of course I wanted it. But on, on.

On Anita's white bed, careless of its fine fabric, pounded this
rampaging smelly naked monster with curly red hair, this muscled
goat of a husband, straddling a little mewling creature who turned
out to be me, thin thighs thrust apart by Leslie Beck's great, en-
gorged, and forever unsatisfied self. "I can't get no satisfaction"—
remember the Stones' song? Always, always satisfied in the flesh;

never, never in the spirit. Poor Leslie. He'd altered the angle of the
dressing-table mirror so it reflected the bed. But a man can have
the biggest organ in the world, and thrust and thrust, and forever
survey and search the soft and convoluted foldings of female flesh,
in and out, in and out, and still not find what he's looking for. Any
more than I was satisfied, than a thousand orgasms would have
satisfied me: each could stop the clock for a moment, suspend time,
unite me to the universe, block out the mind, expand the spirit,
exhaust the will. But strength and sanity return. I have stopped; the
clock has not: two hours nearer death, and mortality is as real as
ever. Time to leave, to go home to Ed, to shower, to fall into that
legal, dutiful, comforting bed, made fresher and more interesting by
what had gone before. We had a percale duvet set in our house—
easy-care, in appropriate pastels—and oblong pillows of the unexotic kind.

When I got to the office the next day, wearing my nice new
earrings and a garter belt that gripped me round my waist and kept
me aware of my body, kept me on my exotic toes, as it were, Leslie
was already there, hovering at my desk.

"Nora," he said, "this is your last week, isn't it?"

"Is it?" I said, taken aback.

"Chloe's home from vacation this weekend," said Leslie Beck,
"so the firm's back to normal. But we've all been so grateful for
your helping out. I think Mr. Agee wants to give you some kind of
bonus. It will certainly have my recommendation."

I could have gone three ways. I could have screamed and wept
and had a broken heart. I could have cut up his clothes, as Jocelyn
did. I could have gone to my mother, in essence, as Anita once or
twice went to hers—that is to say, gone home and suffered in silence,
self-esteem shattered. But I chose the third option—or, rather,
it chose me. I simply fell out of love with Leslie Beck there and
then.

"Well," I said, "I don't think I'll bother to work my notice out. I'll go now."

"You can't leave us in the lurch like this," he said.

"I can," I said, and I did. I went straight home, burned my garter belt and all my defiled panties in the anthracite stove, and said to Ed when he came home, "Ed, I'm not working for Leslie anymore. He keeps chasing me round the office desk. It isn't right; his wife's pregnant. He is not a nice man, and I am never asking him to dinner again, and if he asks us, I'm sorry, we can't, we're busy."

"I wish you'd decided this earlier," said Ed. "We could have managed a holiday," and I knew I was home and safe.

There was no punishment. No baby, no social disease, no discovery, no divorce, no ostracizing, no shame, no self-hatred; only one glorious nervy summer and one holiday deferred. We went in September.

When I got home from Rosalie's, after telling her the full tale of Leslie Beck and myself, it was one in the morning and the kitchen light was still on. I was instantly anxious. Ed had found out. I had spoken to Rosalie, and he had somehow overheard. My thoughts had traveled down Dalrymple Street, across Gossamer Road, back up Hogtie Lane and home, been absorbed by some kind of spousely osmosis, and Ed was waiting up to kill me.

I went straight to the bedroom. Ed was safely in bed and asleep. The episode was in the past. Ed looks very good when he is asleep: calm and peaceful Richmond living; the gentle, regular exercise of the mind; the conviction that books are the real life and world events some kind of hysterical flurry on the other side of a TV screen; an affection for his children which allows him to overlook their various excesses and trust in me, enables him to sleep with the tranquillity of the cherished child.

I supposed that one of the children had left the kitchen light on.

I put my hand round the door and switched the light off and a little voice cried "Ooh," so I switched it on again. A girl with no clothes on stood there: a strong, very white-bodied girl with a red crotch, curly red hair, and wearing braces, which glinted as she turned her startled head toward me. She was eating a big slice of bread, carved from the loaf still on the table. If you go out for the evening, no one ever bothers to clear anything away. It was Amanda, Susan's daughter. Colin came up behind me, wearing a towel to preserve his decency from his mother's gaze.

"I hope you don't mind," says Colin. "Amanda had to stay. She missed the last bus back to Kew."

"Of course I don't mind," I said. "I'm glad to see you again, Amanda."

And so I was. Amanda, Leslie's by-blow. Children tend to stay in the villages their parents carve for themselves out of the hard city rock, marry and procreate within them. Leslie, ruthless lord of the manor, self-appointed, against whose rule the village men forever strained and spoke, begat out of wedlock the beautiful Amanda, and Colin, handsome village lad, had the temerity to woo her.

"I hope I haven't taken the breakfast bread," said Amanda. She seemed unabashed by her nakedness. "I just get so hungry in the night."

"I bet you do," I said.

Leslie Beck would get up in the night to eat sliced white bread. He preferred the crust. In the morning, only the weak central crumb would be left. Susan, who had had the privilege of spending whole nights in his company, had once told me so.

Last time I'd seen Amanda, she'd been twelve, large-featured and plain. Now she was eighteen, I supposed, handsome rather than pretty, and without self-doubt, as the metal diamonds on her teeth proclaimed. Not many girls are prepared to go on wearing them, at her age, no matter what the orthodontist suggests. Leslie's Life Force had entered in; it made her body glow, her skin translucent.

Lucky Colin, I thought, and left them together and went to bed. I
was so tired.

Another time, another place. We're in the mid-seventies and in the
Dordogne, France. The Roses, Vinnie and Susan, have rented a
farmhouse here: a low stone building enclosing a wide courtyard,
stone-walled, wooden-beamed, simple, rustic, comfortable, as it
grew naturally out of a benign landscape. The kitchen is dark and
cool; since it's high summer, meals are taken, for the most part, out-
of-doors, on a long trestle table beneath a canopy of grapevines.
For breakfast there's fresh bread, slabs of local butter, plum confiture,
and coffee; for lunch, more bread, local cheese, fruit, and wine; the
evening meal, unless Vinnie chooses to cook, is eaten in any one
of a number of local restaurants, where the cuisine is French
provincial—the kind of food the world will not see again. Marie
comes up from the village to clean; she is young, fresh, smart, and
vaguely disapproving of the visitors. Jean-Paul comes up twice a
week to do the outside work: hoe the vegetables, sluice down the
courtyard, take away the trash. It is one of the most expensive
villages (properties?) on the agency's list. The plumbing works.

The farmhouse is on a hill and has a view—the high cliff of a
river gorge to the south, its face riddled with prehistoric caves; to
the west, more hills, more vineyards; and farther up the hill, the
yellowy stone walls of a medieval town. Stories of dinosaurs absorb
the children, and the heat of the day dampens arguments and pro-
tests; in the evening, there's a safe river pool for them to swim in.
In the mornings, someone will go to the Périgueux market: plums,
peaches, aubergines, stuffed tomatoes, pâtés, cheeses, poultry (dead
and alive) in a profusion that seems natural to the peasant and is a
source of wonder and pleasure to the city folk.

The farmhouse sleeps twelve. This year Vinnie and Susan have
asked Ed and me, Wallace and Rosalie, Marion Loos, and Antony
Sparvinski—Vinnie's publisher, whose wife has just left him. Every-

one thinks vaguely that Sparvinski, who is thirtyish, unworldly, and foreign, might do for Marion. We are beginning to worry about Marion. We feel she is our responsibility. We snatched her out of her natural place in the world, promising her a better one, and now we suspect she is unhappy. A few lines that look remarkably like resentment are beginning to form around her brow as she peels the cucumber for Vinnie's salad. Vinnie acknowledges that cucumber should be eaten together with the skin, which contains an enzyme that helps digest this otherwise most indigestible of vegetables, but the tender flavor and melting texture of a finely sliced and well-blanched peeled cucumber, Vinnie says, is worth minor digestive distress. We go along with it. Vinnie is our taste-and-culture leader. If he says something's worth minor distress—for example, peeling and chopping horseradish roots dug fresh from the garden—for the sake of its natural flavor, that's it: he fires us with enthusiasm, he chivvies us; he points out to us that a cracked and crazed blue-and-white Minton plate, two hundred years old, is a better thing to eat off than a factory-made new Wedgwood, and we agree. Because Vinnie loves the past, being nervous of the present, all our houses are full of old things, antiques; almost nothing is new. Even our towels are bought in junk shops, Vinnie pointing out that the old fabrics pick up moisture better than the new, and he's right. It's because of Vinnie that we all have white soap in plain white china soap dishes in our bathrooms, and baths that stand on legs and are impossible to clean beneath. Vinnie believes that the functional is beautiful, so long as it's more than fifty years old. None of us would dare use "ease of cleaning" as a reason for buying or not buying anything; only gradually have plastics crept into our houses. There was a time when Susan decanted dishwashing liquid into an earthenware jug. Now that it has become usual for men to share housework, even Vinnie can work a washing machine and will use a dishwasher.

Our lot: see us as the brake-lining classes. That is to say, with our ridiculous impracticalities, our love of the old, our suspicion of the new, we wedged ourselves between the unthinkable (that our history would be buried under rubble) and the unstoppable (that profits must be made) and slowed down the headlong rush of the developers to dispose of our past entirely. While we were on our knees polishing some ancient flaking slate floor, carefully refitting and matching worm-riddled window frames, sneering at our neighbors who couldn't tell old oak from new pine, they, the true revolutionaries, wanted to start over, to seal the cockroaches under concrete, to bury TB along with damp and ignorance, to put the past to the bonfire, as the past put its witches, alive. We were both right. We, in the snobbery of our taste, paved the way, alas (we would see it as alas, of course we would, purists to the bone), for the theme parks and heritage industry which now plague us, with their bonny milkmaids and olde worlde cookies; but if our towns are still discernibly different one from the other, if we have a green field left, it's because we sniffed and looked down our cultured noses at what was new and convenient. The effort wore us pretty thin. The world leapt out of control. We're reduced now to using ecologically sound dishwashing liquid, in nonbiodegradable plastic bottles. Vinnie was our hero.

Leslie was our natural enemy. It being against our principles to have enemies, we fraternized; we did what we could to convert him. Some of us even slept with him, to defuse him.

Marion, with her instinctive response to paintings, was our friend. It was our duty and our pleasure to offer her what assistance we could. What we valued, what we tried to rescue, as well as the old, was intelligence and response. We would open our houses and our hearts to it. I don't think it made us better people. The "deserving poor"—those who would acknowledge the standards of their benefactors, who washed their faces and minded their manners—do well enough from century to century. It is the undeserving poor, who are never likely to reflect credit upon us, or do anything other than despise us, who need us: the undeserving of spirit we should turn our attention to. Marion's brother Peter, for example, who hadn't an idea in his head beyond X-rated videos.

So picture Marion, elegant even in her much-washed orange shift of a cotton dress, long-legged, large-eyed, wearing rubber gloves to peel cucumbers.

"Marion," says Vinnie, "you can't possibly peel cucumbers in rubber gloves. Where's your finesse? Besides, cucumber juice is good for the skin."

Marion sighs and takes off the gloves and risks her nails. She is always obliging, always polite, part friend, part protégée, part help. We trust our men to her without thought: betrayal is not in her nature, nor—and perhaps it is the same thing—is abandonment to the moment. In spite of her looks, there is a chasteness in her that seems to deter. She is unlikely to grip the male imagination. I would never be totally easy if Rosalie was alone for too long with Ed, and certainly not Susan; but Marion could spend a morning shopping in Périgueux with Ed, and I wouldn't prickle, or feel left out, or think that existing secrets were being revealed or fresh ones plotted: I would just know she'd bring back the best and freshest vegetables, the rarest and most perfect cheeses.

This particular morning, Vinnie was preparing a five-course lunch. He had all of us helping. Ed was trimming meat with his fastidious fingers; Wallace was sharpening knives—swish, swish; I was skinning tomatoes; Marion was slicing cucumber; Antony was shelling fresh green walnuts. Susan was excused; she was upstairs writing an article for *New Society* entitled "Charity: System Bolstering or the Answer to Need." The more noisily hedonistic Vinnie became, the more Susan retreated into a remote and chilly aestheticism. The door was open; sunlight shone through, and the smell of basil and ripe grapes and hot hills drifted in. We were happy, except for the slight crease of discontent on Marion's brow. Then the room darkened, and who stood in the doorway but Leslie Beck. It was the

first time I had seen him since I'd walked out of Agee, Beck &
Rowlands, leaving him, or so he claimed, in the lurch, and myself
lucky not to be in the family way. He was wearing jeans, a white
shirt, and a red cravat, and looked like the wealthy bounder he was.

"I just happened to be passing," he said, "in the Rolls. I wondered
if you intellectual folk would put up with me, a mere businessman.
I'm going on down to Cahors. I thought I might take you all out
to lunch."

We were surprised. We stared. No one said anything. He picked
us off one at a time.

"Hello, Rosalie," he said. "Hello, Nora—long time no see. Hello,
Wallace—I was having lunch with Jocelyn; I go over to see her
and the girls quite a bit. She said to remember her to you, how
much she likes the new program. Hello, Ed—I saw you were in
the quotes-of-the-week in my Sunday paper. What was it? Something pithy and witty." Then he said to Antony Sparvinski, who
was small, round, earnest, and nervous, "Hi, Antony. You know,
Antony's publishing a book of mine. Of course, it's been ghost-
written; I'm told I don't have the literary touch. It's in the 'How
To' series. How to read a surveyor's report. Back in the domestic
market, for my sins, but that's where the profit is, isn't that so,
Antony?"

Antony agreed. So he was the traitor.

"I never thought you'd make it, Leslie," he said. "I never thought
you'd find your way down here."

"I did," said Leslie, "and I brought the manuscript with me, just
to give you some holiday reading."

"Thank you very much," said Antony. He looked guilty and
helpless. I couldn't think why we'd thought he would do for Marion.

Then Leslie said to Vinnie, "How's the cock of the walk? It all
smells good. What a pity Anita can't cook. What a waste of France!
Where's Susan?"

"Upstairs, working," said Vinnie, and once one of us had spoken, what could we do but acknowledge Leslie, and even feel privileged he had deigned to call.

"Stay to lunch, Leslie," said Vinnie. "And welcome. Is Anita with you?"

"Anita's in Cahors with little Polly," said Leslie, at which we all sighed gently with relief. "Not so little now. I'm on my way down. Well, well, Marion, still at it? They working you as hard as ever? I'd have thought you'd have got your own gallery by now."

And Marion, instead of turning white with rage around the nostrils, as she was very well able to do, just said, "I need a sponsor first. Perhaps one day I'll find him," and went on peeling and slicing cucumbers.

Leslie said, "Now what am I to do with my hungry chauffeur, since you won't accept my invitation?"

He knew quite well that if he made us confront our egalitarian principles in public, we'd have no option but to live up to them.

"Ask him in," said Vinnie. "There's food and drink for everyone."

"Her," said Leslie, and we all sighed.

Reader, if you can at this tense moment bear to leave these hot, dreamy, wine-soaked, garlic- and olive-oil-drenched salad days for a little, I'll take you back to the wet, cold Norfolk afternoon when Ed first met Marion and brought her home to Bramley Terrace.

Ed had commissioned a coffee-table book entitled *The Artist and Money*. Now he, the picture editor, and a photographer traveled to Norfolk to visit a touring exhibition called "The Bank and the Painter," sponsored by a High Street bank, to catch up with and photograph a minor Rembrandt etching, *The Moneylender,* and possibly a couple of Van Gogh café scenes as well, painted in exchange for a dinner and a glass of wine or so.

The exhibition was not a success. There were few people to get in the way while the photographer, having done with the Rembrandt, was setting up for one of the Van Goghs. The tall, pretty girl who had handed out the warm white wine and limp sandwiches nudged

Ed and said, "Don't make a fool of yourself. That one's a fake. A
forgery."

In those days, Marion had a Norfolk accent you could cut with
a knife, which stood to reason: the exhibition was touring the prov-
inces, and the bank was going through one of the nonelitist phases
banks go through when the credit centrifuge, in low-interest gear,
spins money out in the direction of the common herd, before changing gear and sucking it back in again where it belongs, with the rich
and powerful. The purpose of the exhibition was, as well as touting
for customers, to demonstrate that famous artists were people, too,
and had human problems, and in so doing, by using the cult of the
personality, to make art accessible to ordinary folk. Or such was
their quite laudable purpose. They had asked for girl Friday vol-
unteers among their branches, and Marion had stepped forward; and
because she was pretty, and clearly of the people, she had got the
job. She was paid no overtime for this special project and was
currently working a sixty-eight-hour week. It was the kind of detail
Marion would instantly work out.

"What do you mean, fake? How do you know?" asked Ed, taken
aback.

"Well, look at it," said Marion. "Anyone with half an eye could
tell it's a forgery."

Ed looked and couldn't. But, then, paintings weren't his specialty.

"It's too polished around the edges," she said. "It's too careful
for a man who wanted his dinner. Look at the way the light comes
out of the lamp. Like Morse code—dot-dot-dash, dot-dot-dash. Too
regular. No, it's a fake. The one on the left's okay. That's the Van
Gogh. Same subject, different painter; a hundred years or so in
between."

And she passed on with her plate of sandwiches.

The photographer said, "I'll take the one on the left, to be on the
safe side," and repositioned his camera.

Ed followed Marion into the side room, where the wine was kept, and asked her if she had any special knowledge of the subject, and she said no, how could a bank teller know anything except the denominations of bank notes and how to refuse credit to the unworthy so they didn't ask twice? At which point the exhibition director, a serious man with a cavernous face, came in and suggested that Marion get on with her work and not waste time talking to guests. And thus Ed reported the conversation:

MARION: This guest is talking to me. I'm not talking to him. And I've worked forty-eight hours so far this week, and it's only Thursday, so I reckon I'm entitled to a conversation or two.

DIRECTOR: You seem to have an attitude problem, Marion. It's a great privilege for you to be asked to work here for us, among these beautiful and world-famous works of art.

MARION: They're mostly fakes, Buster. You've been had. Why do you think the insurance is so low? There's a whole lot of people laughing at you up their cultural sleeves.

DIRECTOR: Are you drunk?

MARION: No. I'm just shit-tired. You were too cheap to pay what the national galleries wanted: you rented from private houses and got a load of rubbish. The etchings are second-rate; the plates must have been hacked to pieces. Those poor bloody painters— they have to put up with you when they're alive, and you're still buggering them when they're dead.

DIRECTOR: I hardly think a girl like you is qualified to pass an opinion on art. Now will you get back in there and do what you're paid for, and all you're fit for, and serve the wine.

MARION: I'm ashamed to. It's warm. Even a girl like me
             knows white wine should be cold. And it's sweet.
             They'll all have headaches in the morning. Worse
             than after my mother's tonic wine.
DIRECTOR: Perhaps it would be a good idea if you left now
             and didn't come back.
MARION: You mean I'm fired?
DIRECTOR: Yes. (*Exit Marion*) I'm sorry about this. Head office
             insisted I recruit from the philistine ranks. I told
             them it wouldn't work, and I was right.

Ed, the photographer, and the picture editor passed Marion in
their taxi on the way to the station. They stopped the taxi.

Marion said she had no money until payday and nowhere to live.
No, she refused to go to her parents' house. She would not give in.
No, she did not think the bank would take her on again; if they
offered, she did not think she'd accept. Banking stifled her; there
were no proper promotion prospects for women, anyway. Being
"good with figures" got women as far as bookkeeping, seldom
accountancy. Doing what she was told to do by people stupider
than she upset her. No, she would rather go on the streets.

The taxi meter clicked up. The publishing collective would miss
its train if they delayed further. Marion consented to get in the taxi
and go to London with them, and Ed brought her home to Bramley
Terrace. We had no spare room, so we found her space in Leslie
Beck's basement, and she helped out with Hope and Serena in the
evenings and with my Richard and Benjamin, and Rosalie's Catharine, and Susan's Barney, and did her course at the Courtauld,
melding the households into a yet tighter unit, as she went from
one to another, sopping up the standards of what are now called,
in an attempt to diminish them, the chattering classes, but which I
would rather call the classes with conscience—of whom, I fear on

a bad day, as with French-provincial cookery, the world will not
see the like again.

We belonged to a level of society somewhere between the street
protesters and the bourgeoisie establishment. We were the shock
absorbers of the nation, the swing voters: if our patience grew thin,
we'd change the way we voted. It was our only power—that and
the sense that sheer strength of communal good intent, shared indignation, would somehow magically influence the course of events.
We went to the theater, read novels, talked politics, waxed indignant,
followed the news, listened to the radio, were active men and women
in the PTA, brought our children up to be nonracist, nonsexist—
when that concept presently dawned upon us all—and to empathize
with others. ("Colin, but *why* did little George beat you up in the
playground? No, don't hit him back. Talk to him. Understand him,
and forgive. Become his friend.") We had given up on our generation, finally understood our own powerlessness, our littleness of
vision, as the more desperate and drastic energies of the world swept
in and engulfed us, like the ocean swamping some secluded rock
pool. We put our faith in the future our children would create, if
only we created them properly. It was, I think, and still is, a noble
vision. And I continue to believe Amanda and Colin in my kitchen,
Amanda naked and cheerful, metal teeth gleaming and unabashed,
Colin in his courteous towel, will do better than we.

Ed brought Marion home; we believed there was some sort of
better life she could attain. We treated her like a car whose engine
hadn't fired properly: we thought if we really tried, and pushed and
pushed her to the brow of the hill, and let her run down, the engine
would splutter to life, and she'd carry on under her own energies.
And the trouble was, now she'd run down the hill and was in a dip
none of her choosing, but ours, and the engine hadn't quite fired.
Marion stood at the sink peeling cucumbers in rubber gloves until
told not to by Vinnie; she was nearly thirty; she hadn't married; she
had no children; she lived in a bed-sitting room and worked in this

art gallery or the other as an assistant, until the day she'd tell management what she thought of them and either walked out or was fired. And the gallery world is small, and her reputation preceded her. "Marion? Marion Loos? No, I don't think so." Though she was never brisk and brutal with us. We were her safety and her hope.

She trusted us, and it made our responsibility the greater.

Leslie's chauffeur strode up the path, "crushing ants with every step," as Rosalie later complained. She was forty-five-ish; she wore what looked like combat fatigues. She was over six feet tall. She did not seem the kind to linger over Vinnie's five-course lunch, to properly savor the peasant harshness of the local wine. We sighed in our hearts; our meal was ruined, the serenity of the day gone.

Leslie Beck introduced her as Lady Angela Pettifer. The Rolls was hers: she was driving down through Cahors to Bordeaux; she was giving Leslie a lift. We had wronged her. Leslie Beck tried to bring in champagne; she dismissed it and him. "You can't drink champagne with pork and beans," she said. One of us! She was interested in the story of Marion's life; she had it out of her almost before the fresh, crusty bread was broken, certainly before the tomato-and-basil salad was finished.

"You need to run your own gallery," she said. "You need a backer."

We all turned hopeful faces toward her. A title, a Rolls . . .

"Not me," she said. "I'm always broke. But I have friends."

We were nicer to her than ever.

"I'm not Leslie's mistress," she said, out of nowhere, "in case you think so." And I was glad, and so was Rosalie. Wives one can endure; other concubines can lead to a state of agitation.

Reader, can I remind you of a few things? At this stage, Leslie has had carnal relations with myself and Rosalie; his daughter Catharine, aged eight or so, drinks Orangina with the other children down the far end of the trestle table, politely ignoring these new visitors as they politely ignore the great proportion of the adult world which does not directly impinge upon them. So long as their parents look happy, children are well able to forget them. Did Leslie's eyes drift over toward Catharine, searching through the children to locate his own? Rosalie said she thought so. I doubted it.

Susan was not in a good mood. Of all of us, Susan was the one who was best able to show her displeasure. Wallace would darkly brood, but there seemed nothing personal about it; Vinnie could suddenly lose his temper and be violent, and then be full of remorse; Ed would go white and icy, then pull himself together; Rosalie and I were placators; Marion could look offended and often did; but Susan's displeasure could make a warm sun seem cold. This year she had cut her straight brown hair short and sharp: she was trying to make the transition from young motherhood back into the outside world, and finding it difficult.

This summer she was impatient with our ways; she found Vinnie's preoccupation with food and the relics of the past irritating. She talked to Rosalie and me as if we were idiots; we were always on the verge of believing it, as it was, as if it were our husbands who functioned in the world and we just trotted along behind, clucking and tutting, more like our mothers than we had ever believed possible. It was Ed whom Susan really liked: they would lose themselves in talk of Herodotus and sociology, while Rosalie and I muttered who? what? and Wallace dreamed of mountains and Vinnie poured more wine. It's Ed and Susan who ought to be married, I would think. And that didn't make me right for Vinnie, either. I was too finicky, too precise. Right for no one, not even Leslie Beck— or only for a summer.

During that lunchtime I remember Susan saying:

TO VINNIE: Let Leslie open his champagne. It can't be worse than this awful peasant plonk you keep getting. Do people lose their palate as they grow older, like their hearing?

TO MARION:	So, how do you like Antony, Marion? We asked him down especially for you. Now don't disappoint us.
TO ANTONY:	How do you like Marion, Antony? She's got British citizenship. . . .
TO ME:	I'm asking Ed to the opening of the new gallery at the Museum of Mankind. I hope you don't mind.
TO LESLIE:	So, how many good buildings have you torn down this year?

Culminating with:

| TO LADY ANGELA PETTIFER: | Is there room in your Rolls for me? I can't hang around here any longer. If I can get back to Bordeaux, I can fly back to London and do some research. Then Vinnie can keep the car and look after the children. Do them all good. . . . |

And that is exactly what she did. Susan packed her bag and left with Leslie and Lady Angela, leaving Vinnie openmouthed and humiliated, and the thought of Vinnie humiliated shook all of us, not just me.

Rosalie came into Accord Realtors; she was lunching with Mr. Collier. She had bought a new coat. Lately she had been buying from thrift shops, but this one had a crisp and cheerful air. It looked suspiciously like one I'd seen recently in a store window, its tag saying five hundred twenty-three pounds. I'd wondered who there'd be around these days with enough money to buy it, except I supposed there was always a woman ready to spend her last penny on clothes. It just hadn't occurred to me it would be Rosalie.

"What's the matter?" asked Rosalie. "You're brooding."

Mr. Collier was in his office, waiting for a fax to come through.

"I was thinking about the past," I said, "and the way it catches up with the present. Susan's Amanda and my Colin are dancing about naked in my kitchen."

"Then it's just as well," said Rosalie, "your Colin isn't Leslie Beck's son. If he's not."

"Of course he's not," I said.

"Some people," said Rosalie, "say that once a woman's been with a man, she never breeds true again. Her children take their features from all her lovers."

"That is just not scientifically possible," I said, and refrained from adding, "And some people say you're going out with a murderer."

"When Susan went off with Leslie Beck to Bordeaux, that time," I said, "they had an affair, didn't they?"

"An affair, an affair," Rosalie jeered. She was in an uppity mood. "How romantic you are. I expect they spent a night or two together. If you and I did, why wouldn't she?"

Nor did I point out that Rosalie had spent only a couple of intimate and ridiculous hours with Leslie Beck and had a baby by him only by accident, and he and I had loved each other for a whole summer.

Instead I said, "I love your coat," and Rosalie said, "I know what you're wondering, Nora, poor Nora—are you going to get in touch with Leslie Beck again? And can you bear it if he isn't interested? If you're too old and he's forgotten?"

"You're talking about yourself," I said.

And Rosalie said, "I know. But I'm protected by Mr. Collier, and you only have Ed. I got this coat fifty pounds off because it had been in the window, on display."

"Good for you," I said.

"Anyway," said Rosalie, "I think Marion should have first option on Leslie Beck the widower. I think we owe her that."

"Why?"

"Because if it hadn't been for us, she might be married to some nice bank manager and living happily in the suburbs with four kids and some pretty pictures on the wall."

"Now you're talking like me," I said, "as if marriage were an end in itself. You're slipping. Marion would have got where she is without our help."

"She wouldn't," said Rosalie.

"She's not the marrying kind," I said.

"She would have been," said Rosalie. "She'd have had to have been."

Mr. Collier put his head out the door and said, "Half a mo, Rossie."

"Rossie?" I said. "That sounds very kind of domestic. Supposing Wallace comes home?"

"You just don't want me to be happy, Nora," said Rosalie. "You never have," and I felt again the ground shifting beneath my feet, just as I'd felt when Susan suddenly up and went off with Leslie Beck, leaving me disturbed, angry, and jealous.

Mr. Collier and Rosalie went off arm in arm. I wondered why she had felt obliged to be disagreeable to me. Perhaps it was instinctive: the need to warn others off your territory, when first it's won. Or perhaps women friends are just for when there's no new male upon the horizon? I didn't want it to be true, but at least it meant I didn't have to take it personally. All the same, I wanted to cry. I told Mr. Render I wasn't well, left the office, and took the train to Green Park station.

I walked down Bond Street, past the expensive stores, which had never been part of my life, and now, I supposed, never would be, up Maddox Street, past the furtive fly-by-night carpet and fabric shops, and round the corner to where the streets opened out and became wider and less busy, where the commerce of fashion gave way to the commerce of investment art. I went past Browse D'Arby, past a window containing an old master or so, another with a discreet ship-at-sea-in-storm on an easel, a display of astrolabes, to make a change from the gold frames, and on to the Marion Loos Gallery and the nervier, chancier realm of contemporary art.

I went through the swing doors, and there facing me was Anita and Leslie Beck's bedroom. The tawny curtains, the dun scratchy wallpaper, the orangey chair, the best white linen, the silver-backed comb on the bur-oak dressing table; and somehow the shadow of Leslie Beck was there upon the bed, humping away, defacing and yet enlivening, as if one film were superimposed upon another, and the stronger image showing through. But of course that was only in my mind, and I hoped not ever in Anita's. I thought it was probably not a very good painting, anyway, but what did I know?

Marion wasn't there. She was out at the Tate.

"There's been a nibble for the MacIntyre," said Barbara helpfully. "Of course, it would be now they're all packed up and on their way back to Scotland."

It was a world I didn't understand and said as much. I said I wanted to buy the Anita Beck painting.

Barbara said she wasn't sure it was for sale. Aphra said she was pretty sure it wasn't. I said, since it didn't say anywhere it wasn't for sale, why wouldn't it be? If I was prepared to spend my life savings on a painting in the middle of a recession, why shouldn't I?

Barbara said, "Oh, dear," and asked if I was all right. I said I was, and why shouldn't I be? She took me into the small back room and made me some chamomile tea, and suggested we wait until Marion came back. I have always thought chamomile to be rather nasty slimy stuff, but I drank it, and presently my heart stopped beating so fast. The phone on the desk rang.

"Aphra," called Barbara, "it might be Ben. Can you take it?"

"No, I can't," called Aphra from the far side of the gallery, causing a possible customer, a woman in a turban, to look up, startled. We didn't behave like that at Accord Realtors. "I'm not going to interfere between husband and wife. All that happens is that everyone hates you."

So Barbara took the call perforce, and it was indeed her husband, and he was obviously not happy. She had to hold the phone some way from her ear. "Yes," she said, and "yes, but," "but I can't possibly," "but we agreed," "you're not being reasonable," "I was only looking at paintings," and, growing bolder and angrier, "What difference does it make if you're asleep and I come home at one o'clock, or two o'clock, or three," and then she wept a little.

"Shall I leave the room?" I asked, but she nodded at me to stay, and then put the receiver down hard and fast.

"He's impossible," she said, "impossible." And then to Aphra, "I'm going to have to go home. Ben says he's not going to be my babysitter. He just doesn't seem to understand. This is his baby, too. Why does he act as if it were just mine?"

"Because you stayed out late with Leslie Beck the creep," said Aphra, "when you were meant to be on parole. So your warder is angry. Why ever did you do it?"

"I was drunk," said Barbara, surprisingly. "All that sake."

"I didn't mean staying out late," said Aphra. "I meant getting married and having a baby."

Barbara apologized to me, and to Marion in advance, and hurried home.

"Marriage is a prison," said Aphra. "The husband is the warder, and the children are chains round the ankles. I'm going to be like Marion; I'm going to stay out of the way of the Life Force, as defined by Leslie Beck."

"You'd lose a lot," I said. But I was quite cured of my own surfeit of jealousy; Leslie Beck was simply not a fit subject for it, and I even began to wonder whether I couldn't do very well without putting Anita Beck's painting on my wall. Why, at this stage of my life, did I begin to want souvenirs, mementos? It was absurd.

"Have you ever met this Leslie Beck?" asked Aphra.

"I have," I said.

"And that's why you want the painting?" She had clear, direct eyes.

"Yes."

"What is it about this Leslie Beck?" asked Aphra.

"The size of his dong," I said, getting annoyed with the way her generation patronized mine, and I was gratified when she looked quite shocked.

"Barbara didn't say anything about that," said Aphra, and left me alone. It was like a tennis match, played with someone much better than you. You managed to bat back one terrifying shot, only to receive another.

Marion came back from the Tate.

"Why, Nora," she said, loftily. "How lovely to see you!"

She was looking elegant. She wore a kind of taupe silk suit and a little spotted scarf. Her nails were long and red. If anyone told her now not to wear rubber gloves to peel cucumbers, he'd receive short shrift. I was wearing my comfortable shoes. I thought, "I could publish the story of your life, if I wanted," but not even that power gave me consolation.

"Aphra tells me you want to buy the Anita Beck," she said. She was distant and formal. Rosalie was more her friend than I. She had something against me. What was it? What I had and she had not? Husband, home, kids, domesticity? The sense that I patronized her, as Aphra patronized me? I wished I hadn't come. I wished I'd plodded back to Ed.

"I'm not sure about buying," I said. "Rosalie told me it was here."

"I don't want you to have it," said Marion Loos. "When I think what Anita went through because of you, I'd rather you didn't."

It was one of the more unfortunate days of my life. I should have stayed at work. I should not have told Mr. Render lies. I was being

punished. I rose to go. Marion put out an elegant hand to re-
strain me.

"And where would you put it? On a wall that's shared by you
and Ed? Think about it, Nora. You were shameless, the lot of you.
No rigor, no self-discipline, in and out of each other's beds."

I opened my mouth to protest and shut it again.

"And what is more," said Marion, "you were all so self-satisfied.
You thought you were doing me a good turn, you thought you
were being so generous, deigning to educate me."

What is more, what is more!

"What is more," said Marion, "you thought a damp basement
was good enough for me, so I have asthma to this very day. I had
to use my inhaler in the Tate today. It was embarrassing. Something
they spray in the air.

"You know what you lot did," said Marion. "You used me as a
servant, wiping your babies' bottoms, picking up your dirty panties.
You didn't see it like that, oh no. I stood it for years," said Marion
Loos, "and it was all appalling. But what did I know? You took
advantage of me."

"I think I'd better go," I said. I was cold to my heart. I hate rows,
voices raised, people telling home truths. It was what she was born
to, no doubt. What we'd never saved her from. The fishwife lay
beneath a thin, thin veneer of poise and self-control. I thought I
disliked her. I thought of Ed bringing her home. If she hadn't been
so pretty, would he have done it? Of course not. A plain and spotty
girl talking about forged Van Goghs could be left to her own fate;
a pretty one, not so.

"I don't mean to make you angry," said Marion.

"You have a bit," I said. "Anyway, you've saved me throwing
away thousands of pounds. Your Barbara asked me to say she was
sorry, she had to go home; her husband's angry because she spent
the night with Leslie Beck."

It was Marion Loos's turn to have the color drain from her cheeks. She sat down abruptly. She didn't bother to smooth her short skirt or keep her legs together. She seemed ungainly and young.

"Oh, Christ," said Marion Loos.

"We're all upset," I said. "He's stirred everything up. But Barbara didn't mention the size of his dong to Aphra, so I expect it's shriveled rather with age. I believe they do."

Marion began to laugh. She stretched out her arms toward me. "I'm sorry," she said, "really sorry. Of course you can buy the painting. No one else is going to. I can't afford to turn away trade, just for the sake of principle. I'm not like Vinnie and the rest of you. I have to live in the real world. And as for Anita, I'm just being hypocritical."

Cautiously, I let myself be embraced, and felt my resentment drain away. I am not very good at the new habit of touching and embracing; I was brought up without it. I associate it too clearly with sex. Little Miss Virgo, Vinnie would say. Little Miss Butter Wouldn't Melt.

Marion outstripped her teachers in so many ways; I was proud of her. I didn't say so. I thought she might hit me.

I've had enough of all these true confessions. I've changed my mind. I'm not going into detail about my affair with Vinnie, which has nothing to do with Leslie Beck's Life Force. Vinnie beckons gently, and women follow sometimes. Leslie Beck brandishes his giant phallus, and women lie wounded all around. Besides which, since Rosalie jeered at my use of the word "affair," I feel quite nervous of it. I suppose it has got a kind of old-fashioned ring. What am I supposed to say? The furtive intimate relations I enjoyed for a while with Vinnie? I suppose Rosalie would like me to say "fucking," but I won't. She can do what she likes with Mr. Power-Cable Collier plus Pekingese; but as for me, I don't fuck, I have affairs. I have a husband, a home, children, and many obligations, and I have affairs the better to sustain them. Husbands may have affairs for all kinds of reasons—what do I know? Wives have them not just to assuage the desires of the flesh, but to quell the raging spirit.

But since Marion took me so suddenly and surprisingly to task for my infidelity—if that's an okay word—I feel less sure of myself. So I'll be brief.

It began the day after Susan left with Leslie and Lady Angela for Bordeaux. It hardly seemed her most direct route home, though none of us liked to say so. Nor had she and Vinnie had any particular disagreement. Vinnie had given up his part-time work at the medical practice; *How to Tone Up Your Heart* had done very well at the bookstores, and a longer and more interesting book, *The Nature of Dreams*, had been well received by serious critics. Vinnie and Susan were finally out of debt.

"I don't know which she disliked more," said Vinnie sadly, as we picked out aubergines and yellow peppers from one of the glossier stalls in the Périgueux market, "my giving up on the healing arts, betraying everything we thought we stood for, or the people she admires taking me seriously. Better if I'd stuck to diets."

How mean of Susan, I thought. Vinnie wore a blue-and-white-striped T-shirt. He had grown a mustache. He was tanned, fleshy, and handsome, the way Gérard Depardieu is. We had left the others behind. Ed and I had had a minor disagreement that morning. Ed had said what a pity Susan had left. I'd said oh really, why? He'd said because now there was no one to talk to. I'd said did that mean he couldn't talk to me? He'd said you know what I mean, and I'd said no, I did not. I was hurt and upset. In other words, I was prepared and ready to take offense, prepared and ready to go with Vinnie to the Périgueux market, just the two of us. Long, long ago I lost faith in the sincerity of my own righteous indignation. If you hear it from anyone—whether yourself, a spouse, a boss, a politician, a general—understand some evil is planned.

My eyes were still red-rimmed with tears. Vinnie bought me a
Pernod in a bar. Then another. People stared. It was a hot, hot day.
We went down to the river to see if it was cooler. It was not. I was
still upset. Vinnie had a soft heart. He could not bear to see anyone
in distress. He put his arms around me. He was a completely different
shape from Ed. Ed's belly was concave where it met, or failed to
meet, my midriff. Vinnie's was convex; it butted into me, firm and
blue-striped, offering powerful consolation. There was no one
around. The strong garlic-and-oil fingers tried to push up the narrow
hem of my dress: a rather feeble Indian cotton, I remember, browny-
pink stamped with large orange flowers, hideous in retrospect but
having a kind of flimsy accessibility—no doubt why I was wearing
it. I keep the sash belt at the back of my panties drawer, though
the dress itself, along with all the other garments one once wore
and loved, has long since been sucked up into the maw of time and
vanished.

"It's too hot out here," he said, and drew me into the bushes.

What the romantic (and Ed tells me I am romantic) remembers
of these events is the place, the ambience, the totality of someone
else's being and body, not sexual detail. Unless something is un-
pleasant, or truly remarkable (like the size of Leslie Beck's dong),
actual performance gets subsumed into the gestalt, fuzzy around the
edges like the orange flowers on the browny-pink dress, part of the
whole but not its total purpose. Whether Vinnie was good or bad
in bed, or on the stony banks of the Dordogne, I cannot remember.
Better to be Vinnie, I think, and have your total self remembered
with affection and pleasure, than to be Leslie Beck and have your
sexual prowess recalled, because that must, with age, fail, and as
that diminishes, so must you. But I'm not a man, I wouldn't know.
It can only be speculation, since men are so nervous about sexual
performance, they seldom talk, let alone write, about what really
matters to them.

Mostly I remember the blue-and-white T-shirt stretched over a tight belly Susan nagged him about, and a lizard sitting on a hot stone, staring at me with unblinking eyes, as if the kind of stillness, the suspension of time which can fall like a protection around lovers, had stretched to include him, too. Or perhaps it was a her. Who's to tell, with lizards?

I said it would not, could not, happen again. Should not have happened in the first place. It was beneath his dignity either to agree or to argue. I claimed we had meant, and planned, disloyalty to no one. He asked me not to be hypocritical. I shut up.

I didn't "love" Vinnie as I loved Leslie Beck, though I'm sure that if love is a thing to be deserved, Vinnie deserved it more. I think what happened was that our intimate knowledge of each other, that inevitable component of the friendship of couples, had brimmed over its accepted edge, swollen by excitement, secrecy, fulfillment. But then, by some unlikely good fortune, and I can see it as good fortune, and by virtue of a kind of mutual embarrassment, the heady brew evaporated.

Susan returned unexpectedly. Anita, she said, was tedious; Lady Angela made passes; London would be hot and empty. She'd changed her mind. We, her friends, were the lesser of various evils. Opportunities to be alone with Vinnie were limited. When we could, we took them, Vinnie and I, over the years. But when I quarreled with Susan, allowed myself to be upset over the matter of Ed and she on the bed during a party, I also managed to make it happen that I could not see Vinnie again without invoking comment. Should I take credit for that? I don't know. During the summer with Leslie, I felt faithless to Ed and did not like the feeling. Over the years with Vinnie, if you had asked me about "infidelity," I would have denied its application to myself, and believed it. Ed and I had become one person, albeit with two independent bodies; Ed and Vinnie were friends; what I did with Vinnie included Ed; it was just that it seemed better not to tell him.

There was no serious "need to know."

Vinnie's relationship with Susan was trickier, and a source of grief and worry to him. I think if I had pushed it, he would have left Susan and come to me, but I didn't want that. I wanted Ed and Vinnie; I wanted my cake and the icing, too; and since it hurt no one, why not?

I heard a noise. I looked up from the page. And there, facing me, clear as day at Accord Realtors, stood Susan. For a moment, I was confused. It was Susan of eighteen years ago, back from Bordeaux, back to chaperone her husband, back from her outing with Leslie Beck and Lady Angela, back to kill me. I must have felt guiltier than I thought I did. But no, it was now; it was the nineteen-nineties, not the seventies, and Susan was still brisk, beautiful, and superior. She had got thinner, not fatter; her eyes were still large and luminous. She looked what she was: intelligent, competent, busy. She looked like Glenn Close.

I pushed the manuscript into the drawer.

"Susan," I said.

"This has gone on long enough," said Susan. "One of us has to speak to the other."

"Not necessarily," I said, but I found myself smiling. I was so pleased to see her.

"I'm sorry," she said, and before I knew it I was embracing her. She felt like my mother, which made me feel like a forgiven child: trusted, trusting, and safe.

"What are you sorry about?"

"I can't honestly remember," she said, "but someone has to apologize, and I can't wait around anymore for you to do it. Rosalie's called me. Leslie Beck has turned up again: that's more interesting than us not speaking."

She wanted me to go halves with her, she said, buying poor Anita Beck's painting. It didn't seem right that it should go to a stranger, but she couldn't possibly afford the ridiculous sum Marion was asking. After all she'd done for Marion, you would have thought

NORA   147

she could have made some concessions. And Marion had let all kinds of things slip in the past, which Susan now reported to me.

Both Mr. Render and Mr. Collier were out of the office. I felt increasingly at liberty at Accord Realtors to write my novel (or my memoirs) and to speak to friends during office hours. Since Mr. Collier had been wooing my best friend, Rosalie, I had felt more and more like a colleague and less and less like an employee. I rather wondered whether it was not self-interest which prevented me from warning Rosalie against taking baths with Mr. Collier, but you can be too paranoid, even about your own nature.

"I know all that," I said to Susan when she'd finished. "I've always known."

"But it's totally shocking," said Susan, whose job these days, I remembered, was fund-raising for a child adoption agency. She had discovered in herself, as many of us do, a liking for sitting down in her best dress at formal dinners, and having food put in front of her, and talking to people of importance and distinction. She had done her early shift working with the deprived and miserable, her middle shift trying to lever society toward taking responsibility for the deprived and miserable; now she just wanted some peace and a good dinner, and Anita Beck's painting at a reduced price as a memento of more interesting times. But she was my friend again, or said so. I must take a positive, not a negative, view of her actions and attitude. Look, I was really pleased to see Susan, not to be alienated from her anymore, not to have to cross the supermarket aisle to avoid an encounter. Nevertheless, she had made Vinnie unhappy in a way she needn't have, seeing her own bad temper as somehow sanctified, allowing it full rein, exercising it needlessly: "I'm cross. You must put up with it." That, more than anything, in men or women, makes for unhappy homes.

And why did she want to share Anita's painting with me? To save money? I thought not. She had plenty. I had seen Vinnie's *Midriff Diet for Men* on display in bookshops everywhere for the past year. More likely it was an attempt to resurrect her past and see her minor fling with Leslie Beck, the man with the biggest dong in the world, on a par with my summer of love. Although she, like Rosalie, had gotten a baby out of hers, and I hadn't, theirs had been of no other consequence. Mine had.

I supposed Marion would say that made my sin against Anita Beck worse, but who was Marion to put on moral airs? She must be wondering herself, or she would not have felt obliged to tell Susan how she acquired the Marion Loos Gallery—something I had known for years, and also managed to keep secret for years. I will try to take the sting from it by recording it, as I have done Leslie Beck's reappearance in Marion's life, but not yet my own. Now I will look out of Marion's unfairly large, wide eyes. It becomes quite a relief not to look out of my own. It is pleasant to feel, as Marion feels, somehow better than other people: that she has the prerogative of proper feeling, proper behavior—a full yet discreet sensibility. Oh, yes, it is quite pleasant to be Marion, after all. To have no children, no hostages to fortune, when it comes to it, is quite a relief. I enjoy it here, in Marion's mind.

I find it quite difficult to like people; I think I got into the habit of dislike when I was a child. "Oh, Marion! Marion was looking down her nose when she was born," my mother would say.

Ida and Eric were both large, overflowing people, as was my younger brother, Peter. I was always tall for my age and had large feet, but I was thin. By the time Peter was twelve, the others were all two stone overweight apiece. I was born controlled, and was either born or soon became an organizer. I had to be. If I wanted to leave the house with my hair combed, I would first have to find the comb, somewhere among the dirty dishes and the cigarette stubs and the lottery tickets. All of them smoked, Petey from the age of eight. None of them read books. Both parents would tell friends I had been switched at birth. At first it hurt me; then I longed for it to be true, though I could see too great a resemblance, more's the pity, between my father's nose and my own to allow me to really believe it. My family felt that the day existed in order to be enjoyed; I felt that the day was a mere framework in which one could some-how "get on"—though where I was meant to be getting on to I did not understand, and there was no one around to tell me. Those born, like me, strangers to their family by virtue of their intelligence

usually respond to language and have books to help them out, or
their English teacher takes an interest, and so they more easily find
their proper niche in the world, get to university and start a life
appropriate to themselves. But I had a problem with the written
language: I was, and still am, mildly dyslexic, though excellent with
numbers, and some slight functional disorder left me unable to draw
anything more complex than a cat sitting on a table. It was not until
I was fourteen and plucked up enough courage to go into the local
art gallery that I understood where my passion and my interest
lay—that is to say, in other people's paintings, in alternative visions
of reality. But I didn't know what to do with it, and, again, there
was no one to tell me. Bad at English, bad at art, good at math.
They steered me into the bank at an early age, and even that Eric
and Ida thought was overly ambitious. And I liked no one at the
bank, either: everyone was so plain and ugly; everything you looked
at seemed contrived to root you brutally to the here and now; it
was mean of spirit.

I hated my family. I hated boys, whose messy fumblings under
skirts upset me, and whose only ambition, so far as I could see, was
to get the better of me, reduce me to their own sorry state. Other
girls got loved, it seemed to me; I was the kind boys just wanted
to bring down a peg or two. I hated my job. I hated the Van Gogh
fake worst of all. Not that it had been painted in the first place,
which seemed a compliment to the artist, but that no one even
noticed. What did that say about the curators of this exhibition?

When Ed, the photographer, and the picture editor turned up at
the "Bank and the Painter" show (I knew it was a wrong association
at the time but couldn't have told you why), I felt my heart leap. I
liked the look of these three men; I liked the way ideas seemed to
be in control of their flesh. They were more animated than the
people I was used to, who tended to the pudgy, who had the pallor
of the unenlightened, the thick pale skin of those who are anxious
to keep doubt out—an altogether stolid and complacent look.

To be translated, in the course of a week, from beans on toast with Ida and Eric in Norwich to avocado vinaigrette with Ed and Nora in Primrose Hill, although the price was washing the dishes and putting the children to bed, seemed some kind of miracle. The marvel had happened. What I had always hoped to be true was indeed true: that if you have a genuine liking and an enthusiasm, albeit untutored, for something, just for its own sake, why, then, this counts as a rare gift, and you can become a valued member of society just on account of it. Your difference will be noted and admired; the world will open its arms to you. I lived under the stairs, and I listened and I learned.

"Under the stairs" worried Nora and Ed, so they moved me to Leslie and Jocelyn Beck's basement, where, everyone told me, there was "lots of room." But there was not the same atmosphere. Leslie Beck did not read books; he had safe reproductions on the walls; Jocelyn collected horse brasses; Hope and Serena, for all their dullness, told lies. I did what I had to, to earn my rent: developed asthma and babysat in the evenings and on weekends for Ed and Nora, Rosalie and Wallace, Vinnie and Susan, and picked up what knowledge, what social graces, I could. I meant, after my first week at the Courtauld, to end up at least director of the Tate Gallery. So quickly life can change.

I don't think I was particularly highly sexed. Perhaps it was just that Eric and Ida had been noisy and frequent lovers, and I was determined that what was good enough for them was not going to be good enough for me. Pushing open the bathroom door one day and seeing Leslie Beck's erect organ, purply and mottled, unnerved me; I told the others about it. Perhaps I shouldn't have. But I was really pleased to discover I could tell a good story, be socially accepted, make other people laugh. Giving an account of Leslie Beck's dong, as they loved to call it, liberated me just a little from feelings of inferiority. I became equal to them. I worked for them one by one, but I was from that moment part of the group.

When Jocelyn and Leslie parted and Anita moved in, and I had to help Rosalie with poor flipped Jocelyn, I was linked into the group even more tightly. My benefactors, my friends. I trusted them—they would share their last crust with you for the privilege of helping you—with the exception of Leslie Beck. I understood him too well. I understood that his background was like mine; that he had fought his way out and up; that his talent was for making money and losing it, and it was a talent they marveled at but didn't envy. I understood that Leslie Beck believed he would have to buy his friends, and they let themselves be bought, out of kindness to him. He envied them their social ease, the buzz of conversation that rose from their dinner tables; he wanted to be one of them, and the more he wanted to, the less he could be, because the point was that the only way to be one of them was not to want to be one of them. He had attached himself to them, and they went along with it; me, they had attached to themselves. It was a better position to be in. I was their good work, and I squirmed beneath it, while at the same time—I won't say "loving" them; I will say "not disliking" them. For me, that's quite a lot. Gratitude is a terrible emotion.

Leslie Beck recognized himself in me, of course he did. I failed to find him attractive, as did the others. I knew too much even then about that kind of man: redheaded curly-haired males with biceps, vigorous, somehow bursting out of too-tight, too-bright clothes. You meet them in betting shops and afternoon drinking clubs. My dad had a couple of friends like that; when they came round for a drink and a game of cards, my mum would always put on her lipstick. They like to notch you up, tell the lads about you. But what do the Noras, the Rosalies, the Susans know? They're innocent. They think marriage is all about true love or lust; they don't understand self-interest. Men like Leslie acquire women like Jocelyn if they possibly can—a cut above them socially—and learn what they can until they've learned enough. Or else they go for the plain ones with a good dowry, like Anita, who will work hard and be grateful and

never cause trouble. But to satisfy the demands of self-interest is
not to satisfy the soul; they swagger, but they're never content;
they're restless; they need acceptance. And scheme to get it, because
all they know is scheming. That I understood in him. We were
rivals, and I was winning.

The day after Anita moved in, Leslie waylaid me on the steps as
I was on my way to the Courtauld.

"Marion," he said, "thank you for being such a help with Jocelyn.
We've all been having quite a time with her lately. I expect it's the
menopause."

"She's rather young for that," I said.

"What would I know? Hope and Serena will need continuity. I
hope you can stay on."

The court would need to be convinced, in any custody case, that
Hope and Serena had continuity, that is to say, and I didn't feel
inclined to help him out. I said I'd stay for a couple of weeks, and
by that time they'd be used to Anita. He said it was not certain that
Anita was staying. I said Susan and Vinnie's au pair was leaving,
so I could move into their house; it was comfortable and convenient
there. Leslie said it was time he had the basement treated for dry
rot before it spread to the rest of the house, and had central heating
and a proper kitchen and bathroom installed. Of course, then I'd
have to pay proper rent, but he'd keep it as low as possible. I said
I'd have to be on my way; I didn't want to miss a lecture on "Cubism
and Politics." He asked if he could come down that evening; he
wanted a shoulder to cry on.

And all through the rest of the day I thought about whether or
not I wanted Leslie Beck to cry on my shoulder, and whether or
not, if I did, I would be able to have a centrally heated, newly
converted flat in Rothwell Gardens free. And I let him cry on my
shoulder, and when we went in to look at the old boiler room, and
I showed him the dry-rot spore which he had never wanted to believe
in (a surveyor's house is the last to get seen to, as the dentist's child

has the worst-cared-for teeth), and he showed me his mottled, purply thing stretching up toward the light of day, I began to laugh, thinking of the comparison, and of what Ida and Eric had done to me, that I should make such a comparison, or perhaps it was just exposure to too much "Art and the Symbol" at the Courtauld. Dusty and dirty as it was down there, I succumbed to Leslie, and became part of his fiefdom; he, for his part, felt able to come to terms with and eradicate the dry rot. A kitchen and a bathroom were more or less put in, though the plumbing for both was inadequate. There was no hot water, other than by kettle. The central heating never arrived. But I stayed on and helped with his children, and when Anita was away with her parents, I would join Leslie in the bedroom for the night. It was part of a bargain; it was part of the pattern of my life—part of my revenge upon it. It stopped me having to think about boyfriends or why I wasn't married. It was automatic. It was without effort. I went to his and Anita's wedding and helped look after Hope and Serena throughout the ceremony without turning a hair, merely being glad for their sakes that their lives were to be more settled. Any qualms I might have had about deceiving Anita disappeared completely on her wedding day. She had turned into Mrs. Be-Done-By-As-You-Did.

There was some quality in Leslie's sexual energy, his very in-domitability, the size and scope of the tool fate had given him, which failed to ignite the erotic imagination—or, at any rate, mine. I could take or leave this experience, and it paid the rent.

But one day Anita came down to my flat. She was crying. She was wearing a particularly dreary dress. It was navy blue and had a little white collar. She tried to look authoritative, like Jocelyn on a good day, but always failed. She had told Leslie she was pregnant. She had thought he would be pleased. Instead, he shuddered, said he was already a father, he did not want another child, there was too much expense involved, and asked her to consider an abortion. I suspected it was not expense that made him shudder—he was doing very well at the time financially—but rather the thought of his life being wound even more closely with Anita's. The planning deal with which her father had been connected was long since accomplished, to everyone's good profit; and just as dentists have trouble getting patients to remember to pay their bills once the pain has gone, so Anita, just by existing, had trouble reminding Leslie of her onetime importance in the scheme of his life. Now his need was gone, and she was a fixture to which no gratitude was owed.

"Why don't you just hit him?" I asked. I felt incensed. I felt he had gone too far. I had finished at the Courtauld and was running a small contemporary-art gallery in Hampstead—not very good paintings and not very much money—while the owners, Jane and George Harris, were away; I rather naively imagined they would be so pleased with my performance when they came back that they would ask me to stay. The contrary was true. I was young; I had imagined people sold bad art at the lower end of the market because they couldn't tell the difference between good and bad. Only little by little, as the world worked upon me, did I realize that many people like "bad" art. I try not to make crude value judgments, these days. My taste is like a sharp blade blunted by disappointment; I saw and saw away at "good" and "bad," hemming and hawing like any other gallery owner, trying to keep prices down and commissions up. As it was, when Jane and George Harris returned, they found all the "good" paintings, as I saw them, on the walls, and all the "bad" paintings stacked in the basement, and nothing sold. In retrospect, I have some sympathy with them: supposing I came back and found Aphra's choices all over my walls, and my income up but my reputation down (where it counts, at the Tate, the Metropolitan, and so forth). I would most certainly ask her to leave. But at the time it hurt. It was just before this happened, when my future seemed secure, that I thought I could afford a moral gesture, and moved out of Rothwell Gardens. Anita, of course, saw my leaving as an unkind act, for she had hoped that I'd be able to help with the baby, and here I was, helpful Marion, deserting her. I think she did hit Leslie. At any rate, little Polly was eventually born.

Leslie kept an eye on me after I left his house. He would turn up from time to time at whatever dreary place I happened to be living in, whichever back-street gallery I toiled in—partly to gloat, partly to offer sympathy, partly to use my shoulder to cry on. His mother in the north had died; his father seemed scarcely to notice, just nodded her out of the house in her coffin, the same way he'd nodded her out shopping, and got on with the garden. Leslie wept over that. Jocelyn tried to turn Hope and Serena against him. That annoyed but did not distress him. Anita refused to smile and scin-tillate. That shamed him. Business was bad. That really agitated him. He'd borrowed too much; used the security of Rothwell Gardens for some additional loan; lived in anxiety lest someone foreclose on the property. Anita's father would lend him money, but only if he put half the house in his wife's name. This he refused to do.

"Men earn the money," he'd say. "What do women want of them—everything? Women see marriage as a meal ticket for life. Anita broke up my marriage to Jocelyn. At least Jocelyn's family did their best for her, dowrywise. Anita should think of that."

We'd make love—Leslie's workout, I'd call it, if I wanted to upset him, and I often did. I felt he was right—that my life had run up against a dead end—and I could feel my benefactors thinking the same thing, and hated it.

"You should have stayed with me," said Leslie. "Stuck it out. I'd have left Anita for you in the end." That wasn't true. He hadn't liked me leaving Rothwell Gardens without his permission, that was all it was.

"What, and throw my life away?" I'd say. He was a lonely man. I wanted someone like Ed, or Vinnie, someone companionable, if I wanted anyone. And they didn't come my way. Nothing seemed to come my way. Not even Eric and Ida could be proud of me. Who could be proud of a female shop assistant, with no money, no home, no husband, no children? Dregs, and I had worked my way so proudly into dregs. Better that I'd ironed aspiration out of my soul and stayed home.

What I wanted to do was impossible, because it would cost half a million pounds to do it, and how did someone like me find that kind of money? I wanted to run my own gallery—not to work in some sad art shop in the suburbs, selling prints and cards, but to own and run a proper gallery in the West End, where I'd have enough status and power to be part of the mysterious and ongoing world of the painter, at its leading edge, where the splashing of paint upon canvas—or these days, board—becomes part of the culture of nations. I wanted to play the role of the connoisseur, to be both patron and muse to the world I loved. I wanted to be somewhere where at least a few people would know what I meant if I said "good." I had seen the premises, just behind the Museum of Mankind, and they were empty, and waiting. I had the skill, the training, the business sense, the contacts, the discrimination—everything that was required except the capital. And I remembered how I had jeered at Ida, when once she'd told me she'd have studied music at the guildhall but her parents couldn't afford it; she'd had to go out to work instead. A likely tale, I'd thought; an easy way out; an easy justification for lack of commitment. Now I could see just how real and hard a factor money was—or, rather, the lack of it. How it stood between people and what they could become.

Now I know some women manage to marry a million pounds and much more besides, and I daresay I am as beautiful as they are, feature by feature, but I am not that kind of woman. Anyone who wants a good time would do well to avoid me. I say what I feel, and feel what I say, and both things can be difficult to live with, and neither is the way to marry a millionaire.

I was sitting staring into the half-dark one evening, bemoaning my fate, when Leslie came to my door. I was surprised; I'd had a visit from him only a couple of weeks before; he usually came round every other month or so. He came to me with a proposition. His visit, he said, was for business, not pleasure.

A wealthy South African man, a Mr. Clifford Streiser, had just flown in with his wife. Mr. Streiser headed a consortium which was buying a thirty-acre derelict docklands site with a view to its development. Mrs. Brenda Streiser had come with him, to visit a fertility clinic in Harley Street. Leslie, if he played his cards right, could handle, as agent, the Streiser development, and all his troubles would be at an end. Playing his cards right included wining, dining, and doing the odd favor.

"I am not a call girl, Leslie," I said, "not yet. And no businessman would see me as a favor. I am not the type."

Leslie looked quite shocked.

"I'm not talking hundreds here, Marion," he said. "I'm talking hundreds of thousands, maybe a million. And don't you need half of that million to start your gallery?"

"Whatever it is," I said, "I see you mean to take a fifty-percent commission."

"You'll learn," he said. "Once you have your gallery, you won't sound so superior."

I said I was baffled as to how we were to extract a million pounds from the unfortunate Mr. Streiser, or what particular part I could possibly play.

"If I could forge an old master, I'd do it," I said to him. "If I could bribe someone else to forge it, better still. But what would I bribe him with? My body? I'd be willing, but it would take ten years to earn it at current rates." I wouldn't make a good whore; I wasn't either good enough or bad enough: my heart not golden enough to be the cheerful kind, yet my soul stubbornly nonbiodegradable, being too occupied with mind to achieve a proper semblance of the debased and wretched fallen woman. Hopeless! Who'd want me?

He looked embarrassed and finally told me. We took the Streisers out to dinner at Claridge's. I rented a dress. It was creamy white and dead simple. I did my hair as the pregnant wife in the van Eyck painting had done hers. I made myself look quiet, intelligent, attractive, sane—the qualities people look for in babies. Leslie wore his best gray suit and a tie curiously toned down in color. He looked, for once, honest as well as competent. We made a good pair.

Cliff Streiser was a tall, broad-shouldered, pleasant, ordinary, and rather fleshy man who'd discovered the knack of making money without hurting anyone. All you did was buy up large tracts of derelict ground in overlooked places toward which the city crept, and which had always been despised, and then turn them into glittering shopping malls and office blocks, turn the shame of a district into the pride of the city, and you were honored for it. He looked a little confused, a little out of his depth; his bright eyes darted to and fro. Princess Margaret dined in a corner. "Wait till I tell my mother," he said. I liked that. I thought he was kind. His father was dead, and he mourned him. That seemed to me important, too. Wealth couldn't have happened to a nicer man. His first wife had gone off with a polo player. Well, that happens, if you suddenly grow rich and it goes to your wife's head. Polo players!

Mrs. Streiser the infertile, his new wife, was blond and pretty, brighter than he was and younger by some fifteen years. She had been that day to the "Pride of the Pharaohs" exhibition at the British Museum, and had stood in line to see the newly discovered Leonardo drawing on display there. That was really something. They had three black live-in servants in their large house in Cape Town. She showed me photographs of them, as if they were part of the family, and was even shopping for presents to take back to the cook's little girl. Yes, she let the cook have her little daughter live with them. Anything else, said Mrs. Streiser softly, would be unkind.

One way and another, considering how society restrains and

restricts its members, and the difficulty of resisting its pressures, I thought the Streisers could be described as a good couple, could almost slip through the eye of a needle and go to heaven.

I presented myself to them as Leslie's girlfriend, which was true enough. In fact, throughout the meal I spoke not a single lie, except once, when I said I was pregnant. And that I would have to have a termination, because I couldn't upset my parents. Well, South Africa is still a fairly old-fashioned society, and it seems parents there can get very upset when their unmarried daughters get pregnant. Now, what a pleasant and stable society for anyone, provided he or she is not black, in which to be a parent, if not necessarily a child.

"My dear," said Brenda Streiser, "you can't have an abortion. You have to have the baby. You will always regret it if you don't."

"But I can't do it to my parents," I said. "They don't even know about Leslie here. They're so old-fashioned. They're so proud of me. It will break their hearts."

"A baby's life is sacred," said Brenda. "And not yours to take away."

"Brenda's right," said Cliff. "She's always right about these things. Brenda's a marvel. I've got the brains, she's got the heart."

"I can't have babies," said Brenda. "So I know what I'm talking about."

"Poor Brenda," said Cliff. "She's had a terrible time. All that messing about with her insides, and all my fault."

"In the end," said Brenda, "it's his sperm count. Nothing to do with me. Not his fault, poor darling. Well, only in a way."

"Mumps," said Cliff, "when I was a grown lad. I told you, didn't I, Leslie? How I suffered! But what a man's suffering to a woman's?"

"You did indeed tell me," said Leslie. "What a tragedy!"

After prawn cocktails, we went on to Chateaubriand. I made little mews of appreciation, though I hate red meat. A good appetite's a good sign. I was trying hard not to dislike, not to be disliked. So much counted on me. I was looking very good. Not a hint of the asthma that sometimes plagues me. Other diners were staring at me, even more than at Princess Margaret. If I could dress like this all the time, eat in places like this, I thought, I would feel at ease and at home in the world. Perhaps my error had been to aim not high enough. I had been so gratified and stunned by my goatish leap from bank clerkery to life around the Bramleys that I had stayed upon that particular ledge too long. It was time to leap once again, and I could, I could. If, on one particular day, the dreary pattern of a lifetime changes, and just in the nick of time, the next change will also be sudden, and in the nick of time.

"Why don't you come back home to Cape Town and stay with us?" said Brenda. "Have the baby adopted, go back home; no one need ever know."

"I could never part with a baby once I'd had it," I said. "And besides, they depend on me at work. I can't just walk out, let them down." This baby was going to inherit good moral traits, as well as a handsome and healthy physique and a sweet and pliable nature.

"I'd like to adopt," said Brenda, "but Cliff had this silly prison sentence, before he even met me. They won't let us adopt. He hit a policeman who was beating up a black. He was only twenty-one."

"You could always try surrogate motherhood," said Leslie to Cliff, "but I don't suppose Brenda would fancy that."

"No, I wouldn't," said Brenda. "I think all that's unnatural. I don't want any other man's stuff in me. And I don't want Cliff putting any of his in someone else, and what would be the point, there's no sperm in it anyway."

"Hush," said Cliff, for the waiter was hovering.

"Eat up, darling," said Brenda. "I'm dying for the profiteroles."

I wept a little into my steak as I tried to eat up. Clifford ordered a bottle of claret that cost ninety-nine pounds. They knocked it back. I drank mineral water.

"Oh, dear," said Brenda, and she cried a little, too, because she loved her husband and wanted a baby and didn't see how to reconcile the two.

"The real problem is," said Leslie, "I'm already married. My wife has a weak heart. A man like me can't be expected to live celibate all his life. But I can't abandon her. It's not her fault. She's ill. If she found out about Marion, if there was a baby, it would kill her. What a mess we're all in!"

We contemplated the mess, and the more we contemplated it, the worse it seemed. At last Clifford solved it.

Clifford said, "Supposing you had your baby in secret, Marion, and you handed it over to us, and we compensated you for its loss. Then you wouldn't have to have an abortion, Leslie wouldn't have to confess to his wife, Brenda would have her baby, which would be as pretty as its mother and as able as its father, and I'd have given my wife the best present in the world."

Leslie didn't say "How much?" outright, though I thought he might have. We bargained through the profiteroles. I think Brenda thought we ought just to give her the baby, out of love and friendship, but Clifford thought a financial transaction, and a large one, would be preferable. We were breaking the laws of both nations. He didn't want me changing my mind at the last moment. "What's money," Leslie agreed, "compared to peace of mind?" And he suggested that if Brenda went on holiday for a few months before the baby was born, she could return to Cape Town with it in her arms, and no one would know it wasn't hers. Brenda looked happier than ever.

There is a world shortage of white newborn babies of good healthy stock on offer for adoption. The Marion whom Clifford and Brenda saw was not poor. She had other options. The deal was made at nine hundred fifty thousand pounds. Clifford couldn't quite bring himself to get to the million. I wept a little into my black *café filtre* to think of the baby from whom I would be parting, and said I must think about it; it was all so sudden.

I spent every night for a week at a cheap hotel with Leslie. He told Anita he was in Scotland. Leslie said he was doing this for Anita's sake, not his own; he had somehow to maintain the marital home. I became pregnant at once, and just as well. The week was the most fertile of my cycle. I wondered whether it was a happy coincidence, and thought probably not. Nothing that had to do with Leslie was coincidence. This had been well planned in advance, probably from the moment Clifford had let slip his wife was attending a fertility clinic. I found a paperback entitled *Fertility and Contraception: The Facts* in the back of Leslie's car. He had traded in the Porsche for a Citroën. I could tell things were not good for him.

At the end of the week he said, "We'll only be about three weeks out on your dates. It'll be just a little overdue."

I said, "That's all right. My brother and I were both a couple of weeks premature. It runs in the family."

I asked why he didn't make me pregnant before our meeting with the Streisers; he said to make sure I didn't get any ideas. I didn't pursue it.

He seemed to me a kind of devil man, pounding away at me with his chief asset in life, as if his future depended on it, which it probably did. The hotel was a hellhole. The bed was one of those old-fashioned narrow ones with a wire mesh for a base, not springs; it sagged in the middle. It was no holiday—though I was using up one of my precious holiday weeks.

I asked Leslie why he was so certain I was pregnant. He said there was an eighty-five-percent chance of it, and that was good enough for him. I asked him why he had had to book us into a back-street hotel in King's Cross used by whores at worst and strays from the station at best, and not Claridge's, and he said as he'd be deducting all expenses from my percentage of the Streisers' payment, he'd assumed I'd want the bill kept as low as possible.

I wondered whether the baby would inherit Leslie's temperament. If so, I was not sure I would be able to love it, especially if it was a boy. I asked myself if I would want to rear it, and the answer was no. I would produce the baby Brenda wanted, and she would make the best of it. Vinnie's baby, or Ed's, or Wallace's I could have loved, but not Leslie's. Was it to my credit or otherwise that I never had sexual relations with these three, though I daresay I could have had I tried? I was in and out of their bedrooms often enough. And it seems to be natural for men to want to bed their servants, their domestic or office maids, though not to have babies by them.

I think I was flattered that Leslie meant to have a baby through me, whatever his motives were.

I told Leslie I would have the pregnancy terminated if he did not agree to hand over seventy percent of the Streiser money, immediately, as it came in. One-third on agreement, one-third on delivery, one-third three months after the birth. I argued that since I was going through the actual process, the physical and emotional discomfort of birth, seventy-thirty to me was a reasonable division. He argued that since any baby was half the father's, and the idea and the contacts were his, fifty-fifty was more than kind to me. We settled at fifty-five–forty-five in my favor, and Leslie said the sooner I had my own gallery the better. The money was going directly into Leslie's bank account, laundered into some crevice of the dock development deal.

I called Cliff and Brenda and said that after much thought I agreed to the deal, and listened to Brenda's sigh of happiness, and marveled that something which would make me so unhappy could make another woman so happy. But I expect, like most women, she thought she could grow the baby into her own image, regardless of its genes. It is in this hope, I imagine, that some women have baby after baby: as the infant gets to its feet and begins to argue, displays its own temperament and character, they quickly have another, hoping this time it will work. It never does, of course, but on they go. Rosalie, Nora, Susan—ever hopeful. At least Anita gave in and stopped after one.

As soon as the first installment arrived, I went straight around to the real estate agents and put down a deposit on the premises that were to be the Marion Loos Gallery. I spent the next few months preparing to buy and borrow stock. People were helpful—surprisingly so. I was more liked than I deserved to be. I was moved by the way contacts and colleagues put themselves out in my behalf. For the last three months of the pregnancy I went to Italy and there toured churches and monasteries; the baby kept me good company. I conversed with him; I instructed him; he was completely my friend. He could not answer back, but I knew and he knew that I was doing the right thing. A baby brought up in a pleasant home with kind parents and three servants anywhere in the world has a better chance of happiness than one brought up in some squalid inner-city room, which was the best a single mother on an ordinary female wage could provide. What is natural, careless maternal love, we both agreed, fetus and myself, compared with the love of nonnatural parents who care profoundly, even unto a million pounds' worth of love?

For the last six weeks, Brenda came out to Venice to join me. She was very little and precise and eager. Churches bored her, but she liked sitting in St. Mark's Square drinking the most expensive coffee in the world. I didn't dislike her one bit. She made me drink chocolate; coffee would be bad for the baby. I hoped for her sake the baby would not take after Ida, or resemble its Uncle Peter. We gave birth in a nursing home outside Venice; I used her name.

If I myself couldn't manage to have been switched at birth, I would at least make Ida and Eric's version of my existence true for their grandchild. Switch the mothers, not the child. The baby was a boy, his hair a reddish fuzz. I supposed, from the books I had read, that this would fall out in about three months, and a stronger growth come in, and I was glad it would be left to Brenda to find this interesting, and important.

Brenda gave me an extra fifty thousand dollars after the birth, to make the sum up to a million.

"Don't let Cliff know," she said. "You know how men are. So proud! This is from my pocket, because that's what I feel like—a million dollars!" The original transaction had been in pounds sterling, but I didn't have the heart to tell her so and spoil her story, even for approximately twenty-five thousand pounds at an exchange rate of approximately two-to-one. I am not all bad, merely unmaternal.

I waved her and the baby goodbye from the Venice Hilton, had a good night's sleep, which is difficult when you have a newborn baby—I was sorry for Brenda—and then moved into a cheaper and more romantic hotel, which I thought was my style. For a week I comforted myself with the Renaissance, a period which always helps the close observer put human experience into a historical perspective. Then I went home to London—via Milan, where I bought the kind of clothes I thought women who ran West End galleries would wear—and completed the deal on the gallery.

Oddly enough, Leslie seemed to be far more upset about my lack of baby than I was. He had assumed he would have another girl: had believed he could only beget girls. On hearing I had sold his son, he quite took offense.

"You should never have done it," he said.

"It was your idea in the first place," I protested.

"You should never have gone through with it. I didn't think you would. It was just a way of getting you into bed for a whole week."

And I don't think I believed him. In the end, what does motive matter? I don't suppose God has the time or inclination to divine it before Judgment Day sounds and the dead are raised up in the full clamor of their righteous indignation and vigorous disclaimers. It's what we do that counts, not why. I opened the Marion Loos Gallery. Leslie got himself onto his financial feet again, and someone else brought up the baby. I didn't see Leslie after that for a long time. We had worn each other out, in some way I didn't quite understand, until there he was, standing in my doorway, with Anita's painting under his arm, and dust motes in the air, disturbing the tranquillity of the day.

Okay, out of Marion's head, back to my own. I, Nora, should be better equipped after this practice to explain Marion to Susan, but it doesn't seem to work like that. Just because I understand what it is to be Marion doesn't mean others can or want to.

"What shocks you about it?" I ask Susan, but I know that answer perfectly well. It shocks Susan that a woman should take her life into her own hands without permission from social workers. Since Susan is the one who normally interferes in other people's lives and is not herself interfered with, interference seems fine by her.

"You know perfectly well," says Susan. "Babies can't go to anyone just on whim. You're trying to annoy me, Nora. Next you'll tell me you think it's okay to sell your kidneys to the highest bidder."

I open my mouth and close it again. "No one else's business if I choose to," I want to say. "If I'd rather have a custom kitchen than a kidney, why shouldn't I?" But I don't want to argue with her. I just think she is quite the wrong wife for Vinnie.

We are in her house in Kew Gardens Square, one of the more desirable locations in the area served by Accord Realtors, and readily salable, should Vinnie and Susan ever wish to put it on the market.

In this it is quite unlike 12 Rothwell Gardens in Primrose Hill, though the houses themselves are very similar. In these, the hard times of the property market, location is all-important. In the central-city area, grandiose property above two million pounds can still be sold, as the Middle East empties after the Gulf War, houses with electronic security devices already in situ being in special demand. Anything in an apartment building with a security desk at the entrance and proper surveillance of all callers, and inside the apartment a room (usually a w.c.) already converted to a communications center—steel-walled against bomb and gun attack, with alarm system and radio equipment already installed, into which the dweller can retire at the first sign of trouble—can be sold at once, at the asking price. But good solid family houses in the inner-city area, and the next price bracket down, are now two a penny. Nobody wants them. Nobody can sell them. Only in the suburbs, where citizens still assume they can breathe the air and live without fear of terrorist or personal attack, are such houses in demand.

Susan's front garden was well pruned and tended. Her brass knocker was shiny. Her door key was on a proper ring, easily accessible, in a tidy bag. She and Vinnie had fought over the years, object for object, his tendency toward creative mess versus her determination to be orderly. I could see that some compromise had been reached, but that the terms of the armistice veered in her favor. The old splintery pine had been replaced by good, well-restored pieces, glossy with beeswax polish. My taste, of course, and Vinnie's, ran to dog hairs and old favorites and take-us-as-we-are and let's-eat-in-the-kitchen. Not so Susan.

We went into the drawing room. Flowers had been formally arranged. Bookshelves lined one wall. They sagged. This would have been Vinnie's victory—a battle won, if not a war. Vinnie disliked being dependent on carpenters, plumbers, painters, electricians. He thought every man of honor should be his own tradesman-craftsman. Susan would cry out for professionals: "Please, please, not another botched job!" Vinnie would say: "Oh, that! I can do that." And it might take him years, but eventually he'd get round to it, do-it-yourself book in hand. Why pay pounds when you can do it yourself for pennies? Susan would grit her teeth; her mouth had set into the look of someone who gritted her teeth. It was no longer soft and full, vulnerable; it was firm and thin. But he'd won about the books: they were old and shabby, and very few of them had been published post-1950, which meant they were difficult to keep clean. A duster, swept along the shelf, would catch the bindings, the old jackets, and tear them. It was what we at Accord Realtors call "a most gracious room"—that is to say, there was space for a grand piano, on which were some family photographs and Vinnie's award for Best Food Writer of the Year—something which looked like a copper leg of lamb perched on a brass plinth. He'd spent a couple of years as a food columnist, Susan said, on a Sunday paper. I knew that. I'd read it every week. Vinnie was away. I was disappointed to hear it. Of course. He was in the States, researching the relationship between dairy products and catarrh.

"Poor Vinnie," said Susan, "they keep his nose to the grindstone. I think he'd much rather be writing books on the nature of reality, but that kind of book doesn't sell."

And I held my tongue and didn't remind her of Vinnie's book on the nature of dreams, which had sold but had not suited her view of her husband as a person of the flesh, which left her as a creature of the spirit. In order that she be ethereal, he must be solid. Or so Vinnie had often complained, breaking off more French bread, spooning out more apricot confiture, while Susan sipped her black coffee. That was the summer they weren't getting on too well, the summer she'd left with Leslie Dong the magnificent.

"Nora," said Susan, "there's something I need to share with you." I know this "sharing." It means someone is determined you're going to end up thinking just as she does. She wants you on her side. And she doesn't mind hurting you. I didn't say "I see. And not just the cost of Anita Beck's painting." If my Colin and her Amanda were sharing my kitchen in the nude, she and I might well end up joint grandparents. Vinnie and Susan, Ed and Nora, Rosalie and—who? Wallace, down from his mountain? Mr. Collier the mad electrician? All brought together again, with Anita Beck's painting of Leslie Beck's bedroom on the wall, to keep the past in tune with the present. I did not think Marion would be washing dishes for us; some things change.

"Share away, Susan," I said, and felt almost fond of her again. I had been jealous because her house was twice the size of my house, and because she ran a charity and I worked part-time at Accord Realtors, and because Vinnie still had energy and initiative and Ed liked to sit at home and watch TV. And because she had Leslie Beck's daughter and I, at best, could only have Leslie Beck's grand-child. But there was more that we shared than that drove us apart: a whole past. I forgave her.

And she shared. She shared.

She told me some things I already knew and some I did not.

She told me how angry she had been with Vinnie and all of us the day she left for Bordeaux with Leslie Beck and Lady Angela. Not because of anything in particular we had done but because of what we were, because we were self-indulgent and self-satisfied and could talk only of food and babies. She was not like us; she had things to do, and here she was trapped with a husband and two small children she had acquired almost by accident. She was being sucked down by hot sun and wine, and the crackle of cicadas was making her deaf, and her brain was ceasing to work, and she kept tripping over half-naked children.

"We were on holiday," I said. "We were just being, not doing."

"Nora," Susan said, "you and Rosalie, whenever was either of you doing, not being, unless in bed with Leslie Beck?"

She shared with me. Leslie Beck had told her and Lady Angela, as they took the B-roads down to Cahors, across the river Lot, to the high plain where the hot south begins and the air smells of overripe peaches, that any woman was his for the asking. Lady Angela had laughed and told Leslie Beck he was a braggart and a liar and a vulgarian, and he said every woman could be had, all it needed was a little planning: the only thing women ever needed was the opportunity and a man who wanted them. And he was a man who liked women. And the women he had had never forgotten him.

"Why's that?" asked Lady Angela, and Susan, who was irritated and annoyed by Leslie Beck, said from the back, "Because of the size of his thing, Lady Angela, that's what he means."

"How do you know?" asked Leslie Beck, surprised. "You're not one of my women. Not yet."

"Because Marion saw it by mistake," said Susan, "and she told me, and I told Rosalie, and Rosalie told Nora."

"And now you've told Lady Angela," said Leslie Beck, well satisfied, and then had to remind her to drive on the right, because she'd veered directly into the path of an oncoming truck. Lady Angela said it made no difference to her, she was gay, but she'd heard that the length of the male member was not important to heterosexual women. What did Susan say? Susan said she was in no position to make comparisons.

Susan shared with me that she wished then very much that she was back with Vinnie and the rest of us, talking about food and babies. She hated talking about sex. But the conversation was burnt into her memory.

She shared with me that when Leslie Beck presently saw a hand-printed sign, "Les Ice Caves des Madones," by the side of the road, they followed arrows down bumpy lanes to a makeshift village composed mostly of cafés and souvenir shops. Notices invited them to leave the brilliant day for black cold, to view the stalactites and stalagmites. Lady Angela refused to do any such thing; she preferred, she said, to stay above ground as long as possible. Caves made her think of death. "Don't get into mischief," she said, and Leslie laughed and said he would if he could, but he doubted if here was the place. Susan and Leslie descended by means of a rickety elevator and joined a party of tourists. They were rowed across an underground lake, where the water was black and terribly still and cold. Above them arched a vaulted sky of rock and, glowing all around, intricately wrought pinnacles of icy stone, pink and green and mauve. In the flickering lights provided by a vulgar management, Susan let Leslie Beck hold her hand.

"Cold enough for you?" he said. He wore a white cricketing sweater, the kind with vertical cables, round his shoulders; the sleeves were tied over his chest. Susan had declined his offer to borrow it. She wore only a summer dress. She shivered. "I told you so," he said. She had to lean into him on the boat, just for warmth. He put his arms round her. ("Gorilla arms," said Susan. "They always seemed too long for his body.")

"See, to the right," said the guide, "Mother Nature has fashioned a nun, and over there, look, Mother Mary. Look hard and you'll see she is clasping Baby Jesus to her bosom. Indeed, God is everywhere."

And the tourists gasped with amazement and gratification at these symbols especially sent by the Creator, and the boat tilted a little in the smooth black water as they craned to make out which exactly was the bit of the salty spire of rock that was Jesus, and all except Leslie and Susan were sure they could tell.

The boat beached. The party followed the guide through a tracery of paths, marveling at more stalactite madonnas—see, see the Holy Child's little hand—and Indian chieftains with intricate headdresses, and stalagmite chandeliers and soup ladles suspended over their heads—

"The other way round," I said.

"Don't interrupt," said Susan.

"I'm sorry," I said. "Go on sharing." I did not want to hear this. The reason I had visited the Marion Loos Gallery was not to see

Anita's painting, or to buy it, but because it seemed possible Leslie Beck might show up while I was there. That fate might bring us together once again. Oh love, love; romance etched so deep into the female soul it defies all reason; abandon sense all ye who enter here, and all of us have entered. Romance in the head—nothing to do with lust in the loins. Look, at the time of the hot summer of Berkeley Square I didn't love Leslie Beck at all; I was seduced by secrets, which are to true love as artificial sweetener is to sugar, calorie-free but in the long run carcinogenic, not the real thing, and only a peculiar aftertaste in the mouth to tell you so, to warn you. A cheat. Everything costs. Nothing is for nothing. Fewer calories, more cancer.

Susan shared with me that Leslie Beck said "Follow me," and so she did. And they went down slippery paths through slimy rocks which management had not cleaned up, until the noise of the party was lost, and only a glimmer of light struck through from above. Leslie leaned Susan up against a rock and covered her body with his own to keep her warm, and she quite forgot how she despised him: and feeling not his fingers in her hair, but something which she could have sworn was bats, screamed, and ended up lying on the ground with her back in a greenish puddle.

"We'll lose the others," she said. "We'll die down here. No one counted us. No one will miss us. Only Lady Angela, and that too late."

"I wouldn't mind," he said, "just finishing my life now. Would you?"

That touched her greatly. She was a sucker for sentiment, she said; she'd married Vinnie because he told her making love to her was like making love to the sea, something dark and infinite. He had said the same to me, but I didn't tell her that. I felt ashamed of myself for taking from her something she relied on, grew up with, had her babies by.

"We're hopelessly lost," she said to Leslie, as she followed him farther into the jumbled mass of rocks, so cold to the touch, but trusting him, because women do trust men at such times. Then the path opened up and a blast of light and warmer air met them, and there coming toward them, returning to the entrance, was another party, another guide.

"You knew the way," said Susan. "A shortcut, that was all."

"How could I?" he said. "We were lucky, that's all."

Leslie Beck the lucky.

But when they got down to the villa outside Bordeaux, and Lady Angela mentioned to Anita that they'd stopped off at the caves, Anita, who was suffering from an allergic reaction to the sun, and whose eyes were tiny in a shiny red swollen face, said, "Oh, Leslie and I always stop off there," and Susan thought she must be blushing, but how could one tell? There were baked beans, brought over from England, along with marmalade and tea bags, with hefty pork chops for supper, and Leslie Beck acted toward her as if she were Lady Angela: not an attempt at flirtation, not a flicker of the eye, a move of the hand; so she got a lift to Bordeaux airport.

Susan shared with me that only then did she realize that they had made love "unprotected," as she put it, and it was the most fertile time of her cycle, so she went back quickly to the Dordogne to join Vinnie, to fudge any possible issue. Which indeed there was, in the shape of Amanda, she of the crinkly red hair.

I did not share with Susan how disappointed I had been at her unexpected return: what was the point of my stirring up yet more old wounds, old memories? What she didn't know couldn't hurt her. Anita had stirred up more than enough already, left us reproach as a legacy. Anita Beck's revenge, thus to present us with the truth of our lives: we the faithless, who both claim and demand fidelity.

Susan shared with me her worry that Colin might be Leslie Beck's son, making any liaison between Amanda and Colin incestuous. I told her she had no need to worry. Her own guilt made her anxious; that much I shared with her.

"But Colin is so obviously Ed's child," I said. "You only have to look."

"Do you think so?" she asked, dubiously. "Well, Ed's always wondered."

That shook me. I felt cold. I did not let her see.

Susan then shared with me that when Vinnie told her I had seduced him on the banks of the Dordogne, she, being indignant, had told Ed what Leslie had told her, that Leslie and I had been having it off all one summer.

Kiss and tell, kiss and tell. In a secret liaison, each party believes there is a balance of power, an equity of terror, a mutual deterrent; and how often each is mistaken! Pow! Boom! And there you have it, a wasteland of rubble that used to be people's lives, over which ragged children swarm.

I stopped sharing any more with Susan. It seemed a very one-sided business to me.

I did not bring the matter up with Ed. He had never seen fit, after all, to bring it up with me. I felt diminished and insulted. Either he had gone through powerful emotions and I had simply not noticed, or he was so good that jealousy was not in his nature, in which case it might be possible to reconstrue "good" as "apathetic." Either way, I did not like it. I could see that the kind of cozy, tranquil love I thought we enjoyed together might not be that at all; it could be just habit—Ed's need for someone to live with, to shop and cook and be pleasant, to put aside money for the future, to watch TV with; someone who would try to prevent the children from smoking in the house; someone lying there beside him, night after night, to satisfy such rare sexual urges as he had.

Or perhaps he was doing me a kindness: staying with me, keeping the home together for the sake of the family. Forgiving me but no longer liking me or trusting me—living a half-life with me because of Leslie Beck. Nodding in front of the television, night after night, rather than speak to me; animated with friends, dreary with me.

How many men are like this with their wives? Because finally, word
has got back.

Anita Beck, this is a fine revenge.

I write this on Monday. On Saturday, Rosalie said, "Nora, you're
nuts. Nothing's altered since yesterday, and yesterday you were
perfectly happy, so what are you going on about?"

Rosalie was to spend the afternoon at Mr. Collier's. He had refilled
the swimming pool in her honor. She was not sure she wanted that.
She would have to appear in a swimsuit and was nervous that her
cellulite might put him off.

"My marriage is built on lies," I said, dismally.

"Think yourself lucky to have one," said Rosalie, briskly. "At
least they're your lies, not his."

She was putting strips of wax on her legs: pressing lengths of
fine, sticky paper onto the skin, ripping it off, its surface now darkened by removed, unwanted hair. It was both fascinating and
disgusting.

"I'm going to be late," she said. "Marion was on the phone for
hours. I wish Leslie Beck would fade back into the wallpaper. Everyone's been upset since he turned up. Now Marion's thinking of firing
Barbara. Can you imagine? Where is Ed this morning?"

"He had to go to the office," I said.

"Um," she said, and I thought, well, Vinnie's away, and Susan's
in Kew Gardens Square, and for all I know Ed's not at the office,
he's with her. But this could only be my paranoia. Sometimes I felt
paranoia was the only strong emotion that now possessed me, ren-
dered me irrational. All that was left of love was the fear of abandonment, the child kicking and screaming, lost to all reality in its
tantrum.

Neither Mr. Collier nor Mr. Render is in the office today. I can
shuffle papers as much as I want, do some more work on the scene
at the Marion Loos Gallery, as reported by Marion to Rosalie, and

by Rosalie to me. No doubt errors have crept in, but there's the fun
of it. Truth is too rigid a master not to take pleasure in cheating
him. It is, in any case, a relief to forget my own predicament, at
least for a while.

So let's envisage it. Marion stands staring at the Anita Beck painting. She has the *Guardian* review page in her hand: "Group Show
at the Marion Loos," by Melanie Deutsch. It is not the lead review,
but you couldn't expect that for such a show. And at least it runs
to a respectable length, which is good, though it does refer to a
"little, good-hearted show." There is even a photograph. It is of the
Anita Beck painting, which to Marion's surprise looks remarkably
good in black and white. No doubt that is why it was chosen. Much
of the column is devoted to Melanie Deutsch's particular theory, the
apex notion—namely, that it takes a whole lot of indifferent paintings to produce one good one. By inference, the Anita Beck is the
one at the apex of the pyramid. Marion has no patience with this
kind of thing, but when she looks around the gallery and sees eight
red dots for every ten paintings, she is not too disturbed. And at
least no one has said, as they perfectly well could have, that Marion
Loos has lost her nerve, is playing safe—that as recession bites,
standards fall.

She has had four offers for the painting and refused them all: two
from regular clients, one from Nora, and one from Susan. She is
not usually given to such quixotic behavior—on the contrary. She
supposes she wishes to spite Leslie Beck, or perhaps she merely
wanted to own the painting herself. She could have put it in a darkish
corner at home and no one would have taken much notice of it.
Now that there has been a photograph in the *Guardian,* all this will
change. She has to rethink.

Enter Leslie Beck, waving the newspaper.

LESLIE: You should have marked it up at least two thousand
          more. I told you so.

MARION: You didn't happen to sleep with Melanie Deutsch?

LESLIE: Marion, all that is over. I am an old man. You must come round to the house; I've at least two hundred canvases there.

MARION: She must have worked hard before she died.

LESLIE: She did. I encouraged her. I was her muse. I'm lost without her. To grow old alone . . . don't you feel alone, Marion? The dark edging in? The Life Force fading?

MARION: I have the gallery, I have my friends, I have my work. No.

LESLIE: And your cats; I hear you have cats. It worries me. That's a bad spinstery sign, Marion.

MARION: How do you know I have cats?

LESLIE: Someone told me. Yes, your delightful assistant. Your Barbara. The one with the difficult husband. She tells me she was at college with Melanie Deutsch. Where is Barbara?

MARION: I don't know. She's late in.

Enter Aphra.

APHRA: Hi, creep. How ya doing?

LESLIE: Hi, minilight of my life.

APHRA: Who's the major? Don't tell me. Barbara. Your generation never gives up. It's all the red meat you eat. Disgusting. Do you know what the legacy of your lot is to us? AIDS. I read it in someone else's paper, on the train.

The phone rings. Marion answers it. It's the Tate. They want to know all about Anita Beck: what is the corpus of work; can they view it; who are the executors; is the legal position uneasy? Instead of handing them straight over to Leslie Beck, she says she will call back. She hates Leslie Beck. She asks him if Anita Beck left a will, and Leslie says no, and Marion says in that case he can't dispose of the paintings until after probate, and that can take years.

LESLIE: Whose side are you on, Marion?
MARION: Anita's.

And now she feels better. Leslie leaves, pursued by angst. Enter Barbara, with baby in arms.

BARBARA: I'm sorry, Marion. I didn't know what to do. Ben refuses to look after Holly anymore. I thought he was a proper caring father. But now his office has come off flexitime, and he says his job is more important than my job; mine is just pin money, and anyway, a baby needs its mother. The truth is, it's been all trouble and complaints ever since the baby was born. We've both been so tired, and there's no money for proper child care, and I'd no idea it was going to be like this.

APHRA: Why didn't you ask me? I could have told you.

MARION: Just go away, Aphra. I don't want to hear your marital woes, Barbara. This is your workplace, not a therapist's office. And you should have rung about bringing the baby.

BARBARA: The phone's been busy all morning. We need another line.

MARION: Don't tell me how to run my business.

BARBARA: And I thought you'd be in a good mood, what with the Anita Beck in the *Guardian*. I thought you'd be really happy.

MARION: You are not a little girl, Barbara. And this is not a game.

BARBARA: You're just jealous because Leslie Beck showed me Anita's paintings. And because I can pull strings at the *Guardian,* and you can't anymore. He said you used to be his au pair. Is that true?

The baby starts to cry.

MARION: I think perhaps you'd better take the baby home, Barbara, right now. People come to galleries to be away from babies. I think your husband's right; a mother's place is at home with her child. You are probably too highly qualified for this job.

Barbara starts to cry as well.

BARBARA: But I love working here. I want to work here. It's just how can I do everything? Finish this shift, go home, and the housework starts, and no one ever tells you you're beautiful, or cares what it's like for you. All they do is worry about the baby. And I take one night off, just one, and look what happens. Ben gets hysterical, and you get moody. Why don't you just run off with Leslie Beck, Marion? He's your last chance. Poor man, he's so sad. His wife died. I only stayed to comfort him, and he couldn't, anyway. He said he was like King David, and could I just warm him all night, but I had to go because of Ben. I thought we were all friends.

Aphra has the baby; she has her knuckle in the baby's mouth.

APHRA: I think I'd rather like one of these. . . .

MARION: You're both fired.

But neither of them takes any notice of her, and both go into her office to make themselves some herbal tea, to reduce their stress levels. Marion would like to cry, but the phone keeps ringing, and she has to do three people's work, and she can't.

So much for Marion. Back to Rosalie, finishing her leg wax on Saturday morning, talking to me, myself wondering if Ed is where he says he is, at the office. Rosalie's legs are now smoother than they were, but not so young as they were, and she has a lot more weight to lose. I wondered, if Ed were to leave me, would I find someone else, could I keep someone else, would I want to?

"Rosalie," I said, "there is something you ought to know about Mr. Collier."

"He said people would get round to warning me sooner or later," said Rosalie. "He's a mass murderer. I know. He told me."

"It's not a joke."

"Anyway," said Rosalie, "she deserved it. Fancy doing that to a man, cuckolding him in his own house, in her own bath. Baths are even worse than beds. At least Leslie Beck only did me out-of-doors, not in his wife's bed."

She was angry with me. I knew she would be. She stared at herself in the mirror.

"Leslie Beck or a mass murderer," she said. "What's the difference?" Then she relented, and smiled at me, and pecked me on the cheek. I could smell a thousand lotions, a thousand scents—all the aromas of the past.

"Of course he didn't do it," she said. "He just ran into a perfectly horrible woman, and married her, and now he's met me, and together we'll look after the Pekingese."

"What about Bingo?"

Bingo was Wallace's name for the red setter. Rosalie had tried to call him Hector, but over the years Bingo had won. I wondered if Wallace and Mr. Collier had anything in common and decided they were both open, as it were, to the drastic. Both made headlines.

"I might give Bingo away," said Rosalie, and I thought, well, that's the end of Wallace, and probably Bingo. She'd never liked him. "Don't worry," she said, "I'll take him with me if it ever comes to it, but it probably won't," and she kissed me again. "I don't think Wallace fell," she added. "I think he jumped. We had a fight just before he left. He was looking at Catharine, who had just had her hair cut short, so it curled all over her head, and Wallace said she reminded him of someone. Who could it be? I named an aunt or two, on both sides; but he went on shaking his head. So I said perhaps it was the face he saw when he looked in the mirror, and I reminded him of what Jocelyn Beck had once said—'the spitting image of her father'—and I think there was something about my voice, because Wallace said, 'Oh, yes, the Becks, back in the Primrose Hill days. That's who it is. Leslie Beck.' And then he stopped talking. All that night and all the next morning he didn't say a word to me. And then he went off to the Matterhorn, for this PR race to the top. The Matterhorn's dead easy, any tourist can do it, but it always looks good on film. I think it was for a Diet Coke TV ad."

"How low we all sink," I said. "Once mountain climbing was all about purity and solitude and spiritual endeavor, now it's about Coca-Cola."

"Maybe it was Diet Pepsi," said Rosalie. "We both preferred that. Not so sweet. But 'Leslie Beck' were the last words Wallace ever spoke to me."

And Rosalie went off to Bluebeard's castle to sun by Mr. Collier the mad electrocuter's swimming pool and worry about her cellulite, and I went home, where I found Ed sitting reading a manuscript in the back garden. The lawn needed mowing but I didn't mention it. I just couldn't myself have sat and read with a clear conscience in grass as long as ours, and I was surprised he could.

"It was too good a day to stay in the office," he said, "so I brought some manuscripts home."

I said to him, because I couldn't help it, "Did you see the photograph in the *Guardian?* That was a painting by Anita Beck. Remember the Becks, back in the Primrose Hill days?"

"I thought her name was Jocelyn," he said, but at least he spoke, which was more than Wallace had to Rosalie.

"That was the wife before Anita."

"I think we're remarkable," he said, "you and I, to have stayed married to each other so long, considering how things go in the world."

And he smiled at me so sweetly I felt better, until I thought, perhaps smiles are like flowers and are offered to assuage guilt. Perhaps scowls and empty vases denote a happy home.

The next day was Sunday, and Ed went with Colin and Amanda for a walk in the park. He seemed tranquil, cheerful, and subdued, as usual. I tried not to stare at Colin; no need to reassure myself that he was indeed Ed's child, of course he was, it was just that reason itself was becoming disturbed. There was no way Colin could be Leslie Beck's. Unless sperm loitered and hung about—it was meant not to, but how could you be sure? To think too closely about the origins of these strapping children was distressing; by magic they appeared, by magic they endured. Surely we could leave it at that?

And Colin, as I watched the three of them leave the house, had so much the same build, the same shape, though on a larger scale, as his father, that I was quite returned to my senses. He held hands with Amanda, who had Leslie Beck's bright blue eyes and her mother's straight thick hair. She had her mother's briskness and competence, but not, thank God, her mother's insensitivity. I had decided that though I would be courteous to Susan when and if I saw her, I would not seek out her company if I could help it.

As soon as they had gone, I went to the phone booth on the corner and called Leslie Beck. It took me some minutes to pluck up the courage to do it. I remembered the number by heart. It was like being a schoolgirl again. I felt once again what I had quite forgotten: the sensation of standing at the crossroads of a thousand different paths, adventure round every corner. I understood what was stripped away by the passage of time: the sense of alternative; and the understanding was not pleasant. I am old, I thought, but not so old as Leslie Beck, who can't manage it anymore, and what could I possibly want from him other than that? But there was something I needed, some acknowledgment I had to have, some picture of myself when young, thrown back from his eyes. Nothing of me reflected from Ed's eyes any longer, nothing.

And I went to the phone booth; I did not use my own phone. It was the habit of the past reasserting itself—the excitement of secrecy. I had nothing to hide yet was afraid of being overheard; perhaps, in some mysterious way, I might be recorded on the answering machine. Technology may be man's friend, but it is the enemy of the secret woman.

Leslie Beck answered the phone. His voice had not changed.

"Why, Leslie," I said, as rehearsed, "it's Nora. Ed and I were so sorry to hear about Anita. It must be very upsetting for you."

There was silence at the other end. I prattled on. "Marion told me Anita was painting toward the end. I wondered whether there was any more of her work available, or perhaps you only sell through Marion? I saw the picture in the *Guardian*—of course, that's not why . . ." I was flustered. This was not going right.

Then he said, "You rehearsed that, Nora."

"Oh, God, Leslie," I said, in my normal voice. The other had sounded strained and squeaky.

"Why didn't you come to the fucking funeral?"

"I didn't like to," I said. It was pathetic. I felt guilty.

"What none of you women seem to realize," said Leslie Beck, "was that Anita understood me. Why don't you come round?"

I didn't want to. I had only wanted to hear his voice. It was like taking old family snapshots out of a box: I would remember myself as a different person, a stranger.

"I'm supposed to be cooking Sunday lunch," I said, stupidly. I could have been nineteen.

Leslie Beck said I must use my ingenuity. I had always been good at ingenuity. Anita had admired it. So I went home and left a note on the kitchen table to say I'd gone round to Rosalie's, she wasn't well; why didn't they all eat out at the Golden Friar, they did a special Sunday lunch; I'd try to meet them there—and took the train to Leslie Beck.

Twelve Rothwell Gardens was dilapidated and shabby. The property had a For Sale sign on a board in front of it. So, I noticed, had four others in the street. The kind of people who had recently upgraded their properties and life styles and bought in the Gardens were those now most hit by the recession: senior management, leading architects and lawyers. All business was bad, except for debt collection, which thrived.

Leslie Beck opened the door. He wore his dressing gown. His feet were bare. He apologized. He said he thought he had flu; he was not the man he had been. His face had shriveled in upon itself. The hair was now sandy, not red; it no longer flourished, as once it had. The full mouth had narrowed.

"You're looking good, Nora," he said. "It's a bad day for me. Some days the depression's bad; sometimes it lifts. It's lonely without Anita. I've let things get into a mess."

He had. The floors had not been swept for a time, nor the carpets vacuumed. Things lay where they had been put, in a most disconcerting way. Furniture, for some reason shifted to the middle of the room, just stayed where it was. The dresser stood six inches from the wall; the sofa faced the door—as if Leslie had suddenly lost his zest for life in midpursuit of a mouse. Socks lay discarded, orange peel likewise; old newspapers, receipts, and torn envelopes with scrawled telephone numbers upon them lay on the table, and empty plastic shopping bags lay on the floor where they had fallen, some still full of cat food. All the potted plants were dead.

"Doesn't Polly come and help?" I asked.

"Polly and I have quarreled," he said. "She's a pig. All my daughters are pigs."

Not Amanda, I was going to say. Not Catharine. But I didn't. There'd been quite enough sharing of late. Nor did I ask him what the quarrel was about.

"And, of course," he said, "Anita lost interest in the house toward the end. She just shut herself in the studio and worked away. At the end, she really came into her own."

"What we need," I said, looking round the disgusting kitchen, "is Marion back in here to do the cleaning-up."

"I thought perhaps you'd do it," he said, and laid a scrawny finger on my sleeve.

"You thought wrong," I said.

"You don't have any money to spare?" asked poor old Leslie Beck. "Until the fees from the paintings come dribbling through, I'm going to be in trouble, along with the rest of the world."

I said I did not. I said I had five thousand pounds in a bank, all that remained of my father's legacy. The rest had been filtered into the expenses of our daily living. Ed and I, it occurred to me now, could not afford to be divorced. He had provided the necessities; I had provided the comfort.

"Then why don't you buy a painting now?" he asked, "and save a gallery commission?"

It did not seem quite fair to Marion, but Marion was as rich as Croesus, everyone knew, and Marion had sold Leslie Beck's baby and perhaps didn't deserve too much.

And he took me up the dusty stairs and had to hold the banister as he went. I thought perhaps he was overdoing the old-man act and was making a play for sympathy and it would end in bed if he could, but I hoped not. I had no desire for him left, and it was sad. It emptied out something inside me, a secret dwelling place, as if someone had stuck a Vacancies sign in the window of a small hotel, and it smacked of failure, weakening hope, and shrinking income.

We went up narrow winding stairs, where cat's turds, dried and twisted, lay in the dust, to the loft. I wondered what had happened to the cat; Leslie had never liked them. Leslie opened the door, and color came pouring out as if it were sound, struck through us as if it were radiation. I understood why Leslie Beck seemed so diminished; if you stood in the force field too long, it would simply carry you off. The smell of fresh oil paint and turpentine still hung in the air. The loft had been opened out: three rooms had been made into one and large square skylights had been set in the roof, through which the midday sun shone.

I hoped Ed's walk in the Richmond park had been okay; it can get hot and dusty even there, and the fumes from car exhausts can hover. He must be home by now. They would be getting ready for the Golden Friar, complaining of my absence. They might even ring Rosalie, but there would be no reply. She was lunching with Mr. Collier, who one day I must try to call Sandy, as she did.

The sun struck the canvases stacked against the walls and threw back the reflected light which had so startled me when Leslie Beck opened the door. Here were rugs and books and photographs, dried flowers and painted screens, powdered paint in jars, the paraphernalia of the artist's studio: the overflowing effect which Vinnie tried for, and failed to achieve. But how could he possibly have achieved it, living with Susan? When we were young, I thought, our failings did not announce themselves. They were clothed in flesh, blanketed by fertility, lost in laughter, drunkenness, oil and garlic, peaches and tomatoes, laughter and conversation: all the things we denied Anita Beck because we despised her, and she had saved up what she could and given them back to us.

Anita used strong colors. The painting Leslie Beck had carried to Marion Loos was, of all her work, the most gentle and tentative. I was not sure I liked them, but what did I know? And what did like have to do with it, anyway? Marion never let one say "like" of a painting. It's not subjective, she'd say, it's nothing to do with you. It is something objective, something you have to acknowledge; you either have an aesthetic sensibility or you don't. And if we tried to press her on the aesthetic sensibility, all she'd say was that it correlated with the individual's capacity for moral action. So we gave up, suspecting she was trying to tell us she was better than the rest of us, even Susan.

There was a painting of a half-finished building, with a platform four stories up and a little cage, and the suggestion of small people lost in paint. Anita liked to use paint thickly: color was encrusted over color. There was a bedroom in what looked like one of the wretched small hotels you find round King's Cross station. There was a seascape of a tide creeping round a headland to beat itself against cliffs, just the small narrow strip of brilliant sand remaining. There was an amazing cave with stalactites and stalagmites contorted into terrifying shapes, piled one on top of the other, entangling, like a Hieronymus Bosch. And bedrooms aplenty, mostly quite modest, some almost ordinary, but all pleasant, as if she weren't quite sure about them but had decided to be kind. And there was one of a basement room with a strange mushroom growth inside it. I didn't think that one worked so well.

"I was her muse," said Leslie Beck. "None of you would believe me, but I was. She liked me to get out; she needed me, she used me. It was her Life Force, not mine. I was nothing. Just a kind of brush she used. She stayed here; I left the house. She sent me out."

He was crying. I hated to see it. I thought perhaps I would put my arms around him, but I didn't.

"But, of course," he said, "women don't get the recognition they deserve. I might as well set fire to it all. What's the use?"

I asked him which one he liked the best, and he searched for what he wanted and drew out the one with the unfinished building and the wooden platform four stories out of twenty-eight high. And I was inordinately pleased. I had found what I had come for: a sense of preeminence, of being something special, not the least of all of us; not the one whom Ed put up with or Vinnie could do without, whom Susan despised and Rosalie jeered at, but the one whose energies Anita Beck could best translate onto canvas. I cried, too, and crying no longer suited me, I could not do it gracefully.

"That one's twelve thousand pounds," said Leslie Beck when he had recovered.

"I can't possibly," I said.

"I can't afford to let it go more cheaply."

"It's out of the question."

"Perhaps you could share it with Susan," said Leslie.

"I'd rather not," I said.

"Have one of the cheaper ones," he said. "One of the bedrooms."

"I wouldn't feel satisfied with it," I said, and he had the grace to laugh. We shut the door between us and that peculiar source of power and went down through the dingy, messy rooms and corridors, which set the studio off, as a particularly dreary frame, Marion assures me, will sometimes set off a particularly lively painting.

I went home. When I opened the door, Colin stood facing me. He seemed angry and upset.

"The Golden Friar can't have been that bad," I said.

"It isn't a joke, Nora," said Amanda. "It's terrible."

"Bitch," the usually polite and affectionate Colin said to me, and went to his room and slammed the door.

"What happened?" I asked, alarmed. "Where's Ed?"

I was tired, I was upset, I wasn't sure what more I could face. Life goes on quietly, year after year; everyone smiles, then suddenly everything erupts. I had a headache.

"I think Ed's gone," said Amanda, and I went into some other kind of gear, abruptly. I expect I still had a headache but did not notice.

"Colin and me are brother and sister," said Amanda. "Ed says so. Well, half-brother and -sister. So we can't be in the same bedroom, not under his roof, Ed says. He's flipped."

"But that isn't true," I said. I went up to Colin's bedroom and kicked the door until he opened it.

"This is crazy," I said. "You are who you're meant to be. You're Ed's son."

"Don't be like this, Colin," said Amanda. "Don't upset people."

She wouldn't leave it to me to sort out. She wouldn't just go away. She pointed out that since Ed was totally wrong about her not being Vinnie's daughter, he was probably wrong about Colin not being his son. The problem was that Ed had gone insane. I could see her mother in her.

"Colin," I said, "have blood tests, tissue typing, whatever you like. I won't be offended. But you are Ed's son."

"Then why did Dad say I wasn't?" asked Colin. "And who is this Leslie Beck, anyway?"

I saw the world tilt: it gently moved to the left, then gently moved to the right. Amanda studied me, stopped me. I thought the whole clock would thereby stop, but it didn't.

"And you're drunk," said Colin. He was the youngest. Richard and Benjamin were at college. Colin had always been the easiest, the most cooperative. My impulse was to slap him, but the discipline of decades restrained me; he was, besides, the tallest of my sons. I began to cry. In fact, I remember shrieking and wailing.

"Sorry, Mum," said Colin, but still he stared at me as if he hated me, and Amanda looked as if she were settling in for a good long sharing. I sat down on a chair in the kitchen.

And bit by bit I pieced the incident together.

Scene: The Golden Friar, a cheerful and vulgar eating place in the same arcade as Accord Realtors, which the kids like and where they serve skate in black butter, which Ed loves.

COLIN: I'll have the haddock and chips and peas.
AMANDA: I'll have the grilled chicken and a salad with no dressing.
ED: We'll wait for your mother.

They look at him with surprise. Ed usually goes along with the flow of other people's desires. They wait. Not even Cokes are suggested. Fifteen minutes go by. No mother.

COLIN: Isn't that Rosalie over there?
ED: Yes.
AMANDA: Who's she with?
COLIN: It's Mr. Collier. Mum works for him.
AMANDA: Isn't Rosalie the one whose husband disappeared and no one will say whether he's dead or not? I think it's okay for her to go out with a man. What's she supposed to do?
COLIN: Wait for him.

Ed has risen and gone over to speak to Rosalie. The children confer and quickly order Cokes, fish and chips, chicken and salad, and skate and black butter for when Ed returns.

AMANDA: But didn't your mother say that's where she was
            going? That Rosalie was poorly?

COLIN: That's funny; so she did.

The Cokes arrive. Ed comes back. Ed sees the Cokes and smashes
them across the restaurant, liquid and glass flying here and there.
The buzz of conversation ceases.

ED: Your bitch of a mother. She won't make a fool of
            me anymore. Neither will you two. Fucking under
            my roof. What do you think I am?

COLIN: Dad, let's go.

ED: You're not even my son. Look at you! Bloody rings
            in your nose.

AMANDA: Everyone wears them, Ed. Please calm down.

ED: (Jeering) Ed, Ed. Look at you, listen to you. "Ed."
            You're not Vinnie's daughter, either. You're Leslie
            Beck's. The same way this bloodsucker here is. It's
            incest, and the way no one has the nerve to say so
            disgusts me. Where do you think your shit of a
            mother is? Oh, she's steamy, she's steamy. . . .

Various young people, friends of Colin's, help Ed out of the
restaurant. Rosalie is on her feet, paying the waiter for the Cokes.
Mr. Collier is picking odd fragments of glass out of his trouser leg.
A lot of Coke and glass went their way.

On the way home Ed says he's sorry if he's upset everyone; he's
upset himself, says he's had enough, none of it's the kids' fault, but
he does not retract his statement about their fathering. He goes to
his room. Amanda makes beans on toast. Colin is too distressed to
eat. Ed leaves the house with a suitcase. Amanda and Colin decide
that if the worst possible case is incest, they don't care. They can
live together so long as they don't get married, and the sooner

they're out from under the parental roof, the better. I come home. Etcetera.

Our bedroom seems oddly empty. I go to sleep for three hours. I dream I am in the Marion Loos Gallery, searching in an empty purse, trying to borrow money from Rosalie. When I wake up, Ed hasn't returned. I call various friends, who express surprise and concern but haven't seen him. I try Susan repeatedly but get only the busy signal.

I say to Colin and Amanda what I think I ought to say: that they mustn't let this incident drive them together. They're far too young to commit themselves to anything permanent. This upsets them even more, so I shut up. Anyway, my heart isn't in their lives; it's in my own. I am ambivalent about Ed's absence. Something that feels rather like Leslie Beck's Life Force wells up as an exhilaration, some notion of freedom; on the other hand, the house seems to be a kind of desert, its contents whited out in a heat haze. The television is on and no one is watching it.

Rosalie comes round.

"Colin," she says, "your father is your father. I have known your mother forever. No one has suggested anything different, ever. Your father has flipped. He will be back soon."

Amanda stares in a mirror and says, "I don't look like anyone I know. I never did. I've never belonged."

Colin says to me, "Where were you, then? When you said you were with Rosalie, where were you? Are all women like you?"

Bloody Ed, I think. I'd like to kill him. That makes me feel better.

Rosalie says, Why didn't you tell me? We only went to the Golden Friar because we thought no one would see us. Whoever goes to the Golden Friar?

And so on.

Colin says, If Ed never comes back, how am I going to get a bit of tissue from him to tissue-type?

Amanda says her mother is a hypocrite, too, and who is Leslie Beck, anyway? What do I know about Leslie Beck?

I do not say he is the man with the biggest dong in the world. It no longer seems funny or wistful, or whatever it was, and besides, it is no longer true.

Rosalie puts me to bed and gives me pills. I hear her saying, "Just to add to it, Nora, I think I'm afraid of Mr. Collier. I don't want to go out with him anymore, but I have to. I don't like to annoy him. He has a funny look in his eye. You know the way spaniels look at you sometimes, and it could be devotion or they could be about to bite? That kind of look. Or perhaps I just imagined it."

She hasn't been to bed with him yet; she's trying to put it off. I go to sleep.

I wake with a start, hearing a strange noise. But it is not really strange. It is Colin and Amanda, demonstrating how little they care about the censure of the world. They will probably now have a baby, just to press home their point.

Sleeping pills sometimes have a strange effect: they paralyze the body, root it to the bed, while agitating the mind. I imagine if you had a stroke and could only move your eyes to indicate yes or no, that's what you would feel like all the time. I would rather be dead, but how could you achieve it?

I am cold all down my left side: it is the absence of Ed making itself felt. I take refuge in Marion's head. Open my wide eyes to look at an alternative world.

MARION

*B*arbara brought her baby to the gallery again today. It seems that either I have to pay her more, so that she can afford child care, or she will have to bring Holly with her to work every day, or else I will have to fire her so she can claim unemployment benefits. If she leaves of her own volition she will be defined as willfully unemployed and will not be able to claim anything. Since her husband is earning just over the minimum (£162.25 after taxes), the little family cannot expect family credit. She can't deprive the child of its father; besides, she loves him. They have had very little sleep since the baby was born, which is why, she hopes, Ben is behaving this way. Since he believes it costs only twenty pounds a week to feed a family, a sum his mother once mentioned, this is the amount he has been giving Barbara from his wages, and which she has been supplementing with the money she earns from me. It seems her husband has now torn up the chore-share contract they drew up and pinned to the kitchen wall when they married. He says it is an insult to his manhood, which she has insulted enough.

"All this," I say, "from having sex with Leslie Beck. Was it worth it?"

"I did not have sex with Leslie Beck," she says, "though not from lack of trying. I was sorry for Leslie. He just made me feel so sorry for him. He took me up into Anita Beck's studio. It's the length of the house turned into one room. It is so beautiful and peculiar up there, you have no idea, and he cried because Anita was dead, and I cried, too, and I just somehow wanted to keep the world going."

"And he couldn't get it up," says Aphra. She had her knuckle in the baby's mouth again. "You ought to give this baby a pacifier."

"Ben and I don't believe in pacifiers," says Barbara. She stares at me with desperate, furious eyes. She is quite changed from her usual gentle self. "What am I going to do? I had no idea life was like this. I had no idea it was so unfair."

I don't know what to say.

"*When you look back upon these years,*" is all I can think of, "*they will seem the best time of your life.*" I say it. "That's what people tell me," I add, "young marrieds with baby. The happiest of all." But my voice falters.

Some idiot comes into the gallery. I have to go, though normally it is Barbara's job to face the inquiring passerby, whose only apparent purpose in entering the gallery in the first place is to be able to say, when you give them a price or two, "What? That much? For such garbage?" and walk out laughing. This happens now. For the first time that I can remember, I wish I didn't have to run a gallery. I wish I could just shut the door and go home. Who are the Tate, the Metropolitan, anyway? These idols of mine, the ones whose attention flatters me? For every hundred paintings on any of their walls, only some three percent are done by women. What does that make them? What is it all about? What does the putting of colors on little squares of canvas in certain shapes add up to? It's all some nonsense of my own, some mad way of getting back at Ida and Eric. The worship of mud pies. "Look, look! See what I've done. Aren't I clever!"

The baby wails. Aphra has handed him back to Barbara. It occurs to me that she is a very inexpert mother. I have a glimmering of sympathy for Ben.

"You think you're so one-up on everything, Aphra," Barbara is saying, "but if your boyfriend buys Leslie Beck's basement flat, and you move in without getting married, you're crazy. He'll pay the mortgage and buy the car and the CD player, and you'll do the groceries and the vacations and day-to-day expenses, because that seems fair, and when he throws you out after ten years he'll own everything, and you'll be thirty-three and have only the clothes on your back."

"He loves me," says Aphra feebly. I think for a moment she means Leslie Beck, but of course she means her boyfriend. "If anyone is forced out, it will be him."

"It's happening to all my friends," says Barbara. "They either have babies and problems, or no babies and nothing."

"Then your friends are stupid," says Aphra. But she's beginning to look troubled.

"It's very damp and dark down there," I say. "He never really got rid of the dry rot."

And I refuse to say anything more. This is my staff; I am the boss; we are not a gaggle of agitated girls. They are betraying me, hurting me, but don't know it. The baby is put in the office between cushions on a chair. I send Barbara out to buy some kind of nest for him—whatever they use, these days. The money comes from petty cash. It will be cheaper in the end for me to increase her salary, though she gives me to understand that child-care wages are higher than her own. She thinks this is monstrous; Aphra says it's only reasonable, since working in a gallery is much more interesting than looking after a baby. Barbara leaves, weeping, to shop.

The baby stares at me. I suppose him to be about four months old. When he is not crying he has an unblinking stare. It is hard to believe he is the source of so much trouble. I wonder about my own child. I never gave him a name. I suppose he is all right and has not fallen victim to statistics, the sudden leap in the death rate that stands for male teenagers. I wonder what his political attitudes are? I almost never think about him. I suffered no aftershock when he went off with Brenda Streiser, who clearly, from her marveling gaze, had amply bonded with him. Research on identical twins shows that unless children are subjected to excessive trauma, they grow up to be what they will be, regardless of who rears them. Nature flings the genes together, in its endless experiment, this mother with that father, this father with that mother. The Leslie Beck–Marion Loos experiment is achieved, then carries on into other generations in search, presumably, of perfection. That's all it is: we're just bit-part players in the Life Force drama.

The baby cries. "Run round to the corner shop and get a pacifier," I say to Aphra. "Don't let's traumatize the child." Rosalie's little children, I remember, all had pacifiers. So did Nora's. Vinnie wouldn't have them in the house. Aphra goes.

"Barbara won't like it," she says. I shrug. Aphra pauses at the door.

"I do think you're wonderful, Marion," she says, by the by. "I really do."

I wished Monet and Manet hadn't woken with sticky eyes this morning. I wished my apartment hadn't seemed so dusty and forlorn. I wished the paintings on the wall hadn't seemed like squares of canvas with peculiar colors on them. I wished the weekend hadn't seemed so lonely and myself so friendless. I wished it were not my forty-fifth birthday, or that I had told someone. Who was there to care? I wished that the future were not bound to consist of less, not more—life shrinking to confine itself into old age, a hopeless struggle against loneliness and infirmity, with only a bank balance to keep me warm and a nature too proud and prickly to let me take to drink and be open to the warm and sloppy pleasures of pub and club society, where women like myself, only easier and warmer, abound.

I wished Leslie Beck had never come through my door with Anita's painting stretching his arms, the basketball player who inclines over the heads of his fellow players and just drops the ball in the hoop. Though they say there is more to it than that; there is skill and scheming, too.

I called Rosalie for a chat. Tuesday mornings are almost always quiet. Many people nowadays stretch the weekend through to Tuesday afternoon.

I told her I was feeling low. She told me so was she, but she didn't want to go into it. She told me Ed had left Nora. I said I didn't believe it. And then I had to go, because in the gallery door stood Leslie Beck, smiling at me. I supposed I had become accustomed to his age, for he no longer registered as old. I felt a kind of hurt relief, as if I had been weeping for years and at last, exhausted and purified, I had stopped. I was grateful to see him.

"No Barbara, no Aphra?" he asked.

"No," I said.

"That's good," he said. "I only flirt with them to tease you."

It occurred to me that he meant it.

"I think we ought to get married," said Leslie Beck. "The old Life Force demands it. Our chance, yours and mine, to kick back at fate."

"You mean," I said, "with my money and my gallery you could get a new start in life, now the bottom's dropped out of the development business."

"I'm lucky to have a home to live in," he said. "Don't joke. I'm not."

"Neither am I."

"You're lonely, I'm broke. The only thing is, cats give me asthma. Since Anita's cat ran off, I've been feeling better. Don't I look better?"

"Yes."

"Leslie Beck the magnificent, still?"

"Yes."

He was close to me. His hands were old but elegant. He was touching my sleeve, the way he used to, promising, offering, any number of delightful things.

"Your ambition, after all," he said. "Not to be the servant anymore; to be the mistress."

Aphra and Barbara came back at the same time and broke the spell.

"Take a few days to think about it," he said. "But don't leave it for too long. I'll be snapped up. Widower with large house, central heating; but it's you I want. Always have."

"Creep!" said Barbara and Aphra, united in dismissing him once his hand upon my arm had been seen. Barbara didn't protest when Aphra stuck the pacifier in the baby's mouth.

"You be careful, Marion," said Aphra. "It's a setup. He's after your money. He's asking my boyfriend twice what he should for that flat. It's not even got proper central heating."

"Central heating?" said Barbara. "Aren't you fussy all of a sudden. In your squat there's no heating at all."

"We can burn furniture and beams in an open grate," said Aphra.

"There's no open fireplace in Leslie Beck's apartment," said Barbara, smugly. How did she know?

I left them to it. I called Rosalie again.

"I don't know what to say," she said. "It's difficult on your own. And you can end up in trouble, such trouble! But Leslie Beck? Of all people?"

Leslie Beck, of all people.

NORA

*T*here is no point in remaining in Marion's head. There is no real escape from autobiography into biography. The self has to be faced, or we die.

I called Ed at his office on his direct line. I spoke to his secretary. There was a muffled conversation behind a blocking hand. His publishers are old-fashioned; it seems they cannot afford hold buttons on individual lines. Finally Ed spoke.

"What do you want to say to me?"

"Where were you last night?"

"I go where I want to. If you'd like information, ask your lawyer to get it."

"But, Ed, what happened? Nothing happened. Why are you being like this?" And so forth. You try not to, but this is how it comes out. Ending up with: "You've ruined Colin's life. You've put doubts in his mind from which he'll never recover. You've pushed him into Amanda's arms."

"It's you who've done it all, Nora, not me. I just at last responded. I've had enough. Now go away."

"I suppose," I say, "now you've gone through all my money, you can do without me."

A pause.

"Well, Nora, you would say that."

I am ashamed of myself. I am panicking. Ed has never done anything like this before, said anything like this. He is hard. I understand that he does not mean to come home—for crimes committed against the marriage many years ago, plus my failure to turn up at the Golden Friar.

Mr. Collier comes toward my desk. "Nora," he says, "I think we're going to have to say no to personal telephone calls at the office."

Ed has hung up, anyway. I replace the receiver. Mr. Collier stares at me, his murderous eyes kindly. If Rosalie enters Mr. Collier's bed, will she be allowed out of it again? If Rosalie fails to enter Mr. Collier's bed, will she be allowed to live or be killed for spite?

Without Ed, I perceive, I am unprotected. I am alone. I have five thousand pounds in a bank, and a dependent child who hates me, and a house with a mortgage that increases rather than decreases every month and is unsalable. It is as well I did not buy Anita Beck's painting.

If I can have Colin and Ed tissue-typed, will that make a difference? No, it won't. Ed believes what for some reason he wants to believe. Paranoia. Is he with Susan? I dial her number.

NORA: Hello, Susan.
SUSAN: Why, Nora.
NORA: Was Ed with you last night?
SUSAN: Of course he wasn't.

She's lying.

MR. COLLIER: I did ask you not to make personal calls from this office, Nora.

Do I have to put up with this man? Yes, I can see I do. If I am suddenly deprived of Ed's income, I cannot afford to walk out of jobs, especially not ones which give me enough free time to sit and write, as I do now, what publishers' readers will assume to be a novel, and may pay quite a large sum for. Richard and Benjamin are not yet wholly independent. Ed believes children past the age of twenty-three should be independent of their parents; he has not helped Richard and Benjamin. I have. Which would benefit them most? My public silence about myself, or financial help while they establish themselves in the world?

"Mr. Collier," I say, "I am truly sorry. The fact of the matter is that I am upset. Do you think I could take the afternoon off?"

"I think that would be a very good idea," he says. "And I'm sorry if I nagged. It's just I'm expecting a call on that line from my lawyer. Rosalie and I are hoping to speed up the legal process and have Wallace officially declared dead. Naturally, I'm anxious. We do so want to get married as soon as possible."

Brides in the bath! And Mr. Collier rubs his hands together, as I imagine once did Mr. Crippen, the famous mass murderer, whose wives never emerged from the bath to consummate the marriage; but I can't properly concentrate on Rosalie's troubles.

"I hope I can be a bridesmaid," I say.

I make my way to Kew Gardens Square, parting crowds as a breaststroke swimmer might part muddy and dangerous waters. Ed's car, missing from outside our house, is outside Susan's. It is a strange feeling, when the black anger of paranoia, of jealousy in the head, is suddenly proved justified. The emotion is lessened, not heightened. The sensation is of relief.

Susan opens the door to me. She is wearing black silk pajamas, probably described in a catalogue as a "lounging set"; her hair falls over one eye; she looks absurd. She is too old for romantic dishabille. I cannot believe Ed is taken in. She is wearing her glasses and has

Wilson's Sociobiology, a very large volume, weighing down one hand. No doubt she saw me coming. No doubt she was prepared for it.

The energy of my entry drives her back into her own hall. She leans against the wall mirror, half amused, half alarmed. It is her amusement that gets to me.

"Why, Nora," she says, "are you okay?"

"Where's Ed?" I ask.

"Shouldn't he be in his office?"

"Why is his car outside your door?"

"Is it? He must have decided to go by train. It's easier from here than from Richmond. Terrible to be a daily commuter from Richmond. I don't know how I stood it for so long."

"Was he here last night?"

"Yes."

"Where's Vinnie?"

"Still away. Why, do you want a replacement for Ed?"

She doesn't like me at all.

I ask her how long it has been going on and she says nothing is going on and I am paranoid, and I accuse her of breaking up my marriage and she says my own unreasonable jealousy has done that, forced Ed out of his home. That and my constant infidelity. I am baffled. I am wronged, and Susan claims some kind of moral victory? How can this be?

"He has started divorce proceedings against you," says Susan, and I remember Jocelyn and Leslie Beck and stay calm. Once you start throwing things, you have had it.

She takes me into the living room and starts sharing with me.

She shares with me how unhappy Ed has always been with me, how he has had nobody intelligent to talk to for years, how if it had not been for me and my noisy insistence on having children, he would now be head of his own publishing house and not merely a senior editor.

She shares with me how Ed has stayed with me for the sake of
the children, and tried to keep things on an even keel, treated Colin
as his own, though everyone knew he was Leslie Beck's.

"That's not true," I say. "Colin is Ed's son."

Susan raises an eyebrow. She shares with me how, though
Amanda is Leslie Beck's, Vinnie has always known all about it, and
how she offered to have a termination but Vinnie begged her not
to. By implication, I should have done the same with Colin. What
can I say? I fall silent. She shares on.

She shares with me how I am so noisy and Ed is so quiet. She
shares this very softly. She is being very soft and still.

I understand that I am being manipulated, that Susan occupies
the moral ground and will repel all interlopers, that she has
dragged Ed up there with her, that in her mind, and therefore Ed's
mind from now on, I am dirt. She shares with me how difficult Ed
has found my smoking, and the dangers of passive smoking for
children.

I see that the photograph of Vinnie on the table has gone, and
that there is one of Ed in its place.

She shares with me that if the Golden Friar incident had not
happened, something else would shortly have come along, and that
Ed had been waiting for it, his opportunity to leave me and join
her. That I was now the worthless one, the despised, the moral
leper.

And that, if you ask her, Anita Beck was having her revenge, that
all misfortune emanated from the loft at 12 Rothwell Gardens, by
way of Leslie Beck. And that I had better not say so, or I would be
locked up and declared insane as well.

I rose to go.

"I'm glad I could share so much with you," said Susan. "I think
you'll find this sorting-out is in all our interests. A year from now
you'll be really glad it happened."

I called Marion from a phone booth.

"Oh, Nora," she said, "I was feeling really mean the other day. Was I rude? I'm sorry if I was. Rosalie told me about Ed. She could kick herself for not being more tactful. I hope you're not angry with her. She's got involved with this man, and she's scared stiff of him."

And she told me Rosalie was going round to the Tudor manse to dine with Mr. Collier, *à deux,* and would not be able to keep out of his bed without being impolite, and she told me Leslie Beck was coming through the door and wanted to marry her, and she did not know what to say to him, she was so depressed. She had not been so depressed since she was eighteen. She thought all her life had been a flight from depression.

So I hung up, because I could see there was no one to talk to, no one to help me. I was on my own.

I bought a ticket to Earl's Court. I left the station, found a general store, and bought some bananas, some bread, some firelighters, some milk, and some wax polish. I bought a ticket to Chalk Farm station. I changed trains at Piccadilly and left the bag of shopping for the homeless, keeping only the firelighters. I checked I had my cigarette lighter and that it was working.

I walked up the hill from Chalk Farm to Rothwell Gardens. I knocked on the door of No. 12 and, getting no reply, let myself in with the key I had on my key ring, which I kept in the same spirit as I kept the belt of the brown dress with orange flowers. I am an affectionate and romantic person, and I believe that if you join the body, you join the soul. I was surprised, but relieved, that in all these years the lock had not been changed. My plan depended upon it.

I went upstairs to the loft. I thought I heard a feeble meowing from the linen cupboard on the first floor and opened the door. A thin, thin cat crept out from a jumble of soiled sheets and blankets. I would see to the poor creature on the way down. It did not seem to have much life left in it.

I opened the loft door and the blaze of color and energy leapt out at me and swept through me, and I felt weak. I took the box of firelighters from my bag, broke it in half, packet and all, for it seemed to me this had to be done very quickly, and lit both pieces. The box was stale, as so often happens, and the fumes weak, so it took a little time for the flames to catch. But when they were properly alight, and my hands were in danger, I tossed both pieces into the far corner of the studio, one toward the left and one toward the right, where the brushes still stuck in jars of turpentine, only half evaporated, and watched a little puff of flame and the fringe of some Victorian shawl begin to curl and flare, and, leaving the door open for the air to funnel up the stairs, took myself down them, scooping up the little cat on the way. She would have to take her chances with the kind people of Rothwell Gardens. A woman with a cat attracts more attention than one without one.

It took me a few minutes to catch her. The original scooping up took her by surprise and she was quiet, but then she found such strength as she could and wriggled free, tearing my hand with her claws. I had to coax her out from under the kitchen dresser, though there was no time, no time. Then I had to give her some water.

The front doorbell rang. I had failed. Someone had seen smoke, someone had come to warn and help. Well, it was fate. I had the cat safe and quiet in my arms—she was gingery, old and tough, though skinny. No kitten, she. I opened the front door.

There stood Leslie Beck, except it wasn't. It was Leslie Beck as he'd once been: vigorous and bright-eyed; the hair not so curly, glossy rather than wiry; the eyes, though brown, not blue, wide and startled. Kitten's eyes. Marion's eyes. They looked strange in so young a man, as if life were a perpetual affront to his innocence and he couldn't get used to it.

"Can I help you?" I asked. "I'm afraid I'm on my way out."

"Does a Mr. Pecker live here?" he asked. It was a strange accent. Of course, South African.

"No," I said firmly. I had to get away, get him away. "Sorry, wrong address." I could hear a crackle from upstairs. I closed the front door behind me and joined him on the step.

He followed me down the street. I put the cat down outside No. 6. I remembered pleasant people living there. They had probably moved on long ago, but pleasant people sell to pleasant people, or try to.

"Are you just leaving that cat?" he asked.

"Yes," I said. He looked puzzled. "It lives there," I said.

He followed me, talking. He said that Rothwell Gardens had been his last chance. He was flying back to Cape Town the next day. He was trying to trace his natural parents. All he knew was the name: Pecker, Becker, something like that. His adoptive father had died; his adoptive mother couldn't remember much about any of it—she had a drinking problem. He'd looked them all up in the phone book, rang around; now he was trying Becks as a last resort. It had been a silly idea. They wouldn't want to see him, anyway. But he felt at home here in this country.

"Come with me," I said, "but give me a moment first."

Docile, he followed.

At Chalk Farm station I phoned the fire department. Three phone boxes were out of order; the fourth worked. In Richmond, Accord Realtors is proud to assert, public services work to a high degree of efficiency. There is little vandalism. We may murder our wives in the bath, and their lovers, too, but the public telephones work.

I told them I had seen flames coming from No. 12 Rothwell Gardens. The sooner they came, the better. I wanted the loft to burn and the paintings; I had nothing against the rest of the house. Anita should not have been there, anyway. The house was Jocelyn's by rights. Anita was not entitled to the vengeance she had been exacting.

I sat with the young man, Jamie Streiser, until I heard the fire sirens coming up the hill from King's Cross. Then we bought tickets to Green Park.

"You're a very strange lady," he said, on the way.

"None stranger," I agreed, "except probably your parents."

He was a good-looking boy, and companionable; an excellent return on an investment, I thought. Half a million, and your capital back! I told him about it. I put Marion's case well, Leslie's less so. I felt a great deal hinged on his response. He thought for a time.

"I paint pictures," he said. "That's what drove my adoptive mother to drink." I thought being called an adoptive mother by the child you rear might be the more likely cause, but children twist the world to suit themselves. "This woman runs an art gallery, right?"

"Yes."

He smiled. "That's a relief," he said. "I thought she might be some old hag. Is she married?"

I told him no. He said she probably thought she wasn't entitled to happiness. He was sorry about that.

"Other children?"

"No."

"I can have her all to myself," he said. "I might change my ticket home. It means losing a couple of hundred quid, but it's not every day you find your mother. What a coincidence, you on the doorstep like that. A minute either way—"

I asked him to forget about the step. I could see I might end up in prison. It didn't seem too bad a place to be. I had joined the ranks of the hysterically wicked: the destroyers of art. Cassandra Austen, who tore up so many of her sister Jane's letters. Ruskin's maid, who burned his manuscript, nine years into the writing. Burton's wife, who threw her husband's erotic diary in the fire. Nora, who burned Anita Beck's studio and everything in it. Only no one now would hear about Anita Beck; she would not take her place in the annals of art history, and I did not mind one bit. No, I was on the side of

the destroyers. Art is a cause of much suffering to innocent by-
standers, so they fight back from time to time. Good for them.

Jamie Streiser walked into the Marion Loos Gallery.

"Where is my mother?" he asked. He had a flair for the dramatic.

Marion came out of the stockroom, followed by Leslie Beck. She
was flushed. He looked pleased with himself. Barbara and Aphra,
embarrassed, tried to look at nothing in particular. Aphra straightened the Anita Beck painting. It fell to the ground, stayed upright,
juddering, then toppled back against the wall.

Marion took no notice. Marion and Jamie looked at each other.
Marion sighed. Leslie rushed to the painting, fearing damage.

"Leslie," Marion said, "I'm sorry. It was a sweet offer, but I really
can't marry you. I don't think it would work. My life is so full as
it is, I really can't fit anything more into it. You know how it is
with businesswomen. Busy, busy, busy! I would drive you mad."

There seemed to me a kind of applause in the air. I looked at
everyone's hands, but they were quite still. I took out a cigarette.

"Nora," said Marion, "please don't smoke. It's so bad for the
canvases."

I put my cigarette away.

Leslie said bitterly to Marion, "I suppose this is another of your
young men. You'll be sorry. Don't think this offer will come again.
You're an old hag and getting older by the day. Men last, women
don't," and went back home to Rothwell Gardens.

Nothing happens, and nothing happens, and then everything happens. It's so uncomfortable being Nora, I shall give Rosalie a go.

Rosalie is dressing for her date with Mr. Collier. She has been
on a diet since first she met him, when it seemed that the nothing
happening, and the nothing happening, after Wallace disappeared
into the mountains, might turn into something happening.

There are two dresses in her wardrobe which might by now just
about do, and between which she must choose. One is black with

sequins; one is white with lace around the bodice. You can dress up a little white dress or dress it down, just as you can, mythically, a little black frock. Rosalie is indecisive. But the little black dress has sequins, and are not sequins perhaps metal, and does not metal carry electricity?

ROSALIE: (*Calling*) Catharine, Catharine?

CATHARINE: What is it, Mum? I'm looking for my hockey shoes. If I could only get onto the college team, Dad would be proud of me.

Catharine believes that if only she can be good at sports, by some sympathetic magic her father will reappear in her life.

ROSALIE: Is it metal that carries electricity, or nonmetal?

CATHARINE: Why, Mum?

ROSALIE: Never mind.

Rosalie takes down the black dress, the quicker to die. She wants to get it over with. Death has been hovering, in the form of Mr. Collier's phone calls, in the form of her dreams: last night she was visited by a skeleton, with Wallace's moist living eyes clear in their sockets, dangling Mr. Collier's trousered legs and black shoes. If Mr. Collier is a murderer, she might as well die. If he is not, then life might be worth living. Tonight she knows she will find out. Something has to happen; nothing has happened for too long.

She takes down the white dress. It is the one she often wore when she went with Wallace to mountaineering club dinners. A sacrifice then; a sacrifice now. Brides in the bath. Murder, murder, all the way.

She combs her hair. She tugs. A tangle comes right away. Her hair is not rooted so firmly in her head as once it was. She seems to remember combing her hair halfway up a cliff with Leslie Beck,

when they were on their way back to Jocelyn. He had handed her
a comb. Why? She did her best, but the wind undid her efforts.
Perhaps later he slipped that particular comb into the silver casing
of the relevant part of Jocelyn's brush, comb, and mirror set. Perhaps
later still suggested that Anita paint it. A linking object, as some
objects are even without this kind of human intervention, joining
past to present. A stupid thing like a comb. All women have them,
use them with shared emotion, staring in mirrors.

A phone rings.

CATHARINE: Will you take it, Mum?
ROSALIE: Okay.

She puts on the white dress, since it's nearest, but it's tight. By
the time she gets to the phone it has stopped ringing. Rosalie bustles
off to the Tudor manse in her little car, in a too-tight white dress.
Mr. Collier comes to meet her, beaming pleasure, as she hurtles
down the drive. The division between lawn and drive is lined with
white stones; there are carriage lamps on either side of a brass-
knockered door. He's been picking roses. He opens the car door. He
is not very tall; his face is round and benign; he does not have much
hair. He is as unlike Wallace as anyone can be: Wallace is tall, hairy,
and cavernous. Mr. Collier can rig up a cable from the electricity meter; Wallace is hopeless at that kind of thing. Wallace takes his own
life because his wife was once unfaithful; Mr. Collier takes his wife's
life for the same reason. Rosalie thinks Mr. Collier deserves respect;
she is prepared to sleep with him. She looks forward to it.

MR. COLLIER: I say! That's a dress and a half. I thought we
               might stay in. There's dinner in the oven; the

maid prepared it. It's her night out. A real luxury,
a live-in maid. If the property market doesn't
start looking up, she might have to go.

He chatters on. Wallace used to be silent. He would brood, his
mind on distant mountain peaks. Mr. Collier—he likes her to call
him Sandy, but in her head he's still really Nora's Mr. Collier—
shows her the rest of the house: shiny modern furniture from Har-
rods, Chinese carpets, hideous vases, cocktail cabinets. The Pekingese snaps at their heels.

MR. COLLIER: Not the nicest dog in the world, Rosalie, but my
                wife's dog. It's a comfort to me. You know about
                all that. A Svengali turned up in her life. I know
                they said in court it was the other way round,
                but women always get the blame. You're some-
                thing of a feminist; you know all about that. She
                didn't deserve to die. Women make mistakes;
                she was unlucky.

He begins to look less and less like a murderer; Nora, more and
more of an alarmist. But he pours great dollops of gin into her glass
and not much tonic, and Rosalie sees he puts great dollops of tonic
into his own but not much gin. At the top of the stairs he pauses,
faces her; she faces him. He comes closer; he kisses her; no arms
around her; his tongue goes into her mouth. Well, that's all right.

MR. COLLIER: Oh, Rosalie! I've been so patient. I haven't
                wanted to lose you. I've been through a lot, you
                know. So have you.
ROSALIE: I suppose you didn't hear back from the lawyers?

She wants Wallace declared dead. She wants Wallace declared not dead. What she doesn't want is to dream of Wallace's skeleton, bleached and rattling in a mountain wind, picked over by birds, with Wallace's still-living eyes staring at her, reproachful. Mr. Collier's trousered legs offer reprieve, unless he, too, is death dressed up. It's hopeless.

MR. COLLIER: Not yet. I'm a very respectable man, Rosalie. I take this seriously, please believe me. I don't want us just to have sordid sex. I want a proper relationship with you. Marriage.

Sordid sex. Can she live with a man who speaks of sordid sex? Yes, she thinks she can, in the Tudor manse. They could ask people to dinner. She could live as Jocelyn Beck once lived, long ago: in propriety. Anyway, he hasn't said he thinks sex is sordid; just upheld that casual sexual relationships are sordid. All kinds of perfectly decent people believe that, including Wallace, as do most men that she can see, if far fewer women. She positively wants him now to undo her zipper, free her from the constraints of the dress. She is wearing her high-heeled shoes. They are too tight. If he would show her the bedroom she could take them off casually, fall back on the bed and say, "Oh, Mr. Collier—no, oh, Sandy—of course we'll be married. You and only you, forever more," and open her arms. It is his fate to kill, hers to be killed.

Does she hear a crackling in her ears, as Anita Beck's studio burns, as the flames approach, sweep through the length of the room, embracing the past, destroying it, sucking up the sea, the cliffs, the stretch of sand, sparking and arcing, spitting and steaming? Something, at any rate, deafens her to reason.

Mr. Collier shows her the bathroom before he shows her the bedroom. It is a big room. The floor is tiled; there are scorch marks

on the tiles. The bath is pink, the taps are gold. The toilet has a
pink furry cover.

> MR. COLLIER: Here's where it happened. Here's where he tried
> to kill me; here's where she tried to save me.
> She didn't mean me to die. I couldn't make the
> court understand that.

Mr. Collier for some reason puts in the stopper and turns on the
taps. The Pekingese curls up on the pink furry mat that surrounds
the toilet and looks soulful. Mr. Collier advances on Rosalie and
undoes her zipper.

> MR. COLLIER: Let's have a bath together. I love to take baths.
> I take them at all times of the day and night.
> We'll drink gin together; we'll see what happens
> next.
> ROSALIE: Here? Where it happened?
> MR. COLLIER: Yes. It must be exorcised. She'd want that. She
> wanted me to be happy. She didn't mean for
> any of it to happen. He was after my property.
> He wanted the house. It was the time prices were
> peaking, but he wasn't to know that. None of
> us did.

The bath is full. It is a very large bath, semicircular. He pours in
bath salts. They are scented. Steam rises from pinkish water. Is it
cyanide? Mr. Collier takes off the white dress.

> MR. COLLIER: White, my wife's favorite color. A wardrobe full
> of white dresses. Virgin white. You are so like
> her. Beautiful! The court case, everything: like

a dream. I was so distressed. Smell the scent in
the steam. Don't you love that?

She bends, she inhales. Why doesn't he?

He isn't taking off his clothes. Why not? But it is absurd to imagine
a man will murder not one woman but two in the same bath. One
he can talk himself out of, but two? Of course not. Either way,
Rosalie does not want to turn back. She is dizzy. Something will
happen now.

She hears the sound of sirens. Is it the police? But it's only the
front doorbell, ringing and ringing and ringing, getting the better
of the crackling and buzzing in her ears. She thinks perhaps there
is some kind of drug in the pink powder, the pink water. He is
offering her something to drink; he is adding it to her glass of gin,
which she still has in her hand.

MR. COLLIER: Oh, damn. I'd better go and see who it is. Get
them to go away. This is a night for just the
two of us.

Mr. Collier pushes open the bathroom door. She follows him to
the top of the stairs. She has no clothes on. It doesn't seem to matter.
He opens the front door; she hears Wallace's voice. In her head she
sees his skeleton, his bony hand upon the bell. The door opens
farther; Wallace is pushing it as Mr. Collier tries to close it. The
hand seems as much flesh as bone. She walks down the stairs toward
it. Wallace stands there.

WALLACE: For God's sake, Rosalie, what are you playing at?
If it's not one thing, it's another.

Wallace is back from the grave, and Rosalie, too.

I, Nora, take credit for that. I'm pleased with myself; I have the courage to be me again. I was at home waiting for something more to happen. You can become addicted to event very quickly. I was waiting for the police to arrest me, for Ed to come home. The phone rang. It was Wallace.

WALLACE: Nora?

NORA: Is that you, Wallace? Where have you been?

WALLACE: Is that all you have to say?

NORA: Yes.

WALLACE: Can I speak to Ed?

NORA: He's not here. Try him at Susan's.

WALLACE: Have you been drinking?

NORA: Yes.

WALLACE: Where's Rosalie? I finally get home after all that, and there's no one in.

Wallace has been suffering from amnesia. He found himself penniless and without documents on the China coast; he'd worked his passage from Essen on a tanker flying the Liberian flag. It had taken him forever to get back. Well, that was his story, and he was sticking to it. He might get his job back at the BBC on the strength of it. My own view was that he had met up with some lady from a mountaineering club more his style and type than Rosalie and gone off with her. Changed his mind and decided to come home.

I told him where Rosalie was. I told him despair and grief had driven her into the arms of the Richmond electrocuter; I had tried to stop her, but she was stubborn. He should get round to the Tudor manse and put in his bid before she was permanently gazumped by Mr. Collier.

I sat at the window and waited. Colin and Amanda were out. I was alone in the house. It was tranquil, as a barren landscape is tranquil. I wondered how long Ed had been seeing Susan, how long he had been saying one thing and thinking another, as I had since the summer with Leslie Beck, and whether or not it mattered. The panic, anger, fear, and black jealousy engendered by helplessness, by nonaction, had burned away, shriveled up, when I set fire to Anita Beck's studio. I was left scoured, clean, and trusting in the fate which had held me up over a cat and so given Marion back her son, and punished Leslie in those areas in which retribution were required, and not others, and which had produced Wallace in the nick of time to save Rosalie, and which now brought Colin, not with Amanda, up the path. He looked so like Ed, I thought at first he was. Ed, coming home, forgiving and forgiven.

Colin said, "I hope you don't mind. I'm not seeing Amanda anymore. It's over. She keeps telling me what to think."

I said, "I don't mind."

Colin said, "That's the only reason."

I said, "Of course."

He said, "It doesn't matter whose child you are. You're still yourself."

I said, "That's right."

He said, "I'll speak to you when you're feeling better."

I said, "I feel just fine," but he went away to find some Diet Pepsi. He said Rosalie's Catharine had got onto the college hockey team, and I said that's nice.

I waited to see what would happen next. Perhaps now I would be able to give up smoking. The thought prompted me to open a new pack. There had to be some source of pleasure in life, even though it kills you. Self-destruction is the natural state; anything else is an effort.

The gate clicked. I looked up. Vinnie was coming down the path. I hadn't thought of that. His face was not set and grim; he had not come to talk about Susan and Ed, to be gritty and rancorous. He was smiling. He was coming to talk about us.

Mr. Collier has not been into the office for a week. Mr. Render has been out most of the time. The telephone has scarcely rung. I have written and written and written. I think everyone concerned is in a state either to endure the truth or to deserve it, though I am sure no one ever welcomes it.

Marion calls. She tells me Anita Beck's studio caught fire; they think sun through the skylight, focusing on glass, was enough to do it. Everything has been so dry and hot. Fortunately, Leslie is insured. With the money he can do up the house and buy himself an electronic wheelchair for his old age, Marion says. Aphra has decided against living with her boyfriend. Marion has had to raise Barbara's salary. She can't stand babies, never could. Jamie is staying with her. He thinks he will go to art college in London. What was I doing on Leslie Beck's doorstep? Trying to buy behind her back? Do her out of a commission? What does it matter—the paintings are burned. The Tate's lost all interest, thus saving the nation from further shame.

She does talk. But we have to be patient with long-term friends. They're illustrations—object lessons fate puts in our way, ever hopeful we'll come to a conclusion or two.

"We're all saved from shame," I observe. "I have to go now, Marion. I'm not supposed to be on the phone too long."

I can tell she's offended. I wonder whether to call Vinnie. He is at my house, writing the book Susan would never let him write, on the nature of reality. This is not the fate Susan planned for Vinnie. She wanted him miserable, in perpetual darkness, once she turned the light of her eye away from him. Too bad.

It is so much easier writing fiction than autobiography. I gave up the latter for good the day Ed went. Real life is simply not like this, is it. If Ed goes, Vinnie does not turn up. In the real world Amanda stays around to haunt and disturb. The Tate does not call up about Anita Beck's rather bad, sad painting. Her magic studio does not exist, or if it does, I do not get to see it. But doesn't life in fiction proceed with éclat! In the real world, Marion grows old alone. Once she's given Jamie away, he's gone for good. No one ever knows the truth about Mr. Collier, or what became of Wallace. The children launch themselves into the patternless chaos of their own lives: Catharine does not get on the college hockey team, though this, at least, saves her from muscly calves and tough shins.

Never mind. Leslie Beck is true. Leslie Beck the magnificent; Leslie Beck and his Life Force, moving through our lives, leaping, unstoppable, like electricity, from this one to that one, burning us up, wearing us out, making us old, passing on, its only purpose its own survival. Leslie Beck, enemy of death, bringer of life: the best thing that ever happened to us.

Well, there you have it. Did we do right, did we do wrong? Forget Leslie Beck. Were we good women or bad? I suppose we'll never know, unless there's a Day of Judgment, and we'll find out then. There certainly seems to be a human craving for such a day; but, alas, the needs of humanity at large, like the needs of the individual, are seldom satisfied. We're all too hungry for our own good. I think Marion was right to sell the baby; she'd have made a dreadful mother—though, oddly, of all of us, she was the one most open to moral scruple. A good person. The others of us did all right by our children, more or less, and I suppose must draw whatever moral credibility we can from that. Nor do I think Leslie Dong the magnificent is necessarily a bad man: the cards he deals at least consist of pleasure and children, not like, say, those of General Schwarzkopf, who hands out cards of glory and death. Many seem not to take offense at that, either.

It's in the shuffling of the cards, I daresay, that the whole point and purpose lies, and in the capacity for reminiscence, picking over the past, fictional or otherwise. Since God won't give us a Day of

Judgment, or chooses to delay it interminably, we have to write our own.

This is now going in a drawer. Mr. Collier tells me Accord Realtors is finally going to close its doors. After the boom, the bust; and serve us right.